PEPPER'S GHOST

A NOVEL

WILLIAM AUTEN

FIRE IN HAND MEDIA

Pepper's Ghost
Second edition
©2024 William Auten

All rights reserved. No part of this book may be used, reproduced, or transmitted in any form or by electronic or mechanical means, including photocopying, recording, or any information storage or retrieval system, without written permission from the publisher except in cases of brief quotations in critical articles, reviews, social media, and noncommercial uses.

No responsibility for loss caused to any individual or organization acting on or refraining from action as a result of the material in this publication can be accepted by the author or Fire In Hand Media.

This book is a work of fiction. All characters, dialogues, scenes, and situations are either products of the author's imagination or used fictitiously. Any resemblance to actual events, locales, or persons living or dead is coincidental.

ISBN (print): 9798986092737
ISBN (ebook): 9798986092744

Cover photo and design: William Auten

Published by Fire in Hand Media
Fire In Hand Media colophon is a registered trademark of Fire In Hand Media LLC
fireinhand.com

PEPPER'S GHOST

1

New Job Alert! pings her phone, and she hides it inside her shadow. She skims Duties and Requirements—Still don't qualify for any of that, she thinks—skips over Salary—That's never enough—and jumps to Location where she jerks away. A coworker whose name she doesn't know fake-smiles. "Of course it's here," Charlotte mumbles. "Where else would it be?"

Eyeballs in other cubicles flit her way; keyboards and mousepads click. The AC rattles behind exposed brick, but the humidity sinks on Charlotte. Sweat bubbles under her makeup. She dabs her cheeks and chin before zooming from the job alert's map, dragging it from the blue circle around the city. She changes her search from 100 Miles from Me to 200 then to 500.

The admin from the front strides down, and Charlotte saves her setting and before sliding away her phone stares at her reflection: the black glass abstracts her; half in shadow; half in a light she wishes would show her where to step into and emerge from.

"Brian is here to see you," the admin says.

Charlotte stops herself from asking if he has flowers. "I'll be right out."

The admin stops at an office where a woman behind a computer peeks out.

Brian turns the corner and bumps into the admin. "Never mind. I see her."

"Shit," Charlotte mutters. "Hey. What's up?"

"I thought I'd stop by and see if you can leave."

"I can't. I got work. Besides, what about tonight?"

"Why wouldn't we?" Brian wrinkles his nose.

She can't tell if he smells pot clinging to his clothes or, as he once said, "the stench of late-stage capitalism everywhere." "Don't you have work?"

"I quit."

Her coworker pinches his nostrils and vacates their cubicle.

"I had it with them. Dealing with those customers. It's not who I am."

Brooke steps from her office.

"Is that her?" Brian points.

"Let's go outside."

After they stand underneath the awning, rain dripping off old brick and black metal, he tells her, "That's right up my alley. Be my own boss. Make my own schedule. Work on that stuff then my stuff. I want to be happy."

"I'd like that too. For both of us. But you quit without talking to me."

"We're not married."

"But we got rent and bills every month we're together."

"I got plenty of savings."

"You got your parents. I don't have that."

"They'll help out."

"I don't expect them to help me. Or want them to."

"I'll start my own company. A startup. Like where you're at."

"They don't have that much."

Across the street, women window-shop, lugging their bags.

"I need to get back," she says.

"I'll see you at the apartment." He kisses her. "Then we'll go out and celebrate."

"I'm stopping by my dad's after work first."

He crosses the street and starts for the parking garage but turns for a store where she planned on buying a shirt for him for an interview he said was a goal for the new year. The associate rang up the price, but Charlotte couldn't ask if they provided layaway and slid over her credit card. She steps closer to the rain distorting Brian as he wanders to the front and picks out slacks and a tie and hands over the card his father pays off.

She snatches a weekly and, covering her head, walks to the drugstore where she buys aspirin and a coffee, and when she heads back to the office, sweat and rain chill her as she swipes her fob, trudges up the stairs, and stops short of the cubicles. Her head throbs; her stomach churns. Her stuffed-in coworkers hunch over their monitors and computers—everything and everyone on display in boxes.

"Make the most of it," her father said after she told him about the job. "Something's better than nothing."

"What happened with the nanny gig?" her mother asked

"They were rich white liberals. They moved after the election."

"That's too bad because I bet they had friends with men your age."

"Something's better than nothing, Mom."

"Clarence would say something like that. I guess it could be worse. You'll be indoors."

"Right."

"But you'll be stuck in front of a computer all day."

"I sure will."

"You'll add pounds sitting there. You're so pear-shaped you'll have to watch more what you eat. And exercise. Which you think is walking. But the temp thing will suit you."

Panting and pale, her clothes damp, she steps toward the cubicles where her coworkers watch her return to her desk where two emails from Brooke wait.

Hi Charlotte,

Let's keep personal time to a minimum especially when our colleagues are busy working next to us. Let me know if you have any questions. Thanks!

She scowls at coworkers discussing their clothes or drinks they'll order after work. She reads the second email.

Let's meet before you leave for the day.

The bedhead coworker spins around. "Did you finish Form 313?"

She opens the file she last touched before she searched for jobs. "I had tech problems."

"I didn't see Yumi come by. I've been here all day."

"You always are." She scrolls through her document and pretends caring about "an intake-outtake process regulated by strong-enough data that goes beyond the expected and unlocks potential in what others can't see." Another new-job alert pings her phone. The bedhead coworker's phone buzzes. Charlotte leans forward as he opens a small window in the corner of his screen and pulls up the job. She checks the job's location on her phone. Too close, she thinks. Her coworker opens his profile and clicks Apply. He can have it.

. . .

After half her coworkers leave and offices except Brooke's darken, she stops pretending to work and gathers her things. She calls her father and leaves a message: "I'm leaving work now and will be there as soon as I can." She texts the same to Brian who sends back an image of a woman bursting out of a birthday cake. Charlotte doesn't say goodnight to anyone. No one says goodnight to her, but they peer at her heading into Brooke's office.

"You wanted to see me?"

"Where were you today?"

"I had a personal matter to attend to."

Brooke scrolls her computer. "Did you note that for me?"

"No."

"You didn't with the last."

"I had to…help my dad with something."

"Was the person here today your dad?"

"What's the problem?"

"You're not at work when you're supposed to be."

"I have more than work in my life."

"We all do."

Charlotte's phone rings: Incoming Call – Dad.

"I'm sending you the policy from our employee handbook. I'm cc'ing Teri and Gera from HR so we're all on the same page."

"It's difficult sometimes for me to work the hours here."

"Do you want to drop to freelance? You can take on projects when you feel like it."

"I can't afford that." Her phone buzzes: New Voicemail – Dad. "Did you know there are ghosts of Confederate soldiers here?"

Brooke's chair squeaks as her lithe frame leans back.

"There was a sanitarium here where former soldiers could go. We're on it."

"What does this have to do with work?"

"This building is on top of where they died."

"This is the old waterworks building."

"They built this on top. But the dead aren't dead. Their ghosts may want to be elsewhere. And understood."

"Do you want to speak to Jill, our employee experience officer? I took a seminar with her, and it helped me navigate where we are right now."

"Thank you for bringing all this to my attention, Brooke."

Halfway down the cubicles, Charlotte plays her father's voicemail.

Hey, Charlie Girl, what time you coming over? I got your gift all lined up. See you soon. Love you to death.

She stops at the stairs leading down to the parking garage and looks over cubicles packing in her coworkers who stare into space or at their computers. Their clicking and typing blend with the hum running through the building and through her and neither abrading nor distracting her nor carrying her anywhere else.

⸫

Clarence beams when he opens his door. "Charlie Girl." He hugs her into his big, tall frame. "Happy birthday."

"Thank you."

"You and what's his name do anything special yet?"

"I'm sure he has something planned."

"Maybe he'll take you on a protest march. But after his momma gets him dressed in a nice protest outfit his daddy bought for him." Wrinkles and scars tighten along his temple, cheek, chin, near his milky eye, and his ear like a burned griddlecake. The sunset brightens his silver hair.

"It's OK if he doesn't. I need to kick back tonight."

"Bad day at work?"

"When isn't it? I can't stay long. I'm sorry."

"Don't be. I get to see you on your birthday. What more could I ask for anymore these days?" His hobbles into the kitchen and returns with a faded gunny sack. "On time this year."

"They'll let you into Heaven for sure now."

"Not if the Devil comes knocking for his dues."

She unties the sack and dabs her eyes. "Ah, Dad." She traces his handwriting under the first photo: *Charlotte Alexandra Long, age 11, Virginia Beach, VA*. Waves bubble over her ankles while he holds her hand and they stand in the ocean. She flips to the second: a small black-and-white photo of him playing a mandolin in front of a window. "That's eighth grade."

He reaches into his shirt pocket and clicks a pen.

"I came out and visited you that spring break. Mom dropped me off at the airport."

"You were a pro flying by yourself then."

"I had my first photography class."

On the bottom of that photo he writes *Charlotte Alexandra Long, age* but stops. "How old were you in eighth grade?"

"It doesn't matter."

He scribbles out *Charlotte Alexandra Long, age* and writes *My Charlie Girl & me – Tri-Valley, VA.*

She turns to the clipping from the *Tri-Valley Reporter* and two pictures side by side: the Sunrise Diner where her father took her whenever she visited; and a scar in a landscape where developers tore down the diner, according to the article, for a building that would house a software company. "I guess that's the sunset on the Sunrise."

"Not the first of those places. Or the last." He flips open his lighter and burns the tip of a candle after he stuffs it in a cake. "You don't want these? You look like you don't."

"They bring back a lot."

"Happy birthday."

She hugs and kisses him.

"Speaking of this stuff." He mushes around the cake. "I've been thinking about moving. Not soon or anything. When the time's right."

"Where?"

"Back to Virginia. I want to die in Virginia."

"Dad…"

"I've been smoking and drinking for a long time, Charlie. It's bound to catch up with me."

"Then stop."

He chews slowly. "Nah."

"I'll have to come visit you. I haven't been there in so long."

"It's that time of year, isn't it? Your birthday. I thought I did pretty good this year. Like then. The ocean."

"You did." Her phone rings. "You want to talk to Mom?"

He quickly stuffs his mouth. "You tell Janet I got too many dates lined up to talk to her. My dance card is full."

Charlotte clicks Ignore. Clarence coughs sipping whiskey. She rubs his arm while he leans back and wheezes.

"I'd sing to you but… Better not."

"Next year. I should get going."

He struggles standing and grabs the chair's armrests. "I'm an old chunk of coal today, but I'm gonna be a diamond someday."

"You and me both." She clutches her photos. "I'll see you soon."

"I love you, Charlie Girl."

She pulls out of his driveway but idles on the other side of the road. His silhouette cuts the windows of his small house as he lumbers across his living room. The busted-up gutter drips; rain dampens the siding like deep spots in a green pond and rots the wood of his front patio that he said would never hold an oxygen tank. "It'd fall straight through. Which is why I can't get one." She told him Veterans Affairs could help; they would know he has a Purple Heart. "No one over there knows anything. I've seen what they've done to us. When my buddy Dave Gomez got back stateside, he couldn't get help. Last I heard he's holed up in a cabin in Wyoming drunk and waiting for God or the Devil to knock on his door."

Clarence peeks out and waves to Charlotte, but she pretends listening to her mother's voicemail and, as he closes the curtain, plans on that lie if he asks her why she idled outside his house.

On her drive home, his voice from years ago comes to her. "The ocean." He waited for her to focus on what he said over the map between them after he said he had her birthday present. He tapped Virginia Beach.

She turns for her apartment—Brian's car in the lot; their apartment half lit.

"The ocean," Clarence repeated, leaning in, ignoring the crowd around them and the TV in the corner of the restaurant. Sweat and shaved metal clung to him. The table across from them stopped eating and drinking. He glanced at the TV, downed a whiskey, and set the plan: roll into Virginia Beach, spend the weekend there, return. "What do you say?"

"What about Mom?"

"She and her new friend Jeff are going to Honduras. She said I could have you while they're gone. It's for your birthday."

"I thought you forgot my birthday."

"I had to wait." He turned the map toward her as she checked out the TV. A reporter avoided crowds, fights, tear gas, flashes; stores burned along a street; figures in black lined up. He slid between her, the crowd, the TV. "Just you and me, Charlie. And the ocean. It takes away everything."

Her car rattles after she turns it off; the console buzzes; the radio blinks. "Please die on me today. That would be the cherry on top." She plays her mother's voicemail.

I guess you're not picking up your phone on your birthday. It's hard to believe you're as old as you are. I'm thankful I had you. And I know Clarence is too. I'm sure you've talked to him before me. I mailed you a present. I don't want it anymore. I thought you'd like to have it. It's OK if you don't. I hope it arrives in time.

She pulls out the usual from the mailbox: bills; junk mail; an insurance agent wishing her the happiest of birthdays; a real-estate agent telling her "now's a great time to buy if you're a renter or sell if you're looking to make good money in today's market." She dials the agent and asks how much houses are going for anywhere outside the city.

"Are you a first-time buyer?"
"Yes."
"Are you qualified for a mortgage?"
Charlotte snorts. "Sure."

"Are you interested in single- or multi-family homes?"

"What's the difference?"

"Why don't you come in and talk with me?"

"I want to leave where I am."

"Now's a great time to make that happen. Banks are the most stable they've been, and interest rates are…"

Charlotte hangs up and drags herself to the third floor and the apartment in the middle of a hall where long black-blue bands streak on winter nights and mornings. The stench of pot hits her when she opens the door; Brian's pipe smolders on the kitchen table. She opens the drawer next to the refrigerator and, digging around wine-bottle corks, breaks off a ball of marijuana and stuffs it in the pipe. She takes a long hit but snuffs it when, from the sofa, Brian rises and gums the air.

"There's a package for you. It came the other day."

She pushes aside a dying houseplant and reads the sender's address.

J. Rutherford

Falling River, MN

"You get that Maple Luv? That's the good stuff Bei Bei sent."

"Looks like you got it all since you got here." She tears into her mother's package.

"You want a glass of wine to go with it? Bei Bei said a merlot pairs best with it. Brings out the Vermont soil."

She holds up a jade pendant—smooth; the size and shape of an almond; strung from a necklace—and reads the note.

Charlotte,

Your father got this for me when he was in Vietnam. He bought it from an old couple who sold it from a rickshaw they pulled. If you don't want it, donate it to a shelter for families struggling to make ends meet or for pets who can't find a home. That's how Clarence and I found Zazou Peekaboo the Third before we had you. If you sell it, I don't want to know. If your boyfriend sells it for drugs, I certainly don't want to know.

I hope you have the happiest of days.

Love,
Mom

Brian peels off the couch. "And my parents wanted to do something for your birthday. We're going over there."

"When did they say this?"

"Maybe when that package came." He kisses her shoulder. "What was it?"

She stuffs the jade in her pocket. "Nothing."

"A box o' nothing." He picks up the empty box. "Man, if I was back in grad school, we'd do something crazy with this. Glue it to canvas. Melt it. Use it for negative space. Discuss the discourse for its application in a fascist, ever-approaching theocracy."

"It's like you never left grad school."

"Hello? What was in there?" He pulses the edges gaping like a mouth.

"Maybe we could be delivered someplace else."

He rips off an end. "We could go in one way and come out another." His arms *Ta-da!*

"There aren't enough rabbits in this city for me to follow."

"I'm ready to go."

"I need a minute." As she walks toward the bedroom, Brian tells his smart speaker to play "Charlotte's birthday playlist." The first song comes on. She opens the closet but doesn't change clothes or douse perfume. The singer sings that love can't be chased after but can be found. Straightening before the mirror, she sucks in her gut, squeezes her hips, and tucks away strands of gray hair. She kisses the folder from her father and places it inside her safe stored in the closet. The next song starts—synthesizers like time having no border. She ties the pendant around her neck —the jade cools her—and curtsies to her image and turns for the door while her image moves off the mirror and disappears in darkness.

2

They exit the highway—past the suburbs and out in the county and its sprawling properties, private schools, and country clubs—and wind up a long road ending at a gate, a panel with a keypad, and a sign.

Cherry Hill Estates

Private

All Guests and Visitors Must Be Approved

Brian punches in the code; the gate swings open; his BMW—"It's vintage," he clarified—rumbles through. The street signs change from green background and white letters and numbers to an off-white background and black cursive with sprigs of cherries. Houses roll by: old; pristine; covers for tourist brochures or parades of homes. They pull into the driveway of a two-story Tudor with stone and wooden gables across the street from a three-story Victorian while evening comes on.

After they started dating, she said to Brian, "I thought you said you family struggled with money. Like mine." Snow topped the lawn, but the walkway leading to the house had been leveled off, and she realized his father did not level it off but someone like her father did. The structure Charlotte assumed was a detached garage was his mother's garden shed. "This is a castle compared to where I lived."

"I said my parents still live in the house they bought when they first got married. This is it."

"They're rich, Brian."

"I'm not."

"You're not poor."

"My parents like you. I told you my mom thinks you're cute."

"My parents don't have this. You saw my dad's house at Thanksgiving."

"Your dad works hard."

"Did you tell me this to sleep with me?"

"No. I like you, and I'm trying to tell my story. My version. I'm not happy with everything in my life so I guess I'm picking what to tell. You know where I work, and you've been to my apartment. Which is yours now. My dad got a new job after being out of work for a year."

"If my dad lost his job for a month, he'd be in bad shape."

"That's one of the reasons I connected with you. We're here figuring stuff out."

"I was nervous for you to meet my dad. And he didn't fail to deliver."

"I never heard so many epithets in my life. He had some zingers."

Brian pulls into the driveway and turns off the engine. "We don't have to stay long. They want to say happy birthday to you. Feed and water us. That's it." He smells his tie and squeezes in eyedrops.

"Did you forget they asked us to come over? Or did you keep it from me?"

A man in a yellow polo jogs toward Brian's car. "Hello, you two. Coming it? Or do you want the food and cake brought out?"

"We're coming in, Dad."

"Hello, Miss Charlotte."

"Hi, Bob."

"Dinner's all ready. You want a beer?"

"That'd be great."

"Charlotte?"

"No thank you."

"Something stronger for the birthday girl?"

"We'll be in, Dad."

Brian leans over and kisses her, which she accepts like someone stepping onto ice.

They walk into the kitchen where Marla tells Charlotte happy birthday before stirring pasta and dashing in rosemary. Brian's sisters come in from the parlor. The youngest wiggles down her skirt and sashays to a chair; the oldest clicks her wheelchair over. Brian pulls out a chair for Charlotte, but she opts sitting next to Chloe and ensures she doesn't nudge her wheelchair. Bob waits until Cameron puts away her phone and checks her lip gloss.

"Let's pray." Charlotte and Brian make eye contact while Bob asks for "blessings beyond count, especially for Charlotte on her birthday, and for peace for those of us suffering and for Your hand to guide everyone into prosperity at this table."

"How old are you?"

"Cameron, you don't ask that." Marla offers a bottle of wine.

"I only ask because Brian isn't allowed near playgrounds or grade schools anymore."

"Still telling the same joke," he says. "Good to see your six years in college are paying off."

"You're one to talk."

Bob helps feed Chloe and wipes her chin.

Marla slides an envelope to Charlotte. "Happy birthday."

Charlotte unwraps the ribbon and pulls out a gift certificate.

Athena Spa and Boutique
~Be a goddess on your terms~

"A lady needs that in her corner." Marla tops off her wine.

"I've seen them come up in my job searches."

"Are you looking for a job?"

"The best advice I ever got," Bob says, "was your job is looking for the next job."

"Can we do cake now?" Chloe asks.

"OK with me. Charlotte?"

"Sure."

"I'm out." Cameron stands. "I don't want to eat that stuff."

"The stripper pole can only hold so much."

Cameron flips off Brian and leaves. A door closes down the hall.

After dinner, Charlotte excuses herself and strolls toward the rooms flanked by a stained-glass window that inspired one of Brian's pieces: a collage of a naked female floating in grays and creams; scratched-over sequences, spirals, broken-down DNA helices; painted-over quotes: *I want to understand. Found the secrets of life. It was so easy.* He overpriced it, telling her it would "expose the intersection of capitalism, artists, and patrons."

She opens his bedroom; his parents preserved his first studio in the corner. "You have a place to go to."

Brian comes up behind her. "What'd you say?"

"Nothing."

"You ready to get out of here?"

"Yes."

He caresses her. "Do you want to stop by Devil's Tunnel and relax?" He mimes smoking a pipe.

She adjusts her pendant. "I have work tomorrow. I'll see you at the car." She stops at Cameron's door and knocks—no answer. She sneaks in and sets the gift certificate on the bed and writes on the envelope *Enjoy*.

They return to the apartment where Brian fills a pipe, pours a vodka, and turns on the TV. Curled next to him, Charlotte scans jobs and cost-of-living calculators and tells herself nothing's changed. Brian dozes off. "Nothing's changed." She says it again —louder. He doesn't budge; his tattooed arm flops to the carpet; the flames across his forearm don't scamper over the floor and force them out onto the street. She takes the pipe and pot, grabs her camera bag, and slips out for Devil's Tunnel.

Brian said to her at his show, "My buddy over there is this writer. He dedicated his first novel to all the girls' hearts he's broken. *Without you I wouldn't be here today* he wrote under *Thanks Mom and Dad for believing in me*."

"Which one is he?"

"The one with my ex-girlfriend."

"Here's to them."

After they toasted, he leaned closer. "To new beginnings."

She glimpsed his name on a card next to his work: Brian Salisbury. "Is that really your name?"

"Yeah. Why?"

"You need an artist's name."

"And you are?"

"Charlotte. But I want to go by Alex."

"Why aren't you?"

"All these things to change. People to tell. Some day I will."

"You should do it. Start now." His tone cut into her before he asked her if she knew about Devil's Tunnel.

She pulls into the dirt lot by the trail threading along the river. She continues up a slope to the textile factories and shines her phone's flashlight on branches and vines wrapping around the brick building and its smokestacks and rafters—all the windows blown out. She turns for the back, near the railroad tracks built on a concrete bed aged black-brown, spots the door, handle rusted off, and slips behind plywood covering it. She photographs here and there, leaping over gaps in the floor, stopping when moonlight backlights the building's skeleton and the silver-black space and rubble and chalk white within.

She moves to the in-building the size of a tunnel propped up on one end but sunk under its bricks. Something within breathes. She stops at the door and brambles and branches folded around.

"Old man Taylor sold his farmland," Brian said the first night they were here. "He took the cheapest, quickest deal. He lost money on the sale, but he wanted off this land. He said he couldn't sleep. All his crops and cattle died. He heard voices and saw ghosts. He said the ground bled. Turns out his land was on land the Creeks said was cursed. They said no crops would grow here. No water would stay after the hardest rains. The horses that grazed here died, but the horses and crops on the other side survived. And they said they saw a man walking at night who had horns and smelled of burning fire. When the textile companies moved in they built these tunnels."

She pushes open the door. Dust flickers among moonlight, graffiti, beer bottles, cigarette butts. A stale smell smothers her. A staircase winds into the ground, sections of handrail missing.

"These workers went missing," Brian continued. "They found their bodies in a field near here. I went there when I was in high school. It's on the other side of the interstate. You have to walk through all these trees, and there's this big field with an altar in the middle with 666 on it. Pentagrams. Goat face and horns. Inverted crosses. They found their bodies there. They had been decapitated and flayed. The four of them laid out like a star. Then they found more bodies. Older. They found dog and cat remains." He leaned over the handrail. "Down there."

A noise pops below. Charlotte's pulse quickens. The temperature drops. But she sets her camera near the edge and poses in front of it. The camera fires off. The temperature drops again; a chill scampers over her.

Gasping, she runs back to her car and flings open the door. She takes hits from the pipe as she reviews her photos: she's erased in the smoke and moonlight.

3

"I got a notice about this job fair today. Do you want to come with me? It might be good for both of us."

Brian shovels up his cereal. "Nah."

"The office was quieter last week. I printed off a new résumé." Charlotte slides it over to him. "I downloaded it on my phone."

"They probably got a tracker on everything you print."

"I could care less if they find out."

He sets his phone to his ear. "Charlotte Long? Never at her desk. Most of her projects were sent back to her. And we have records of her printing off documents not approved by management. And her web searches? The girl never figured out private mode. I wouldn't hire her. But her boyfriend's a diamond in the rough."

"Funny." She dumps her coffee and scrapes her breakfast into the trash. "I ran into three people from high school yesterday."

"Where?"

"Getting gas, the bakery, and returning a book. One was a basketball player, another was in my speech class, and I forget the other one, but he was known for wild parties."

"Did they see you?"

She pats puffs under her eyes. "I don't think they saw me, but I overheard one of them say he was going on this road trip before coming back and hitting the job search hard. I felt small when I saw them. But I also could've walked past them, and none of them would know me." She stops applying makeup. "Don't you want to do that?"

"What?"

"Get out."

"Where?"

"Anywhere but here."

"You say that, but you'll find out you have to come back. Everything's here. Your dad's here." He strides past her. A stench drafts around him while he scribbles paint and charcoal on a canvas he started in the middle of the night.

She emails Brooke.

I won't be in today. I'm feeling ill. Should be back tomorrow. Fingers crossed. Thanks.

. . .

She drives to the expo center and parks in one of the last two rows; dodges vehicles honking and waiting for an open spot; apologizes to a driver when she steps in front of the city bus after it drops riders slinging on backpacks or handling briefcases; and merges with the crowd until people peel off to companies and wave to representatives in booths.

Charlotte scans the floor plan and list of companies and booth numbers. She strikes the ones she recognizes from her job searches and heads for the long row of squares tucked in against the side where she turns around as the lines lengthen behind and around her and their talk sounds like her meetings, coworkers, and job-search forums: salaries, bonuses, on-site perks, work-life balance, managers who "lead from behind," and challenges that "enrich the experience for employees." Before she bails from the line, she imagines copies of herself moving down each company: —"I don't have that experience, but I welcome the opportunity to get that. Would that come with more pay?"— until one of her stops and the rest fade away.

She ducks behind a booth when a coworker turns the corner and greets a man whose computer loops code.

A woman in a suit peeks around. "Would like you to be interviewed?"

"Do I look hard up for that?"

"Here."

Charlotte takes the woman's card.

D'Angela Wittmer

Recruiter

eVows Inc.

"We're in a high-growth phase right now. We're close to securing series A money. And we think differently. We're always looking for talent. Maybe that's you." Her teeth gleam. "I can tell you can bring something to one of our teams. Design. Logistics. Analyst. Maybe an accountant?"

"None of that. But I like hearing you think I can do something for you."

"You can. And we can show you how to grow. We don't think of ourselves as a company. We think of ourselves as investing in people."

"Do you pay well?"

"Your starting salary will pay above the cost of living here."

"What's the office culture like?"

"Read them." She pulls up reviews from employees—all average four-and-a-half out of five stars.

"What does your company do?"

D'Angela slides over. A video and voiceover start on her laptop:

Couples spend an average of three-hundred hours over twelve months to plan an event that lasts a lifetime. They'll browse photos, check out vendors, hear songs in their head they want played at their big day, but life gets in the way of all this.

A woman throws up her hands while searching websites.

Existing wedding sites offer inspiration but can't make it happen. Here's where we come in. Our teams take all that off your shoulders and figure it all out, helping you create that dream wedding everyone else will search for.

Two rings join at the end of the video. The woman who earlier threw up her hands smiles and drinks a mimosa.

"That's not for me." Charlotte hands back D'Angela's card. "My parents divorced when I was young." She heads for the exit but pauses: a man and woman alone at a small booth tucked among larger booths, crowds, big bright logos and signs, and a drawing for one year's worth of free bagels. Charlotte walks toward a model of a big top on the table and silhouettes of a roller coaster; a Ferris wheel; cotton candy and popcorn; and top hats and wands flanking Kopolski Traveling Amusement Company – One Smile at a Time.

People file past the plain-looking stout woman and don't say anything or look her way. She waves at Charlotte who walks over.

"Hello there." The woman's smile deepens her wrinkles—no makeup; her torso's weight pulling down her shoulders; her hair more salt than pepper. "I'm Julie Herndon. I handle all our acts, talents, and performers. That's Chris Kopolski our chief operating officer and a member of the family who started it all."

The middle-aged man—thick but not obese; boyish with rosy cheeks; stubble—nods, returns to his laptop and phone, and opens a can of espresso.

"He handles our finances."

Charlotte looks over their display: brochures; articles about new rides and shows; photos of awards—Chris and Julie dressed up alongside an older man resembling Chris and leaning on a walker; clowns; and a man dressed as an eccentric scientist—and games and sideshows; customers' reviews; a sign **Win Four Tickets to Any of This Year's Venues** under a toy gorilla looping the tickets around its fists; and a map.

"You go all over this region."

"We do. Top to bottom."

"And side to side."

"You have to go top to bottom and side to side."

Charlotte looks up. "Yeah, you do."

The crowd next to them cheers. A man yells, "I got all the cream for all the bagels!" His buddies high-five him. A woman in a suit pushes her way through.

"And this is still a thing? These companies are still around?"

Chris shoots up, cradles his phone to his ear, and slams open the door.

Julie smoothes her flowered dress. "He's doing his best to make it so. There aren't many of us left these days. I've been here for seventeen years. Before here, I was a creative assistant for amusement parks in the region."

"Where?"

"I started in Dallas then Houston. New Orleans, which shut down soon after I got there. I was supposed to transfer to Georgia but didn't. I did consulting in Branson. Now I'm here, and I love it. I have a smaller budget, but I call the shots and hire talent, which I enjoy. Tell me about yourself. What are you looking for?"

Charlotte hides her résumé behind her. "I like a lot of different things, and I want to do a lot of different things. More than what I am now."

"That's worthwhile. Lots of different things to learn and experience."

"Yes."

"I want someone like that. Outside the box is good. What are you doing now?"

"I'm a temp at this tech company. It's a startup. I can't stand it. And everyone there. If I may be honest."

"You should."

"Before that…a sales associate at a shop that sold high-end women's athletic clothes. Hated that and the women who came in."

"I can imagine."

"A coffee shop. A nanny."

"My kids could use a good nanny."

"Is that why you'd hire me?"

"Why don't you tell me why you'd like for us to hire you?"

Charlotte steps back. The model of the big top on the table clicks on. The top spins; lights flicker; cheering and laughing and a calliope ring around the base under small horses, clowns, a woman levitating near a magician, and acrobats sliding up and down. "It'd be something different than what's expected of me."

"We're need talented and curious people. Those two things are the most important. I don't care about résumés. I think you have what we're looking for. I go on feeling and seeing someone in person. I have a good feeling with you. And we get to travel and give people wonder. Who doesn't want to do that?"

"I want to travel."

"You may get sick of it."

"I doubt that."

Brian texts. <Lunch at Paulo's? I'll be down by your work in about 30 mins.>

"Thank for talking with me, but I need to go. Thank you for your time."

The big-top model slows, darkens. Chris slips in for a binder he pulls from a backpack and strides into an empty booth. The crowds thin as the expo center's clock ticks toward noon.

"I hope to hear from you. I've been talking this whole time, and I didn't catch your name."

"It's...Alex."

"Nice to meet you, Alex. We're hiring for the upcoming season. Contact me when you can."

Charlotte fumbles her keys while reading Brian's last text: <Where are you?>. Traffic out of the expo center and into downtown ties her up. <I'm on my way to you.> she texts him.

<You weren't at work when I stopped by.>

A truck lays on its horn when Charlotte doesn't roll forward.

<I left to run an errand. Headed back now.>

<They said you called in sick.>

<I'll see you at Paulo's.>

She reaches downtown, parks, and jogs for the pizzeria but stops outside its door. Brian leans against the counter and smooth-talks a girl curling her hair behind her ear; they type on their phones and compare what they saved. The girl squeezes Brian's arm on her way out and stays on her phone as her high heels click past Charlotte who texts Brian. <Something's come up at work. I'll see you tonight.>

Brian checks his phone and orders.

Charlotte takes the long way to the parking garage and, halfway, cruises to her work where she and her reflection in the long panes of glass march toward each other then look at the third floor where most of her coworkers refuse to leave for lunch. "Do y'all not leave?" she once asked one eating at her desk. "Something may come in when we're gone," the woman replied. The woman changed her shoes—heels to runners—and walked the hallway between the building while nibbling a protein bar. Charlotte imagines her reflection scaling the side, penetrating the brick and iron beams and wood, turning on her computer, and applying to jobs while everyone in the office stands back—the believers not shocked at this ghost; the non-believers sure this is a server overload.

She returns to the apartment where she opens a smoothie and her laptop, and as it stalls after she logs in, she pulls out her pendant and her father's gift and hovers over both. She peeks in the other bedroom where Brian tossed sketches he started after waking late, smoking pot, drinking rum and coffee until that buzz overtook the pot, and by afternoon, switching only to rum.

"Dad," she says in her voicemail, "I'm calling to say thank you again for the birthday gift. Part of me didn't want it at first, but part of me did. And does." She dials another number.

"Hello, Charlotte," her mother answers. "I'm finally hearing from you after your birthday."

"I wanted to thank you for the pendant. I love it."

"Have you worn it?"

"I have."

Charlotte checks her laptop. The browser churns. "How are things up there?"

"We had snow and below freezing last week. It did a number on my flowers and on my back. They say that's the last of it for spring."

"It's humid here from rain. My hair is frizzy."

"You have your father's hair."

"How's Ted?"

"We're together. For now. He wants to go to Hawaii on a coffee tour this winter. But I don't know if I can stand being with him that long. He snores. A lot. I've given him herbs, tea, a nasal strip, soft music before going to bed. I'm losing sleep because of him."

"Does he still like teaching?"

"His gig is up at the end of June. He'll have to figure out what to do. He's like you with that."

Kopolski's webpage loads. Charlotte clicks Employment. "I have an opportunity I'm looking into."

"You sound like your father. But they were hunches and bad bets."

"It's different this time."

"He said that every time."

"He's not perfect. But he provided a roof, clothes, and food."

"He was fired twice for drinking on the job. And, God, his time in Vietnam. Poor soul."

"I've been thinking about going by another name." She scrolls through jobs.

"Why would you do that? You've been Charlotte for years."

"Something different."

"Your father and I would have to change documents."

She lands on Entertainers and Performers. "I need to go. Thanks again for the gift. I love it and won't get rid of it." She fills in Today's Date and, wiping her palms, Name: Alexandra

Long. But when she reaches Earliest Date You Can Start, Brian unlocks the door.

"You're here."

She shakes her smoothie bottle. "Quick lunch."

"Feeling better?"

"Getting there."

He peels off his shirt and shorts and chucks them against the hamper and shuffles through the apartment. "You working now?"

As he draws near, she blacks out her laptop screen. "Finishing up."

"Working here?"

"Before I head out, yeah."

He loads and lights his pipe. "My parents said they had a great time with you. Looking forward to it again."

"And your sisters?"

"Chloe can't wait for your birthday 'next week.' Cameron could care less."

She brushes off the pipe.

"You used to take a hit before work or when we met up for lunch before you went back."

"I got stuff to focus on."

He flops in a chair by an all-black canvas.

She checks her application: everything blank; Internet connection wavering. "I'm off."

He motions to her dark screen. "You talking to one of those guys from your high school?"

"Who was the girl at Paulo's?"

"You spied on me. Of course you did. Running an errand my ass." He takes a long hit; smoke curls from his mouth. "She wants to model for me." He taps ashes onto the black canvas; rubs them around; draws wings. "You got to have a muse. You know?" He glares at her.

She snatches her keys and storms out.

. . .

Clarence doesn't answer. She knocks again. No answer. His frame doesn't cast a shadow on the wall by the front door; the floorboards don't creak. She stumbles down the slope leading to his garage, reaches under a beam, and pulls out dog tags taped together—a key between. She opens the door from the garage to the house and touches the hood of his old truck as cool as its blue paint.

"Dad?"

The house stays silent. No gun clicking.

"Don't shoot. It's me." She steps into the living room—no one; the kitchen—empty; the bedrooms—nothing disturbed. She sets her laptop on his table. The WiFi connects, disconnects, connects. She imitates the sound of the first modem he had like water slushing from a busted pipe. The application page loads slowly.

Boots thump the front patio; the screen door squeaks open. Clarence hooks his ball cap by the door.

"Hey, Dad."

"Peter at the Gates. What are you doing?"

"I need a place to stay. I don't know until when."

"Where is he?"

"Dad, don't." She tugs down his arm as he slaps back on his ball cap. "We need time apart."

"Like before?"

"It might be worse than that."

"Did he hit you?"

"He's not that way."

"They all say that until they're not." He slides a new whiskey bottle and a six pack of beer across the table. "The spare is yours. Let me wash bedding for you."

"I'll do it."

He cracks open a beer. "You working?"

"I'm applying to a job."

He chugs the can. "What is it?"

"It's an entertainment company."

"Oh, God, you're going into porn like your cousin Lauren."

"She does make good money. When she has good WiFi. No, it's like a circus."

"We had one of those. Came every April and August."

"Did you go?"

"You bet your bottom dollar I did. I won prizes when I was a kid and stuff for Mary Wilkins. She was my girlfriend when I was in the Army. Before your mom's time. Her dad was a pediatrician. Her mom was my teacher. She'd send her letters with her perfume on them. She stopped doing that after a while." He crushes a second can. "I think she was told not to. Gramps and Grams thought that. Dar did too. Dougie thought I was too dumb and ugly for her. When I got back from Vietnam, she was married."

"I'm not sure what I'll be doing." She refreshes the stalled page. "I'm thankful I found it."

"I won't interrupt you." He grabs another beer, a glass, and the whiskey. He turns turns on his TV and slouches in the living room. His hands quiver while unsealing the whiskey.

"I may go by Alex when I work there."

"Yeah?" He swigs. "They can call you Alex, but you'll always be Charlie to me."

"If they hire me, I'll travel. A lot. Up and down the region. Side to side."

"Remember when I told you I went all over, everywhere I could after the war?"

"I do." She sits across from him.

"If that bullet hadn't grazed me, I wouldn't have." He spins the bottle. "Like a big ol' bee sting. I felt it before I heard the gunshot. And then the explosion. Somebody put me on the chopper." His eye stands still like fog.

"We can talk about something else."

He pours a glass but doesn't drink it. "Dougie picked me up at the train station after I got back. His hair was over his ears, down to his collar. 'Dirty hippie,' I teased him. He had on these fancy loafers. I asked him if Dad and Dar put him in sales. He teased me about my eye patch. Called me a pirate. But that's when he told me about that Challenger in town." He downs his glass.

"Do you want to...?"

"Doug got 'em down below asking. It was the last model. It had this grille up front. Such a sad, sad mouth we joked. But making it go real fast made us smile. Real fast. We went down the old loop we cruised in high school. There was this statue of Lee riding Traveller, head raised, over by First Baptist and Main. I'd seen it many times as a boy. I'd spot the ears of Traveller. Then Lee. And I would say to Doug, 'General Lee is watching us.' And Doug would say, 'Sit up straight, boys. Stop chasing tail and be respectable gentlemen.'" His scarred crooked finger scolds shadows in the hall. "They've taken that statue down."

"Yes, they have."

He chases the whiskey with a beer. "We spent all summer working on it, fixing it up real nice, making it ours. We stripped it, primed it, painted it cherry red. We changed the exhaust. Added wider tires. Dropped a new engine in it. Real fast." He gasps faster and returns to the whiskey. "We was going along this old highway. Ain't nobody around that time of night. And I pushed the pedal to the metal. I lost control. Spun and hit a tree. Passenger's side. Doug's side. Real hard." His voice fades. "Did you like your photos for your birthday?"

"I did." She covers his glass. "Why don't we…?"

His head jerks. "I'll never forget that trip for your birthday. You were lost in it all, watching the waves. I remember the first time I saw it too. I felt small in front of it. But I got in and left everything about me." He leans back and wipes his sweat.

"Let me start dinner for us." She strides into the kitchen and turns on a stovetop knob; the blue flame pops on in a circle.

"Your mom made this cream for me and would smooth my face, and it would feel like all those scars were gone. I gave her a pendant I got over there."

Charlotte touches her neck.

"This green jade I thought was expensive. It was a cheap thing."

"It's not."

"I gave it to her as my wedding ring. She gave me a ring her friend made. I still have it. I don't know if she has the pendant."

"She doesn't. I…"

"We got married at the courthouse. Her brother showed up. All the way from Minnesota. 'Couldn't wait to leave that place,' she said to me. She was beautiful that day." He twitches. "After you were born she couldn't wait to spend hours with you drawing or painting. The two of you making whatever it was. This one time you had on an old T-shirt of mine, and you were trying to paint the same thing she was. But this light… The two of you had this light in front of you." He slumps and stares at sunshine in the room. "This was after the war. Before the ocean."

Charlotte tops off a glass of water and helps him as he slurps it. He asks for another; she fills it; he drinks until he gasps. She helps him into bed and checks his temperature, blotting his face. She turns on the ceiling fan and turns off his lamp. And as she dumps his beer and washes out his whiskey glass, she recalls what she asked him that night after school. "Did you carry something when you were over there?"

"I had a gun and my pack and ammo. And a knife. A vest. Cigarettes. Weed. Mosquito nets. Christ, the mosquitoes. A shovel, a…"

"No, I mean symbolic. Did you carry something like a talisman?"

"A what?"

"Something lucky."

"We cut up VC-gook bodies we found. We kept some of their stuff."

She grimaced. "Dad, don't call them…"

"You asked. I'm being honest. What's this for again?"

"English class. We're reading a book about Vietnam. It's based on the author's time there."

"Who'd want to write about that?"

"He did. It helped him."

"Oh for God's sake. You live with those things. You don't sit around and write about them. What was that word you used earlier? Something about a lucky charm. A symbol."

"A talisman. Why?"

"Never mind."

Charlotte leaves the bedroom and checks the application page on Kopolski's website—frozen—as pixels flicker across her screen. After shutting down her laptop, she fills the glass of water and sets it on the table next to her father if he becomes thirsty in the night.

4

The application page loads quickly. Charlotte peers over her monitor, behind, and in front of her. Two developers working at the back loop arrows on a whiteboard. She scrolls down.

Are you a hard-working individual who works well with others? Are you a self-starter? Are you creative and an independent thinker? Do you enjoy a fast-paced workplace? If your answers are yes, we have employment opportunities in the following departments:

Administration

Animal Handling

Concession, Games, and Vendors

Logistics (CDL drivers)

Performers, Shows, and Talents

Rides Operations/Maintenance

There's nothing like the excitement of working with one of America's premier traveling amusement companies. We've provided family fun and entertainment to state, county, and outdoor fairs, carnivals, and organizations for over 110 years—One Smile at a Time. We place a lot of stock in our employees and throw out the stigma of "carnies." Our staff is highly skilled, incredibly talented, and extremely professional. Wages are good, and the fun is free! Ready to join us?

Charlotte fills in half her application before a coworker stops by on the way to the break room. She shrinks the page until her inbox glows behind it.

The woman shifts her handbag. "I think you helped with the APP account. We were in a pinch, and you stepped up."

"I did."

"But I'm sorry…" Simone cringes. "I never caught your name. Caroline?"

She expands the application page. "Alex."

"Short for Alexandra?"

"It is. My mother was fascinated with Greek culture. But Alexandria was too many syllables for her. So…Alexandra. Alex."

"I love it."

"I'm sorry to be rude early in the day, but I need to catch up on things here."

"Girlfriend…" Simone leans in; her handbag thumps the cubicle. "Totally understand. Kortney has been riding me since Thursday about performative measures they need for Q3 estimates. For that conference in June."

"Oh my God. That conference in June. It'll make or break us."

"Right? I'm like, Kortney, let's get a room if you're gonna ride me this hard."

More coworkers file in. One of their yawns sends a chain reaction of yawns down the desks.

"Make it a great day today, Alex."

"I plan on it." She finishes her application and, reviewing it, leans back as Brooke flicks on her office. She creates an account for Alexandra Long and transfers emails. She keeps the application page up and opens a new tab for Kopolski's homepage and its images of rides, concessions, awards, the midway lit at night, and the logo of a lion and a clown flanking a trapeze ladder. She clicks Schedule Archives: Big Pines Fair, Azalea Days, Wilton County Fair, Mississippi River Expo, Fall Days, West Range Music Festival, Rocklahoma, HallowScream. She clicks News and reads President Glen Greenwald "is pleased to announced Avé Asset Management has finalized its purchases of Kopolski assets that Terri Frimm, Avé's entertainment-portfolio manager, will handle. Greenwald added, 'This will bring stability and future growth to us, our employees, their families, and most importantly our customers who rely on us year after year for our family-centered, high-quality entertainment.'"

Brooke breezes past Charlotte who doesn't hide the Leadership page loading.

Christopher Kopolski, COO

Chris's first job at the company his family started was selling popcorn and candy. He moved into Logistics where he showed key insight into management, organization, and cost efficiency before earning a spot in Accounts. He was then shortlisted by the board and Avé Asset Management to be the next COO. Under his leadership, our company has won all the industry's major awards, received more awards and accolades from industry organizations and peers than the competition, and retained membership in the Traveling Amusement Business Association's Circle of Excellence, the organization's highest honor. Thanks to Chris, we have been awarded Best Regional Amusement Company from TABA five years in a row. His wife Stephanie is active in the community and serves as family ambassador for our company that has made us an industry benchmark. Chris loves to play on the Bomb Squad, the company's softball team. Chris and his wife have three children: Toby, Tyler, and Tammy.

Julie Herndon, Talent and Shows Director
The look and feel of our shows, which remain more popular than ever, are all thanks to Julie. She has blended old-style carnival fun with modern touches for our shows —everything from costumes to performers. *Carnival* has nominated Julie three years in a row for her entertainment and creativity. She has extensive industry experience spanning thirty-five years. She and her husband Gary have two children, Nolan and Emily, both of whom have been summer interns for us!

Brooke cruises into her office where she stands at her monitor and looks toward Charlotte who beams before she selects one of Kopolski's departments for her application. Noise from coworkers setting up for the day swells and fades. She says no to Administration and Logistics but imagines her father would show her how to earn a CDL. Animals would be fun, she muses, but nixes that because of an online forum she read called Dream Jobs That Weren't. She clicks Our Shows and Entertainment.

Lose yourself in the wonder of our shows! Relive the excitement and enchantment of sideshows. Revel in our newly expanded Big Top show performing throughout the day and into the night. Singers, musicians, acrobats, animals, clowns, and our classic shows such as Fleming's

Animal Showcase, the Amazing Illych Family, Punch and Judy's Puppet Show, Ruby the Mermaid, Bonnie and Junebug's Bug Parade, Pandemonium House of Oddities, and Princess Salina who changes into a gorilla before your eyes.

She rereads *Lose yourself in the wonder of our shows!* and the last sentence about a girl changing into a gorilla and selects Performers, Shows, and Talents. Her cubicle mate sets his lunch in the corner; the brown-green glob in the container nauseates her. She confirms the email listed on her application is the new one she created, clicks Send, and feels like she releases a balloon with a note tied to it.

She hits Refresh on her new email—nothing. Again—nothing. She returns to the Employment page—the application template blank. "Damn."

"Everything all right?" her coworker asks.

Her new email confirms her application. "It is now."

Brooke steps over. "My office, please."

Charlotte trails her in.

"What are you working on now?"

"I joined the circus."

Brooke cackles. "Funny. Simone reminded me you helped her team with the APP project. Would you like to join them in the next phase? It's data-timing and client usage. It would look good for your evaluation."

"That sounds exciting as usual, but I'll be having my head in the mouth of lion. Or maybe breaking off chains after I'm dunked in a tank. Either way I can't."

"Is this another story from you?"

"No. I used my computer to join a circus."

"I don't appreciate this behavior."

"I don't either. Which is why I'm resigning. Today. Effective right now." She checks Brooke's clock. "At least I can say I accomplished something before lunch." She tosses her fob on Brooke's desk and cleans out hers but pauses when she comes across a photo of her and Brian she took of them snuggling in the back of his car. She said, "I love you." He whispered the same. And both of them laid there, amid rain and thunder and gray light, holding each other. She sweeps the photo into the trash and pivots her monitor toward the cubicles while a video loops a roller coaster slinging up and down behind a banner for Kopolski's Mighty Midway.

. . .

The apartment stinks—pot, food, sweat, turpentine, dust. She rummages through drawers and cupboards, pulling out her silverware and glasses, and lifts a shirt off the sofa—neither Brian's nor hers, but it would fit her—and peeks at his easel and sketchpad: ink, charcoal, and paint outline a female torso. Charlotte throws the sketchpad down when she reaches this body and a male's in bed. She bursts into the bedroom where she grabs her birthday gift from her father but can't find the pendant. She tosses dresses and blouses—not hers—out of the closet, pushes off the mattress, dumps nightstands, and yanks open the bathroom. She stuffs her clothes into her backpack and double-checks she has the photos from her father. She scours the bedroom again but no pendant. She snaps open the other bedroom and drags Brian's art supplies into the living room.

"Dad," she says in her voicemail, "I need to stay longer with you. I'm sorry. We can figure out my share of utilities and food." She dumps Brian's bottles of rum and vodka down the toilet, grabs his pipe, and pockets a bag of pot. "I quit my job. But I applied to one today, and I feel good about it."

In her car, she lights the pipe, takes a long hit, and as she exhales, wishes the smoke would part like a curtain and behind it her pendant like a lantern.

. . .

"Morning, Dad."

"Morning, Charlie Girl." He quickly stops pouring whiskey into his coffee and hides the bottle. "I made us waffles and sausage. And coffee."

"I smelled it getting ready." She wakes up her laptop and glances at her new email account and cringes at the low connection. "But I can't stay for breakfast."

"Where you off to?"

"A coffeeshop or maybe the library." She cuts a bite of his waffle and drags it through syrup, butter, and chunks of sausage. "Why are you standing? Are you OK?"

He mumbles and steps back.

She takes the bottle.

"Just a drop, Charlie. It's not like the last time."

"It's always like the last time."

She rubs his shoulders and helps him down. "What time will you be done at the site today?"

He opens the window by his table and lights a cigarette. "Around five. Depends if Carlos brings in the sheetrock delayed from last week."

"And a drink after?"

"Maybe."

She tastes his coffee. "Cut it with Coke. A lot. OK? Promise me?"

"Maybe I'll cut it with a sno-cone on a day like this. I hear state fairs have those nowadays. Back in my day we had to sneak in a bottle and dump it over a sno-cone." His knees crack. "Remember that sno-cone you had at the ocean?"

"I do."

"Turned your lips, teeth, and tongue blue."

"Mom said, 'He gives you too much sugar.'"

"It was in that old arcade by the boardwalk. And that thing that spun around like an old movie. With the horse in it."

"A zoetrope." She slings on her backpack. "I'll see you tonight."

"You were obsessed with that thing. The way it moved. Those horses inside it."

"Cut whatever you have with a soft drink. Please. Don't splash it in. Dump it in. I'll see you later."

. . .

You must purchase food or drink to use our WiFi.
Thank you – Mgmt.

Charlotte moves the sign after she grabs the last free table and faces the door if Brian were to walk in. "Come on, ol' Bessie," she says while her laptop whirs. Missing pixels flash in before flashing out, but all the bars for her connection fill, and her new email account loads—but only spam and change-of-email confirmations sit in her inbox. She eats her danish but can't taste the apple.

The front door chimes open; a man scrapes his shoes on the mat. Charlotte does a double take—not Brian. She verifies Julie's email is not listed on Kopolski's website and the response to her application does not list it or anyone's from HR.

Do not reply. This is an automated email acknowledging Kopolski Traveling Amusement has received your employment application.

She digs around search engines and websites listing names, ages, residences, credit scores, court records, and emails and comes across Julie B. Herndon and a work email: j*****h@*******entertainment.com. The cafe glances at her when she laughs at the price for accessing this information and the Click Here! link she assumes will eliminate the rest of her pixels then her bank account.

She purchases the cheapest notebook in the store adjoining the cafe and puzzles out the letters behind the asterisks. When one answer clicks with her, she types it in an email from Alexandra Long.

Hi Julie,

It's me Alex. We met at the job fair. I applied the other day to the talent department you're in charge of, but I haven't heard back. I'm interested in it—anything you have. It doesn't have to be talent, but nothing else lined up with me.

I'm free anytime to come in and talk. Let me know as soon as you can. Thank you. I hope to hear from you soon.

Alex Long

She pushes Send and eats her danish. The apple reminds her of an orchard her mother took her to in Minnesota. She rode a tractor and was allowed three apples, but Janet said they had to be different. She grabbed a blood-red one, a green, and one like the amber leaves fallen around her.

"No snake, Mommy."

"What do you mean?"

"No snake talking to me like in the Bible."

"None of that's true." Janet cut the apple down to its core and shared the slices with Charlotte. "I'll talk to your father about that."

Her inbox updates.

Mail Delivery Fail

Returning message to sender. The message you sent could not be delivered to its recipient. The following address(es) failed.

She closes her laptop, buys another coffee, but peruses the store, starting at the shelves of LPs, tapes, and CDs and, above them, posters, stickers, hoodies, and shirts. "It's one of my favorite places in the city," she said to Brian when she took him there. "Small on the outside. But it goes on and on inside. Like an illusion." She thumbs through classics and rarities and recalls her parents switching on a turntable. Her mother played Americana and singer-songwriters; her father picked his mandolin and sang about a "home over the sea waiting for you and me." Charlotte sat close to him while he played. His hair dangled over his scars, and he popped back his head, swinging his hair, and Charlotte giggled, believing her father was on stage. She pulls out a plastic-wrapped LP of a band her father loved and takes it to the counter.

"Look at that." The employee points to the left corner. "Somebody used this for a coaster. But the record's in decent shape." He rings her up.

His coworker says, "The bassist in my band knows a guy who buys them that way. Says it's more legit than the corporate crap out there."

"As long as it plays," Charlotte says. "Are you hiring by any chance?"

"Not in this economy."

"Pretty bad?"

"The owner keeps saying this is the year we go under. He can't keep up. We're cutting back on store hours next week."

"I'm sorry to hear that."

"Things here get better, progress, then go back to God, guns, and apple-pie ways of living."

"They'd put us all back in chains if they had the chance," his coworker says.

"We're geeks, not jocks. Lovers, not fighters. We use art and heart, not our dicks, to change hearts and minds."

"My dad wouldn't like you. But he'll like this. Thank you." She takes the LP and returns to her table—nothing in her inbox. She logs into her job-search account and pulls up saved results while patrons arrive and leave.

. . .

Her phone wakes her. She rolls over: Incoming Call – Brian. He texted and left voicemails throughout the afternoon.

"Your dad was over here."

"At the apartment?"

"He wanted to know what's going on. Was this your idea?"

"Were you by yourself when he stopped by?"

"You wanna talk, let's talk. Like adults."

She shoots up and peers out the window: an ice-cream truck's calliope somewhere in the dusk. "I want my stuff."

"Come and get it. No one's stopping you. You were here. Thanks for trashing my work."

"There's a pendant that's a family heirloom, and I want it. I didn't see it when I was over there."

"I have no idea what you're talking about."

"You saw it the night of my birthday before we went to your parents. I want it and my stuff." She checks the clock. "I can be there by seven."

"I won't be here."

"I have my key. I'll come in and get my stuff. I don't care who's there."

"Don't touch my work. Or take my weed."

"I'm leaving, Brian. For good this time." The floor chills her feet as she dashes to the kitchen and refreshes her inbox—nothing.

"You can come by and get your stuff whenever. I don't care. I got stuff to do. You got your key. And you can keep it."

Clarence's truck rumbles into the garage. He lowers the American flag in his front yard, saluting it; waves to a neighbor who perches on her walker; tidies up tools, gloves, and his denim jacket, setting them in their places in his workshop; takes his boots off one at a time and with a wire brush scrubs the soles; and staggers inside.

She meets him halfway between the garage and living room.

"Hiya, Charlie Girl. How was your day?" His speech doesn't slur; he doesn't wobble. His hug smothers her; alcohol doesn't seep from his skin. "Did you the hear ice-cream truck down the street?"

"I did."

"I bet they have sno-cones. You wanna get in my truck and catch 'em? It could be our dessert tonight. My treat."

"I got something for you."

"Look at that." He puts the record on his turntable and, when the first song comes on, pretends playing the mandolin. He kisses her forehead, rubs balm on his joints, helps start dinner, and pours them glasses of water as the sunset becomes the sole light among people coming home for the evening.

5

She reaches the end of her list and can't recall any other places she visited since losing her pendant. She reviews what she crossed out: restaurants, coffeeshops, the library, the apartment, her father's place, her car. Her phone rings.

"This is Mark the manager. I'm returning your call about jewelry you lost. I have something here, but describe yours." After she does, he tells her, "That's not what I have."

She rubs her collarbone, opens the kitchen window, and lights the pipe. Don't call him, she promised herself. Show up and get your stuff. But she dials and assumes his voicemail will pick up when he sees she's calling.

"Yeah?"

"I'm coming by and getting the rest of my stuff. And I want time there to search for my pendant."

"Take as much as time as you need."

She blows smoke out the window while a fly scuttles over her father's liquor cabinet. The stories he'll tell if he has it, she thinks. Spin it however he wants. My pendant as proof he had me. The fly buzzes off the handle, returns, buzzes off. She imagines Brian photographing her pendant and sending the image to his artist-friends, and they would collaborate about "bourgeois relationships and the pressures of heteronormative monoculture." She hears them say this as he said it to her while the fly crawls into a gap. She snuffs the pipe and checks her email before sweeping crumbs off the table, stovetop, counters. She searches under the sink: spray, rubber gloves, steel wool, wipes. Nothing in her father's kitchen needs cleaning, but she wipes the refrigerator shelves and dumps food. She finds his vacuum and attacks the floors and rugs that have no dust. Before leaving, she dumps her coffee in a to-go tumbler. She opens the liquor cabinet—no fly inside—and splashes in rum but tosses it all out.

• • •

A car, not his, is in Brian's spot when she pulls up to the apartment. She knocks twice before unlocking the door and announcing she's coming in. The music inside stops; the door jams.

The woman from Paulo's peeks out. "Brian said you were coming over for your necklace."

She steps in. Brian's mixed-media paintings hang by the front door: dripping, diluted, impasto; the figures in the background destroyed, revised.

"My name is Cassie."

"Where is he?"

"He's interviewing for a web-designer position." Cassie walks about Charlotte's things lined up. "I'll get that necklace for you." When she returns, the pendant dangles like game shot and skinned. "Here you go."

Charlotte pulls the pendant toward her heart.

"We're pretty sure we got all your things. Let me give you a hand down."

"I got it." Charlotte slides over the first box.

"I had this one boyfriend who broke up with me after we bought a condo together. I was halfway across the country. He turned out to be a jerk, and I up and left. I don't care about my clothes he has, but I wish I could get back the pictures from when I was a kid my mom sent after I moved there. I know where they are. You send emails. Make phone calls. Plead." Cassie slides over the next box. "At least Brian's a good guy."

Charlotte loads her car while neighbors gawk. The apartment door closes. She refrains from screaming—no air left in her. Pain drills her chest and stomach. She shivers under her pendant and the weight it comes with.

· · ·

She warms her lunch in her father's microwave but can't eat. She pulls loose hairs that fell in her meal. And this is why I got fired from the coffeeshop. She slathers gel on her chest and forehead and considers slathering her entire body like she's been dipped and preserved and her pendant is the string to pull her up from the past. As she curls on the bed for a nap, her email buzzes.

Dear Alex,

Thank you for application to Performers, Shows, and Talents at Kopolski Traveling Amusement. We would like to interview you at your earliest convenience. Please let us know the days and times you're available.

Devon
Human Resources Coordinator

Her fingers can't type; her connection fades. Her laptop struggles powering on, and after it does, pixels stay put, but the connection is no better. Come on, she begs while her browser and email load. She clicks her phone into a hotspot, but her laptop can't find it. She cuts open a box from the apartment but can't find her robe; she cuts open another—no robe but finds her work clothes smashed under books and Brian's pint glass. After chucking the glass in the recycle bin, she snatches her father's robe and runs outside, jamming her phone into the air—the power lines humming above her—but trips on the robe and skins her knee and loses more bars on her signal. She double-checks her pendant is still on.

Blood dripping, dirt and rocks in her wounds, a breeze tangling her hair, blinded by sunlight, clutching her phone, she hobbles to the liquor store down the road.

"Your day getting started?" A man jiggles a handle of gin. "What do you say to making it better?"

She nods at his RV. "You got good internet connection in there?"

"Is that all I'm good for?"

She marches into the store. "Can I use your wifi?"

The employee stops stocking shelves. "Ma'am?"

"I have an emergency. It won't take me but a minute."

"I can call the cops for you." He glances her up and down. "Or an ambulance."

The manager walks over. "May I help you?"

"I need your wifi."

"It's for staff only. There's a Home Depot down the road."

She trudges into Garden & Landscaping—no signal—then Lumber & Building Supplies—slow signal—then Windows & Doors where her phone's bars jump as she connects to the wifi for customers. The email from Devon loads. She wipes her sweaty hands on doormats and replies.

Thank you for letting me know you'd like to interview me. I'm available on these dates.

A lift behind her beeps while it backs up; it lowers a glass door to a floor display. The lift drives off. Charlotte slogs to the door, opens it, and steps through before heading into the bathroom where she cleans up and walks back through the glass door.

6

Clarence taps her car. "I'll see you tonight. And we can celebrate. Crack open the top-shelf hooch." He loads tools and gloves into his truck and, cigarette dangling from his lips, winks.

She rubs her pendant and punches in the address Devon sent. The satellite images and street views from her search show a large field, gold at the time it was captured; off-white buildings; ropes and nettings tied to towers. She took screenshots, anticipating little to no connection on her drive. Leave by 7:00, she planned; cross the river; pick up the interstate; get on county roads leading to the entrance; park, walk, tell Devon "Alex Long is here to see Julie"—all this by 10:30, her interview time. She laid out her clothes and at the last minute added a sweater and recalled she bought it from a secondhand shop. She thought, They will have to take me as I am.

While her car struggles cranking on, she devours her bagel, slurps her coffee, and pockets joints she rolled. The morning commuters slow her down before she crosses the river and hops onto the highway and the long stretch east among hills, forests, flea markets, plants, truck stops, twenty-four-hour restaurants, and porn shops.

A small headache bubbles near the back of her head; she eyeballs the joint but says, "Hi, Julie. Alex Long. Thank you for seeing me today." The radio fuzzes out. "Hi, Julie, nice to see you again. I'm Alex." Bugs slap her windshield. She massages her neck. "I applied to your company because I think working here would be awesome. I'm here because I want to travel and experience things I can't in a cubicle job. I'm creative and a free spirit but can do anything I put my mind to." She checks a sign and her map. "I'd like to be part of your company. I have a personality that would fit here. I'm creative, smart, adaptable. I love change. I like to be in situations that change me."

She turns onto a county road leading to the offices, trees thicken, and the light-blue sky flickers. She taps her phone—blank screen—and as she taps again, the screen glows and a truck honks. She swerves and crosses back into her lane but dips into the ditch. Her car rises onto the road—*chop-chop-brrr!* underneath. She clicks on her hazards: a large branch wedged in a rear-tire well. She pulls—nothing—then, bracing against the tire, pulls. The car rocks, scares her; she jerks away. Out comes the branch.

But she can't stand straight. Her side burns and tightens. Heaving, she collapses but pulls herself up on the door. A lump between her ribs and hip swells as she puts her car in gear; her leg tingles. "Damnit." She finds no painkiller in her purse. A piano sonata fades in and out on the radio. She checks the time, curses again, and fingers the joint. One large, drawn-out hit, she reasons, to numb the pain. She dials the number Devon provided; no one answers. She flicks on the lighter and takes a long hit. She dials the number again—no one answers—and leaves a message. "Car trouble. Maybe fifteen minutes away." She eats half a snack bar, swishes water, and pops mints. She scrounges through her purse but finds no eyedrops and drives the rest of the way with the windows down and her bloodshot eyes staring at her from the rearview mirror.

When she reaches the front gate, her pain neither tighter nor looser, she doesn't feel anything. She pulls into the space reserved for visitors and, smelling her cardigan, removes it. She tugs her T-shirt and pushes the sleeves up her biceps. "Sun's out, guns out." She eats the other half of the snack bar, finishes the mints, and wobbles into reception at 11:17. "I'm Alex Long. Here to see Julie Herndon."

. . .

"I'm glad you made it." Julie moves a chair. "I heard you had car trouble."

"Something got jammed. I think. My tire. Or…" Her high drizzles through her. "Who knows?"

"Those things happen at the worst times. Like before a job interview. At least you got here safe and sound." She pours a cup of tea and squeezes honey into it. "Can I get you anything?"

"Water." She downs one—and two more.

Julie slides the application into a folder. "I enjoyed meeting you at the job fair."

"Me too."

"And I think you'd be perfect for one of our sideshows. How does becoming a gorilla sound?"

"A gorilla?"

"You step in as you. You step out as a gorilla."

She imagines drinking a potion from a beaker, doubling over, and as the beaker falls and shatters, rising hairier and with fangs and yellow eyes. "Is that all?"

"You have lines you have to memorize. Wear a costume."

"I can do that."

"You'll have to help out with props and your castmates Don and Pete. They're great guys. They started the show. And you may from time to time need to help with rest of the company."

"Like the animals?"

"Let's stick with sideshows and entertainment for now. Sound good?"

She titters. "Yes."

"Fantastic. I'll walk you down to meet with Chris. It'll be formalities. If you get past me, it'll be no problem with him."

"Thank you, Julie."

"You're welcome. I knew when I met you you'd be someone we need. Welcome aboard, Alex." Folder in hand, Julie leaves her office.

Step into a box, she says to herself. What does that mean? She snickers but covers her mouth when the office hallway bustles. Alex Long Girl-Gorilla. Or Gorilla-Girl? Maybe if I'm good at that I can be Snake-Girl. Or Girl-Snake. She flaps her arms and tweets. Bird-Girl. Maybe they'll let me operate a roller coaster. Or touch a tiger. She slumps in her chair and imagines a striped tent, a Ferris wheel, and a haunted house in the field behind Julie's office. A train of clown cars taxi her to the tent and its blood-red font: BEHOLD THE GORILLA-GIRL! A little person in a striped jacket and straw hat shouts through a megaphone, "Amazing Alex will astonish you with her primal power!" The crowd grows. On stage, Alex curtsies. The crowd grows silent as Alex stands there, her arms in a V, welcoming something yet to arrive. But she steps off the stage, out the tent, and into another field where an arcade sits near an ocean, and somewhere inside, shadows and light gallop after each other.

Julie pops her head in. "He's ready. Go on down."

She passes offices, the supply room, the break room. Employees work on computers or talk on phones inside cubicles with pictures—families, weddings, dogs, cats, a gerbil wearing a bowtie—quotes tacked on walls and doors, and clippings praising the company. At the end of the hall: a standalone office and a nameplate etched Chris Kopolski – COO. The baritone inside says, "Come in."

From his large desk, papers all around, he stands and shakes hands. "Chris Kopolski."

"Charlotte. I mean, Alex." She spins around and trips. "Lots of awards."

"That's right." He pulls a can from his mini-fridge.

She stops at one award framed as the centerpiece: the Circle of Excellence presented at the American Association of Fairs and Expositions. Next to that is a photo of Chris, Julie, and an older man cradling the award.

"I'm the proudest of this one. Only three other amusement companies have been awarded this. That's my grandfather Glen Kopolski."

"Kopolski." She blinks. "Like you."

"That's right." He looks over her bloodshot eyes.

"Totally forgot about that. He's dead now, right? Like, a long-time dead. Right?"

"Have a seat. Thanks for coming in. I know you got here later than scheduled." He cracks open the can. "I'm the taking-care-of-business guy. I like numbers. Numbers reflect employees and the company. I focus on making us profitable and efficient. Julie will be your supervisor, but I like to make sure we hire the best candidates." He swivels his computer screen. "This is the number that means the most to me. We have entertained millions over our years. Profits, expenses, employees…these are all necessary, but that number is all that matters. I don't believe in waste. Wasting time, personnel, or money. We cut anything that isn't up to snuff. Anything that's a poor return on investment." He opens the folder Julie had.

She rubs her pendant under her shirt. Pain in her back and ribs jab her.

"You said your name was Alex?"

"Yes."

"You came up in our background search as Charlotte."

"I go by my middle name."

He writes in her folder. "And it says here you're from Virginia?"

"I don't live there now. I have family there."

"But you don't live there now."

"Correct."

"Maybe that's why you were late today. Coming all that way."

She forces a chuckle.

"You must be in the area, or my HR department is doing one helluva job."

"You were at the job fair." She squirms. "I must have…" She leans over his desk. "That's my old résumé. It was a practice one I had…practiced with. I left it as is. Virginia. That's my fault."

"You gave us an oldie but goodie."

"Yeah." She squirms again.

"Why do you want to work here?"

"I think it would be great to work for a circus. Fun. A learning experience."

"Amusement company. We're not a circus."

"I'm talented." A headache drills her. "And curious. Responsible with many things."

He glances up and down her folder. "You've done all kinds of jobs. Most of them for a short time."

She grips her chair's arms to avoid crying.

He writes again in her folder. "Working in our shows division can be crazy. You have to know your lines. You have to have on the right costume. You have to practice so neither you nor your fellow performers are hurt."

"Julie and I already talked about that."

"Sometimes we'll do five venues in a row. They're demanding."

"No problem."

"What skills do you bring to our shows?"

"You can give me anything, and I'll make it happen."

"And you're comfortable on stage, memorizing lines, all that?"

"Yes."

"Julie wants you, and I don't like to get in the way of Julie. She has a great eye. She knows what works and what doesn't." He sets aside her folder. "Welcome to Kopolski. I'll have Devon handle details with you. And I'll see you at our season-launch meeting. Don't be late. Alex."

As she limps back to her car, she swears he wrote an asterisk in her folder. She takes a hit from the joint and stares at the rearview mirror until her eyes disappear behind smoke and pain.

7

Official-official she calls the email and its attachments sitting in her inbox: a welcome letter, forms to sign, a directory, schedules, maps, and a cartoon of a clown unicyclist and a tiger unfurling a banner that says WE CAN'T BRING ONE SMILE AT A TIME WITHOUT YOU, <u>ALEX</u>! SEE YOU SOON! She dances around her phone; the other coffeeshop patrons gawk at her. She calls her mother again.

"I got a new job. I'm going to be a performer for a traveling amusement company."

A faucet turns on in Janet's background.

"I start soon."

The faucet turns off.

"Mom? Are you there?"

"Is this a summer job?"

"No."

"For extra money?"

"It's a salary."

"Are you paying fees for something because your boyfriend can't?"

"I'm a full-time employee. I'll send you the link. If you want."

"What are you doing there?"

"I'll be a girl who turns into a gorilla."

"How does that happen?"

"I step into a box."

"Does your father know you joined a circus?"

She gazes around the packed coffeeshop: talking, playing board games, reading, working. "I'm telling you before him."

"Not that he would talk you out of it. Lots of criminals work in places like that. Rapists. Men will go after any woman. She doesn't have to be drunk or in a revealing dress. They don't have to be pretty."

"What's that mean?"

"It's not about looks."

"I'll be fine. I got a new job. They want me to work for them. And I get to get out of here."

Janet's garage door rattles open. "It all sounds exciting for you, Charlotte."

"I'm going by Alex when I'm there." She clears her table and motions to a couple her table is theirs if they want it.

"You'll be always Charlotte to me."

"Maybe I can come visit you when I'm on the road."

"Are you coming up here?"

"No, but I get time off. Like a real job."

"I'll let you know when you can visit."

"You can visit me, you know. Maybe see one of my shows."

"That would take me days to come down. A week. Tell your father I said hello. Bye, Charlotte. Hugs and kisses."

"Hugs and kisses, Mom."

. . .

When she pulls into the driveway, her father staggers turning toward her and unloading boxes from his trailer pulled into the front yard.

"What are you doing?"

"I bought these for you." He holds up the boxes. "And I cleaned out my trailer so we can load it and get you to your job."

"But I haven't told you if I got it."

Whiskey weighs down his mumble.

"I did get it."

"I knew you would." He hugs her. "I'm happy for you, Charlie Girl." He slaps his trailer. "I'll miss you, and…" He slumps. "But you got your room here if you ever need it."

She helps him up.

"I got this too for you." He pulls out an envelope from his truck. "Just in case."

"Have you eaten?"

"No."

"But you've had something to drink."

"You're leaving." He forces a smile.

"Let's warm up those leftovers from the other night and sit outside."

He pauses before the sunset. "Red sky at night…"

"Sailor's delight," she finishes.

"That means it's a good time to cast off."

"Let's get those boxes. You can help me pack."

"Just not your girly stuff."

She lets him go into his house first as when they moved here, and lightheaded after her first weeks at her new school, she sat on the edge of her bed. What's wrong with me? she wondered, crying. Putting on her pajama bottoms, she slipped, gashed her arm on her nightstand, and thumped onto the floor.

Clarence ran to her door.

"It's nothing." She crawled into her bed. "I can get a Band-Aid, and it'll be fine."

He stood in her doorway, his body blocking the light. "You OK?"

She ripped off her headphones and glared at him; the song buzzed. "I'm in my pajamas, Dad. Knock. Please."

"What's that?"

"It's Moby."

"*Moby Dick*?"

"A musician."

"So what's going on? The move? School? Girl stuff?"

"Dad…"

"I can get your mom on the phone, if that would help. But she'll probably tell you to drink this or that. Something that looks like a weed out there in the yard and to stick it out until your time of the month is over."

"Dad, please! It's a lot of stuff, OK?"

"I thought we'd been doing pretty good since we got here."

"It'll go away."

"Things have slowed down for the rest of the week at work. I would take you to the doctor, but you should drive yourself." He flung car keys on her bed. "Happy birthday. I know I'm late with it. Months late. And I know it's no ocean."

"You keep saying that. Every time. You don't have to."

"I thought maybe you being sick and all was me missing your birthday this year. Or the move. I told you your present was on its way. I had to get money after we moved."

"You always do." She pushed her door close.

"I got my own too. Another used one. Looks like yours."

"Great. We have the same car."

"I could switch it while you're at school, and no one would know."

"Bye, Dad."

"I hope you feel better, Charlie."

She closed her door and wished for a lock on it. She grabbed her notebook and pen and slid under her covers and imagined her mother was right. She would come home one day from school and her father's car would be on concrete blocks in the front yard—her father waxing it or changing the oil, engine parts scattered about; smoking and shirtless, farmer's tan; drinking a beer; whistling "Dixie." She wrote a poem.

> Fire in an Open Palm
>
> the euphoria
> of not knowing
> where I'll wake
> when all
> the angels
> have passed
> over me
> like clouds
> so quietly
> I must say it
> in a whisper
> so you listen
> to me

She thinks of this as she sets the table and her father washes up and promises he's done drinking for the night. "I'll miss you, but I'm happy for you." He whistles a jig that a calliope would play.

After he leaves for bed, she opens the envelope he gave her: a card with a mirror on the front and inside the phrase You're Looking at Success!

Charlie Girl,

I'm proud of you, and I will see you bright and early on the day of your move with my truck, trailer, and muscles all lined up for you. And to get you going on your new chapter in life…

She unfolds the check he put inside and sniffles at the amount.

P.S. I can get used to "Alex." But give me time.

8

She follows Julie through the field outside the offices and toward storage units and rooms with two-headed pigs floating in jars, carnivores stuffed and mounted, snake handlers, horse wranglers, tractors and chainsaws rumbling, musicians warming up, and in the largest room, stilt walkers hoisting themselves. They walk down a hall and arrive at an interior room with two men, tables, instruments, bins, and a sign THE AMAZING DR. MANDRAKE AND SALINA THE GORILLA-GIRL. And looming in the corner: a matte-black box like a telephone booth but with a single pane of glass on the front.

Julie walks up to the slim man arranging papers. "Don, this is Alex Long, our new Gorilla-Girl. Alex, meet Donald Haskett. He plays Dr. Mandrake."

He bows and, in an over-affected English accent, says, "The Ah-ma-zing Dr. Theodore Henry Mandrake, professor of anthropology, holder of three PhDs, speaker of fourteen languages, world-traveler, and collector of the odd, the curious, and the demented. A pleasure, my lady."

Alex curtsies. "The pleasure is all mine." She locks eyes with Don until he rises—shorter and skinnier than her; liver-colored spots under wisps of white hair; his voice booming above his stature. "I like your accent."

"I watched a lot of PBS to get it right."

Across the room, the other man, kneeling and unwrapping plastic, clears his throat.

"And thanks to Petey over there." Don's real accent drawls out from Mandrake's.

"Your mustache is cool too." She nods at his handlebar.

"Aren't you a peach? The last girl was a snob. Pete and I were never up to her standards. But she had no room to talk. She was horrible to work with. Always showing up late. Never listened to cues. Inappropriate behavior. Put an embarrassment on us all."

"Alex will be a good fit for you and us," Julie says. "Fresh start for everyone. I've got to run."

Pete rolls up plastic and stuffs the head of a gorilla mask under his arm. "Peter Arrojas. But you're welcome to call me Pete." He adjusts his ponytail; the rest of his jet-black hair falls into a mullet. "Did Julie tell you about the act?"

"She said I'd be an assistant for the two of you and I need to know when to be seen and when not. And I change into the gorilla."

"Pretty close."

"Julie's doing her job."

"Better than Chris."

"Easy, Petey."

"She also said I needed to be able to scream. A lot."

"Now that's true." Don fogs and wipes his glasses. "We go on about every four hours so you've got to keep your scream in tip-top shape."

"Lemon and honey."

"And you can never talk to us. Never ever. Under any circumstances." Pete waits until Alex catches on he's teasing.

She picks up the gorilla head. "Do I wear this?"

"I do. I become you. You become me."

"You are Salina," Don joins in with his English accent. "An Amazon princess on the surface, but underneath you harbor a dark ssssecret."

"I'm a gorilla."

"Julie does hire the best."

"But I'm the literal guy in the gorilla suit," Pete says. "And wait for it. It gets better. The Mexicano in the gorilla suit. Do you know about the trick?"

The three of them move toward the box.

"It's called Pepper's Ghost. Only we don't have a ghost. We have a gorilla. It's an old theater trick."

The box chills her. The edges smudge her reflection, but her image superimposes Don and Pete's.

"That's where the magic happens. You step in. Don closes the door. The audience waits. House lights go out. Don does his thing. You have a convulsion. Then poof! I take over."

"Poof? Like smoke?"

"No smoke. Lights. Like turning off a light in one room then on in another. Slowly." Pete opens the door. "If you look inside, you can see this space where I wait until the light makes me appear."

"I'm the reflection, but you're real."

"You're off in this secret side. You have to disappear in order for me to appear. The light above you slowly goes away. The light above me comes on at the same time."

"The audience watches me get into this?"

"Yep."

"And I have to scream?"

"It hurts to become a raging beast."

"I play it cool at first, like a gentle giant, then something snaps." Pete's chest spreads. "And I go bonkers."

"What about you?" she asks Don.

"I brought this all upon us. So I must face the Fates and die for my hubris. The Gorilla-Girl goes berserk and kills me before lunging into the audience."

"Is there blood?"

"I have this under my collar." Don opens up a bin and pulls out a dark-red capsule. "After Petey strikes me, I squeeze this." He places the capsule near his jugular.

"We like to change it up. Sometimes we can get it so the blood squirts out like a fountain if I keep my mitts on him. Sometimes I bite him, and Don will give it a good pump. And sometimes we each have a capsule. I squeeze one after I rip his throat. Then Don will get his going. It's great with the strobe light on us."

She sloshes one of the capsules in the room's light.

"Try one."

She squeezes it—like a bag popping. Thick red trickles between her fingers and over her wrist. Don pumps her hand until the fake blood arcs onto the floor. Pete grunts and lumbers about the room.

"I see you're back in the groove." Chris side-steps the drops.

Don wipes off. "We're getting ready."

"Same program as last year and the one before that?"

"And the year before that." Pete straightens. "And the year before that. And the year before that."

Chris scans the room and lands on Alex. "Your first day, and you're drawing blood from us."

Alex grips the capsule; more drips fall.

"Are you doing anything else, or is this it?"

"We'll definitely practice after we get our gear out and set up." Don moves boxes. "And after the meeting."

"Don't let me keep you." Chris slicks his hair and resets his hat before stopping in other rooms and buying something from a vending machine near the motor pool, motorcycles, and sequined riders.

Alex asks, "Is he watching us?"

"Ignore him, that s.o.b." Pete tosses aside a towel. "He's all about the bottom line."

Don shuffles papers. "Julie's not. She wants the best out of everyone. Chris looks at everything as either a moneymaker or a money-suck. He cut a family of stunt dogs. The Warshes."

"No." Pete snaps his fingers. "The Welshes. The Welsh Wonder Dogs."

"That's it."

"They had this RV and an SUV, and they would meet us at venues."

"John. Kay. I forget the kids."

"Brandon and Breanna."

"One of the dogs was Rex. Sheep dogs."

"They also had side gigs. Televisions shows. Pet shows. Chris couldn't stand paying them what he was and watch them do their act outside the company. He found out they were using the Kopolski brand and connections to pump their show."

Alex stacks a bin. "What did he do?"

"He got the lawyers to threaten a lawsuit against them. They backed down, but he then upped their vendor fees and made them sign a new contract. He drained them dry and put them at his mercy to keep performing. They left, but they had to buy themselves out. He did it all legally and financially."

"They were a nice family," Don adds. "It was sad when they went away. I had lunch with them, played with the dogs, and Gloria and I were invited for Thanksgiving one year. Chris was brutal. But he had the backing of his family and the company that gave us a lifeline."

"What about Julie?"

"She defended them. Brought out the numbers to show they were a popular act and it was family friendly. But Chris said they cost too much and training someone in-house to do that act was cheaper."

"Is that what happened?"

"Yep." Pete pulls out a bag with the rest of his gorilla costume. "They told younger trainers and Julie to make up a dog show. She spent the rest of the season sketching, tracking down costumes, music, space. She pulled it off."

"She always does." Don checks the time. "We should get to the launch meeting."

"I'll get the lights," Alex says. After Don and Pete exit, she slides over to the box. The room's white roof and walls and the outside light coming in trough transoms backlight the box like a skyscraper. She blinks after believing it pulls her across the floor, closer to its surface, and grows taller and wider.

"Alex, you coming?" Pete asks.

"I was checking it out up close."

"It'll be here when we get back."

• • •

They head toward the field, warehouses behind it, the parking lots, and the administration building. Workers load and unload semis, warehouses, and storage sheds, moving structures, extension cords, generators, crates, lights, girders, backdrops, ropes, chains, speakers, microphones, cages. As Alex and Pete approach the building attached to the offices, Don stands near donuts, drinks, and cups. Chairs unfolding and skidded into rows echo inside where the light tints everything beige. Chris fiddles with a slideshow remote and a microphone. Julie chats with two little people and a purple-haired woman. Don finds seats near the middle of the room. Alex checks out her coworkers: different shapes and sizes and ages remind her the website said generations of families work for the company. A grandfather-looking man rests one of his boots in a chair; he tips back his cowboy hat with large feathers tucked in a blue bandana wrapped around the band; his turquoise necklace glistens. Alex touches her pendant.

Don asks, "Whatcha looking at?"

"That man over there."

"Luis Quesada. He's been here as long as I have."

"Longer."

"How do you know, Petey?"

"He's Latino. We know everyone." He winks. "He started here when he was thirteen. Barely spoke English. The company was in Texas that year, and he kept showing up at each stop along the way. He hitched his way on the back of one of the trailers. He told them he knew how to wrangle. They gave him a job. He was head wrangler for decades. Now he's emeritus. Big award they gave him. That was my first year here. All of his family members work here. Cooks. Wranglers. Maintenance. Eight children and fifteen grandchildren. And they're all here." Pete sips his orange juice. "Chris tried to ditch him because he was, in Chris's opinion, going to suck the pension account dry. Back when this place was going to piss and everyone was threatening with walkouts and lawsuits, Luis calmed everybody down and brought management and workers to the table."

"He's a good man," Don says.

Pete lowers his voice. "Special K is on stage."

"Showtime." Don slides his plate under his chair.

Chris clicks on his microphone. "Gang, I think we're ready to begin."

The crowd silences. Julie sits next to Chris.

"Another season is here. Can you believe it? And I can't wait until we're on the road."

The crowd cheers and hollers.

"We've got another fantastic lineup, thanks to everyone in this room. We've got plenty to discuss. Scheduling, performances, new policies. Let's get to it. Are you ready?"

As cheers and hollers swell, Chris clicks through bulleted lists and plows on with a sermon about expectations and the company's mission and values; new or revised policies; food allowances and per diems; healthcare; overtime; and the new discount-tickets system. He's greasy when he finishes. Not sweaty from nerves Alex notices—greasy.

Chris resets his ball cap. "Now for the good stuff."

The slide flicks: Schedule of Fairs and Events.

"We are weeks away from hitting the road. We should be working hard to tighten our shows, rides, food, everything." He highlights venues, dates, demographics. "And all of this is thanks to our partners at Avé Asset Management."

Pete and Don duck down and gag.

"For the first time in our history, again thanks to Avé, we'll be partnering with restaurants and brewers at select venues, which will be a win-win for us, them, and our guests who love those things from their area. We're promoting we're one of a handful of amusement companies with EPA-approved generators. We are again setting a new standard for the industry. Ron and his team have installed energy-saving lights on many of our rides. We've come a long way since the days of refrigerated train cars and gas-powered generators. It'll be truly unique and groundbreaking, but hey, we're all Kopolskis."

The crowd cheers.

"Let me pass this off to Julie."

Julie takes the microphone from Chris, steadies on her chair, and waddles to the front of the stage.

Alex beams with Don and Pete who whispers, "She's our Main Street against his Wall Street."

"I don't have a whole lot to add because we all know our team is great," Julie says. "And I can't wait to see the amazing talents we'll put on day after day, night after night, stop after stop." She holds up a piece of paper. "This is an email I got from *Showtime* magazine. We're shortlisted for Best Sideshows."

The crowd claps.

"Teddy and Madeline and their crew in acrobatics have wowed the audiences again with their stunts. Everyone involved with that, stand up for us, please."

A thin man and woman rise from the middle of the room; twelve others stand with them—all short and lean.

"The Flying Isgriggs, everyone. And we've rebranded our sideshows, giving them a more old-fashioned feel." Julie clicks a slide: Victorian-era fonts; vintage circus posters; clowns; a strongman; the Matsumoto Samurai Warriors; the Great Zorbak; Drew the Illustrated Man; the Automated Future. "What a great job."

Don taps Alex and nods at the next slide. A scientist-looking man shields himself from a gorilla bursting through a ghostly image of a woman; the audience before them scrambles from a laboratory.

Behold The Gorilla-Girl!
~You Have Been Warned~

Alex blushes. Pete scrunches into a gorilla face that causes her to laugh.

"That's our new Gorilla-Girl back there. See how ferocious she is?"

The crowd turns toward her.

"Let's hear it one more time for this season." Julie lowers the mic and claps with the crowd.

Pete cheers and claps. Don whistles. Alex hoots—the crowd is noisier than with Chris; their energy charges through Alex.

"Petey and I are grabbing lunch. Would you like to come with us?"

"I'll take a raincheck. But thanks."

"After that he needs to run to the post office, and I need to cross off things before we practice. See you at the room this afternoon."

"See you then." She strides toward the stage. "Hi, Chris."

"Hi…Charlotte?"

"Alex."

He leans against the stage. "Your first day is now official. The start of the new season is among my favorites. I remember sitting in the grass and my father or uncle telling everyone how much fun we were going to bring to our guests."

"I wanted to say thanks for letting me be here. I'm looking forward to traveling to all these places."

"Glad to hear that. But you're not going to all of them. Not all the venues require the whole company."

"I thought I'd always be traveling."

"It depends on the venue. You're also brand new with us. You'll probably hit about three-quarters of these stops. And we have to respect what these places want. Some of them don't want sideshows. It's still the Bible Belt."

"What am I supposed to do when I don't go?"

"Relax. Read. Eat. Lounge by the pool. Go home and kick your feet up. Was it Virginia?"

A woman hands papers to Chris.

Alex scans the room and crowds, but Julie leaves the warehouse and, cradling folders, walks with two employees toward offices. The warehouse doors creak open. Engines start in the distance. Workers take down the stage. The crowds break up and file out—all of them familiar with each other and briefly with her.

. . .

She buys food and a water from the cafeteria and walks to her car where she reads the script, scribbles notes, highlights passages. She pulls out a notebook she bought with part of her father's check and, marking the day and time, writes.

Focus on this new part of your life. Ignore him. Stick with Julie, Pete, Don. You are doing this your way. You are part of a circus. Even if you don't travel to all of those places, you will travel. You get to be the Gorilla-Girl.

She gets into her car and digs out the pot she took from Brian; she scours the parking lot and, in the distance, the practice areas—no Don or Pete—then the offices—no Julie or Chris. "How's my first official day so far?" She blows smoke toward Chris's office. "I'll be seeing you on the road. And I'll be seeing the ghosts of all your family members who walk the earth because you've embarrassed them."

A security car pulls onto the road. The car slows in front of a vehicle down from Alex before stopping at hers. She snuffs her joint.

"Are you an employee or a visitor?"

"Employee," she answers the guard.

"Do you have your permit?"

"It's my first day."

"You need to get it."

"I will."

"Name?"

"Alex Long."

He jots in his notebook. "Your division?"

"Shows. I'm a performer."

"Julie Herndon's group?"

"Yes."

"There's no smoking of any kind on the premises."

"Please don't file anything. I'll get my permit. I promise. It's my first day."

"Get it from the front desk. Ask for D'neese. I'll give you until the end of the week. Otherwise, I'll tow you."

"What's your name?"

"Sherman."

"It's nice to meet you. I'm Alex."

"I know." He waggles his notebook.

• • •

Show them you got a lil' gumption in you and get there first, she rallies herself, trotting toward the practice room. But as she rounds the corner, the door is unlocked, and Don sits behind the desk, his feet atop, drinking coffee and flipping through a magazine.

He peers over his glasses. "Hey there, Alex."

"You beat me here."

"I'm catching up on an article." He slides a company-branded mug her way. "I got that for you. Help yourself." He toasts her with his stained and chipped mug.

She pours a hot cup from his thermos. "What are you reading?"

"The Salem witch trials. They were nuts."

"Especially if you were an outsider, poor, mentally ill, or a woman. There are these theories, too, about how it was about gender, wealth, and land. Not so much about religion. But religion may have been a tool to get things done. There's this theory about infected rye bread that may have caused hallucinations."

"I was just reading about ergotism in the rye before you came in." He flips back a page. "'A fungus naturally found in LSD.'"

"They never executed the slave who was the first accused, but they executed a dog."

"I'm impressed. How do you know all this?"

"I related to it. Plus I like things that go bump in the night."

"I'm glad you know real history." He stretches and fumbles a container.

She helps him open the lid. "Like the American Dream is a myth?"

"Pretty much." He pulls out rolls of tape. "Religion and social control make funny bed partners. Grab that tape measure." He unfolds a tattered floor plan penciled on graph paper showing stage, audience, props, actors. "I grew up in a Methodist house." He counts off space, starting from the desk. "I lost all that when I got to school and could think on my own." He measures twice. "Something greater than us exists. But is it personal? I don't know. Is it a watchmaker? I don't know. Is it creative? In a sense. Is it judge, jury, executioner? I sure hope not." He asks her to make four L-shapes using the tape.

"Where'd you go to school?"

"Georgia Tech. I was there during the Sixties and the Civil Rights movement."

Alex marks off the invisible stage's edges.

"I didn't blow up anything, but I was anti-establishment. Vocal about it all. Protests and marches here and there. But not so much now."

"You sold out."

"Yep." He measures from the table to the Pepper's Ghost box.

"You sound like my mom. My dad is the opposite. Still is."

"Where'd you go to school?"

"The School of Nowhere." She keeps her head down but glances at Don who doesn't press.

He tells her to mark the rear of the stage. "Petey should be here soon, and we can move the box. And practice." He dusts off a CD. "Load this and set it in front of us."

An organ pumps out a slow, heavy, melancholy tune. Grinning, his eyebrows bobbing with the beat, Don gestures while the voiceover speaks.

> Ladies and gentlemen, take your seats, for you are about to experience firsthand the mystery of evolution and the powers of science. Witness Princess Salina the Gorilla-Girl. On the surface she's an innocent young woman, but underneath lies her horrid secret. Take your seats, please. The show is about to begin.

He steps back. "Volume is good for us to practice with. When we do this we'll have speakers. You should have seen Chris when we asked for more money for speakers. We used to have two on stage, but they weren't enough. We were missing cues. Or the audience wasn't hearing the soundtrack and our microphones. Hey, Petey."

"Don. Hey, Alex."

"Hi."

"Nice." Pete checks the marked-off areas. "You two set up the stage."

"Alex was a big help."

"Let me get a cup of coffee, and we'll get to it."

"Are you going to wear the costume?" she asks.

"Not on these first few runs." He tops off his mug with Shakespeare on it. "Home roast, Don?"

"Yep. Gloria got me a new drum roaster. This thing looks like an I-tal-ian sports car. Good news is I can see the beans for the first time with this window it has. And it's quieter. The dog cowered when that previous one went off." He raises his cup to Pete. "Enjoy, mi amigo."

Pete toasts Don and Alex. "Let's get our scripts."

"I looked at mine over lunch," Alex says. "Started memorizing lines."

"The last girl didn't do that."

"Excellent."

"And I have notes."

Don crosses his arms.

"Small stuff. We can talk about them when they come up."

The intro begins again and finishes amid bubbles and blips.

Don waits before coming onstage; he opens a briefcase on the desk and pulls out papers. He says in his English accent, "Ladies and gentlemen, boys and girls, welcome to my la-bor-atory. Thank you for coming. What you are about to witness is what many in society would consider reckless. Science gone mad. A complete disregard for safety and the Natural Order." He picks up one of the papers. "But I'm here to tell you what you'll see is Nature itself. Raw, unbridled evolution, red in teeth and claws. A reminder of what we have, always lurking within us." He points to Alex and tells her to stand on the X he taped; she obliges. "This young lady Salina is not who she says she is. On the surface she is a charming, beautiful princess, but underneath she harbors a dark, dark secret."

A cello increases.

"I found her deep in the Amazon."

Alex bursts out laughing. Both men stop; Don glares at her.

"This is one of the things I want to talk to you about. It's different hearing it in person. Plus I'm not Amazonian."

"No one here is," Don says. "But that's part of the fun. It's role play."

"I know, but…"

"Roll with us, Alex," Pete says. "Let's get through this at least once then we can talk."

Don puffs his chest. "Deep in the Amazon I was working on my third PhD at the time, studying lost civilizations and rituals, when I came upon a rumor of a Gorilla-Girl. I thought surely the locals meant a female gorilla. 'No, no,' I was told by the great village elder Bumbinko…"

Alex laughs again. "Bumbinko. Yeah, so…"

Pete shrugs at Don.

"That's something else. It ties in with the Amazon thing. What if we change that?"

Pete says, "How about 'told by my guide'?"

"Sounds better. Don?"

"OK," Don grumbles. "I was told by my guide it was a girl who transforms into a gorilla." Don steps to Alex. "I found her in a village one rainy day looking at my boat, books, and reading glasses. She reached for them, and I stopped her. It was then, my friends, I saw her true nature, for she became agitated and became a raging, snarling gorilla." Don motions *That's your cue.*

Improvising on the spot, Alex flutters her lashes.

"Fortunately, I had a serum with me that made her sleepy. I gave it to her. She drank it and fell asleep." Don swirls blue liquid in a glass bottle. "I knew then and there I had to study her. She has helped me understand our animalistic drives, and I have helped her become a member of society. But now…" He paces. "I shall show the beast within with the help of my serum. What do you say?"

Pete and Alex mime being the audience. "Yes!"

"Very well. Salina! Drink half and please enter the box."

Alex drinks and, recalling the script, waits until Don grabs the key to the box. She turns toward the audience and, making sure Dr. Mandrake does not see her, spits out the blue liquid. A nasty smile cuts across her as she curtsies.

Pete claps. "Yes, Alex! Very nice."

She feigns weakness and staggers for the box. Don unlocks it and helps her in.

"This box is made of the strongest metal known to man. Completely impenetrable to a tired Gorilla-Girl. It will allow us to observe Salina's natural state without risking our lives." Don switches back to his drawl. "At this point you're in the box, our effects guy would take care of the lights, Pete shows up, and, poof, magic. Pepper's Ghost."

"Can we do that now?"

"Let's stick through this part of the show until we're in sync."

She thumbs through her script. "I can see where this can go. But we need to alter the story."

Don and Pete glance at each other.

"It's convoluted and asks a lot of the audience to suspend their disbelief. We don't have to cut it all. Change her name. The Amazon thing. And you had your serum on you?"

"How else do I calm you? That's part of the joke and why Petey breaks out."

"Maybe that doesn't matter. Maybe she isn't from the Amazon. Maybe she's Dr. Mandrake's daughter and has this condition. She's born with it. He's a scientist. He wants to study why she's this way. But he's passed a flaw to her. And he wants to protect her from society because society would never accept her. He understands her."

"That sounds like a lot of movies and TV shows," Pete says.

"That's not who we are, Alex. We're our own thing. And we like it that way."

Alex presses, "We should be our own thing. But society and companies want to alter humans. Like we're broken and an experiment for them. And if things go wrong, who'll pay for it?"

"Never us."

"Never the little guy."

"Exactly. We could tap into something. And why does she have to be exotic? Look at me. I'm plain and very American. No one in the media would talk about me unless I was barefoot, pregnant, and without a college degree. Or someone like me votes for 'the wrong candidate.' Someone out there coming to this will relate. We can keep the shock and fun. A girl turning into a gorilla is something to see at a place like this."

"What's her name?" asks Don.

Alex looks around the room, out the door, into fields where a breeze sways flowers. "Daisy."

Pete stomps his feet. "I like it."

Don crosses his arms.

"She could be an average girl on the surface but have this condition. Or talent. Depending how you look at it."

"Maybe Mandrake helps her channel it," Pete suggests. "Control it. Maybe he's the reason why his daughter is the way she is. Genetics. Inherited traits."

"These changes won't take away from your stage presence or the nature of the show." Alex scribbles. "What is it, Don?"

"Nothing. Let's carry on. Let's go with the father-daughter thing for now." He returns to Dr. Mandrake. "Now, I shall ask lovely Daisy to step into the box."

She grins.

"And now I shall hypnotize her. Daisy, fall asleep. Feel very relaxed. Imagine going back in time, far back in time. Gorilla, gorilla, gorilla. Come out, come out." He turns toward the pretend audience. "No need to fear. I have complete control over this. But this show is not for the timid or weak of heart. If you feel unable to experience what you are about to see, I beg you to please leave now."

Giggling, Pete scampers off.

"Everything is fine as long as she remains in the box."

. . .

"Great practice today." Pete claps. "Lots of changes. But we'll get them. That's what we do."

"Yeah. We do." Alex rolls back her shoulders as she stocks bins.

"I'll get there." Don keeps his back turned as he checks off props. "I came up with this long before either of you had shown up. I got laid off from a job and decided one night to write. I expected nothing to come of it. I had an itch and told Gloria I wanted to scratch it. I felt like a kid again sitting at that typewriter. It was a complete antithesis to that job. I thought it was perfect circus material, taking me back to my childhood."

"It is," Alex says.

Don examines his lab coat. "I recorded my voice. I helped Julie hire Pete, and he added technical elements. He helped me build a better box. He suggested a light and sound operator and timing the dialogue with music."

"I wanted to contribute to something theatrical." Pete unzips his bag and pulls out a bottle of ale. "Until this, I'd been working on stage and had small roles in movies. Cheers. And to Alex for coming onboard."

She tips back the bottle and hands it to Don. "This is going to be an awesome show."

Don swigs. "We'll have to tell Julie about our changes."

"Do you think it'll be a problem?"

"No. She wants us to be creative and own our shows. Within reason. And budget. But what we're changing isn't drastic."

Pete smirks. "Special K will have to pony up the money to change them."

"We'll make his day once more."

"We'll have to put on a good show." Alex focuses on them then the box.

"In the early days we'd switch roles. But Petey is the better gorilla. I don't have the physicality he does."

"It's fun playing him. There's not a whole lot of motivation to a raging, confused beast."

"But you add depth, Petey. He studied the movements of gorillas."

"They build up slowly." Pete hunches his back; his knuckles graze the ground. "It's uncertain when they'll strike."

"And pompous scientist I am, I brush it off, offer my hand, trusting the gorilla. Who is now my daughter."

"The first time we did that, after I studied gorillas, Stacy, our Salina at the time, freaked out."

"But she had it coming to her."

"That she did."

"When we were on tour Julie told us she had feedback from our audiences about the lifelike gorilla," Don says. "Negative and positive."

"And I was auditioning for other roles at the time," Pete says. "So, I was, like, That's great, good for us and the company, give me my paycheck, but pretty soon I can't tour with you because I'll be in New York or L.A. But the years passed."

"Do you still audition?" Alex asks.

"If there's a chance."

"Maybe we can make the show more immersive for the audience," she says. "Spray water in the dark when Pete attacks."

"They'll think it's blood."

"Exactly."

"This is why we hired you." Don tears out a page from his magazine and scribbles. "More strobe lights. Maybe those poppers in spots on the stage. Posters and media. Name change to Daisy. Water in audience. Anything else?"

"That's it for now."

"I'll type up something for Julie. She'll be fine with this. We still have pull. We should burn a new soundtrack."

"Alex should be the voice."

"Me?"

"You are the Gorilla-Girl."

"I like it," Pete says. "The room is dark. Something like 'You are now about to experience the most amazing metamorphosis ever. What you are about to experience is true.'"

"Scientifically true," Alex adds.

Don check his watch. "It's after five, and Chris is done paying us overtime."

"Yeah, I should get going." Pete gathers his things. "It's my weekend for Cecelia. Her mom took her bra shopping the other day."

"My dad did that with me," Alex says. "He said he'd be around the corner. 'Just in case.'"

"I will too. Goodnight."

Don packs up his thermos and magazine. "He's a good father. I have two sons from a previous marriage and a daughter from Gloria's."

"I'd like to meet them."

"You will at the cookout." He heads for the door. "And then it's the Jefferson County Fair."

"I hope I can go."

"Why wouldn't you?"

"Chris told me my tour is restricted. Because I'm new. And it depends on the area."

"He always does this. It's never Julie."

"But no matter where I am, I don't want to simply be standing on the stage."

Don hums. "You want to bring a spark to the role. A life to it."

"Yeah."

"Like you're living it. Even it's make-believe."

"Exactly."

. . .

Her door closes behind her, and she tosses her keys on a table, unpacks groceries, and flops on her futon. Holding up her phone, she considers calling Brian and showing him her place. "Check out my efficiency. Like back in college. And after that. For years. Until I met you." She dials her mother instead, and as she anticipates voicemail, she rambles about "like my first week at school when Dad and I moved, and I called to tell you how miserable it was and at the same time excited because no one knew me, and I could be anyone I wanted to but couldn't because..."

"Charlotte, who are you talking to?"

"Mom, you answered."

"I just got back."

"Me too. It was my first day at my new job."

"How was it?"

"I met a lot of people, went to my first staff meeting, and had my first rehearsal."

"That's a lot for a circus. What's next?"

"Hit the road."

"Where?"

She clenches. "I'm not going to every stop."

"Did you fail their drug test?"

"No. You might appreciate this. There are still areas that don't welcome shows like mine to their towns."

"A little tight in the Bible Belt?"

"Yes."

"Why do you think I ended back up here?"

"You were here when you were with Dad."

"What can women like me say that hasn't been said or done?"

"Anyway… It was a good day for me. I gave the two guys I work with my ideas, and we're gonna tweak our show. Don and Pete are their names. I'm looking forward to it."

"In the approved town."

"And when I'm not in one maybe I'll come see you."

"It can't be this week. I'll be in Santa Barbara. One of the wineries is hosting a mindfulness retreat. I haven't been since I've been with Ted. His mother is going into Alzheimer's care, and he's helping with that."

"And you're not."

"Why would I?"

She turns on her hotplate and plugs in the microwave she bought with her father's check. "I need to go and make dinner."

"Night, Charlotte."

She moves books from a box onto shelves and on top sets one framed picture: a collage of the photos her father gave her, a trail covered in autumn leaves, and her father with his mandolin. She tastes the soup but slides the bowl aside.

Clarence answers his phone. "Charlie Girl. I was going to call you this weekend and see how it all went for you this week."

"I have a party to go to this weekend."

"Do you now?"

"It's with my work. But today was my first day."

"And?"

"Good spots and bad."

"Why's that?"

"I may not be going to every stop."

"Show 'em you need to be at every stop. Smash bananas on their windows. Grunt. Poop on something if you need to."

"You sound tired."

"Ah... Long day."

"Because you've been drinking?"

"I've had one beer."

"More lined up?"

"Not beer. Hey...let's go back to the start. Pretend calling me."

"Really?"

"Just do it."

"Ring. Ring. Pick up the phone, Dad. You can't be that drunk yet."

"Hiya, Alex. I meant to call you Alex earlier. How was your first day at work, Alex? Did your boss end up being a jerk like mine?"

"Goodnight, Dad."

"I'm glad you got out there to your new job when you did. And every day after."

9

The Marcuso cousins tell Alex about a young, pimple-faced Chris dropping crates of light bulbs off a lift.

Vince sips his cocktail. "He had no clue what he was doing. Glass everywhere."

"This was when we had the animals nearby. Too close," Manny adds. "The horses freaked out."

"Those poor things," Alex says.

"My wife at one point asked our insurance company to up the coverage on me. Her next step was picking out a casket and plot for me earlier than I'd planned. She wore down her rosary."

"We were willing to pay him not to show up. We were willing to borrow our year-end bonuses from ourselves and give them to him to sit in the office while we worked."

"This was when they still did bonuses."

"Not anymore?"

Vince demurs at Alex.

"We were about… What do you think, Vince, one week away from saying something to his dad?"

"More like by lunch the next day."

"But now look at him."

They turn toward Chris in a company-branded ball cap and Hawaiian-print shirt and standing next to his wife as their kids run around them on the back deck under a string of lights.

"Pays to be family."

Vince leans in. "Yeah, but they don't have that much anymore. That company owns the bulk now."

"Maybe they'll reinstate bonuses."

The cousins guffaw at Alex.

"I looked them up," Vince says. "They pump and dump. They took out Coleman and Sons. They're older than us. And national." He walks to the grills and jokes with Don.

"Do you smoke?" she whispers to Manny. "I smelled it. It's cool."

"Yeah."

"You got stuff?"

"Not here."

"Whenever I need some?"

"I got you. Yeah. But never around them." He nods at Chris and the execs. "Not even a whiff on your clothes." He raises his beer at her and heads over to his wife and kids talking with other employees.

Julie strolls over, and when Alex sees her vest—smiling suns, birds, rainbows stitched on it—she thinks she's a grade-school teacher without a classroom.

"I've been reviewing changes for the season. Including yours. Those are big changes."

"Too big?"

"Not at all. I'm glad to see you bringing fresh ideas. It's overdue. Don and Pete have worked hard over the years to get it stable, and I think they built a box around themselves."

"Don wasn't receptive at first, but we talked, and he softened."

"That's Don."

"It's not too late, is it?"

"For some of us. But we'll make it work."

"Chris?"

"Among others." Julie drinks her wine. "I've heard good things about you from Don and Pete."

"Good." She downs her beer. "I want to talk to you about something."

"Sure. Hold on." Julie receives a plate from a robust man in khakis and a plaid shirt. "This is my husband, Gary."

He stammers telling Alex he's pleased to meet her and, his one leg flopping every step he takes, rejoins a group of men.

"All of them have been with the company for decades. Honorable men. I'm thankful for them all. What do you want to talk about?"

"Chris told me I won't be traveling to every stop."

Julie sighs at Chris who lifts his youngest child onto his shoulders. "I'll talk to him about that." She leans closer—alcohol on her breath. "He didn't agree with me about you, but I knew you were a good choice."

"I don't want…"

"He gets out of bounds. He misunderstood you when he met you. But it was the first time for you and him. Being nervous is expected."

"Yeah."

"He's heard things through the grapevine about the show. That doesn't mean he's unhappy. Once the season gets under way, he'll focus on other things. I'll say something. He needs to hear it from me." She tosses away her wine. "I'm going to make the rounds. Good to see you, Alex. We're going to have an awesome season."

Alex wanders to the edge of Don's property where trees fill a slope leading to a stream. The strings of lights warm the deck, house, and people eating, drinking, talking, but the sunset backlights it all, and Alex imagines Brian lasting one minute here and her father chatting up everyone. Maybe Don will get so drunk he'll grill in his boxers, sandals, and Gold Toe socks, she muses. Maybe Pete will take a swing at Chris. "Go ape-shit." She snickers. Maybe after more wine Julie will unbutton her vest and squeeze out. She looks up. Maybe a police helicopter will fly over because neighbors complained about noise and the smell of pot and strobe lights and fights. She rubs her pendant and walks toward Don.

"Alex, I want you to meet my wife Gloria."

Bracelets clanging, dyed-black hair down to her waist, she kisses Alex's cheek. "You're lovely, dear. Thank you for coming. Don talks and talks about you."

"What do you like on your burger, Alex?"

"Ketchup and mustard."

"Nope. Won't do. Around here, we're all about flavor. Right, Glor?"

"Don loves showing off his cooking skills. But when we first met he could only unthaw frozen pizza."

"Add a little red-pepper flake and parm, and boy, you're set." Flames jump under Don's cleft chin.

"He's become a culinary wizard. He'll take over cooking duties sometimes on the road."

"I make some mean blueberry waffles. Might have to whip those out soon. Go to the farmers' market wherever we've stopped and get fresh blueberries."

"You'll have fun. Pete's a great guy. A little odd, but who isn't when working for this place. You have to be. I used to tell people all the time Don and I first met at school. Which is true. I was his student in Intro to Computing. I was nineteen. He was sixty."

"I was thirty-two."

Gloria splashes vodka in a glass, squeezes a lemon, and helps Don organize food. "I don't come from a good background. My mother raised me when she could between jobs. My father was a sailor and never around. Very New England. Very dry. Very much about restraint and appearances even if there was no money.

Which there never was. But manners were expected from everyone." She grips Alex's arms. "Who cares what people think? It's your life. Live it the way you want. I mean, for God's sake, you probably don't have an Ivy League degree if you're working here. Do you own your skin? Or is it borrowed?"

Don slides Alex's burger off the grill. "What do you think?"

"Damn, Don."

"It's the herbs, isn't it?"

"Dr. Mandrake would be pleased."

He chimes his utensils.

Chris sets down his daughter and walks over. "Great party as usual, Don. Thank you, too, Gloria. Always a gracious hostess."

"Well, Chris, thank you for coming." Gloria forces a smile.

Chris faces Alex. "Julie tells me you've made an immediate impression. I'm glad to hear it."

"Thank you."

"And you've made changes to the show."

"I had ideas. Don and Pete helped."

"That's unprecedented for a first-timer, but that's great to hear. And I hate to bring this up here and now, but I got word from our first venue that they're asking for the thrills rides, the kids' pet farm, our clowns, and some acrobats. But we can't take the whole company. Including your show."

Alex sets down her plate. Gloria drinks and glowers. Don turns toward his grill crackling; the crowd around it swells. A small circle off the deck sling back shots. Kids and dogs play.

"We thought this might happen. That county has taken a big hit since last time we were there. We wanted to give them a chance. We were hopeful. But we can't control it. But we have the next stop, and our contract with them guarantees the whole company. Thanks for understanding." His daughter runs into his arms; he lifts her and, saying goodbye here and there, leaves with his family.

Alex spits out her food in a napkin. "He did that on purpose."

"They took us all for years," Don says. "Last year they flipped and flopped between having all of us. Half our shows stayed put."

"Christ, he's so fake."

"Glor…"

"He's been after you and Pete for years. He thinks he's the CEO of a mega-corporation. It's a circus that puts on shows for kids and families. Clowns and rides and treats and popcorn. Memories made from that. Bottom line." Gloria marches to the group and invites everyone inside.

Don drinks his beer. "He's tried stopping us in the past. Blaming ticket sales or logistics. The pressure's on him with that hedge fund breathing down his neck. Ours too."

Returning to the deck, Gloria lights a joint. "Knocking up his girlfriend during their senior year is what got him into the company."

Don takes a toke and passes it to Alex who glares where Chris exited before inhaling and exhaling long smoke.

"He married her rather than leave. He's a good man for doing that. But he magically gets a warehouse job with no experience during a recession and a low point for the company."

"Lot of layoffs then."

"Then he moves into HR, again magically, and his ego swells. He knows everyone's background and lies in their work history and why they were written up. Anything that could be a red flag. First thing he does as COO is cut the staff by ten percent. The board had no problem."

"Glor, come on." Don extinguishes the grill.

"Julie applied for that position. But they shafted her. Didn't give her a chance. Not one person on that board supported her. Glen and his sister Roberta. Idiots. Julie puts up a front with Chris. She can't quit her job."

"Why?"

"Her boy has severe Down Syndrome. Her husband is on disability. She's the bread-winner. Sweet Julie looks Walmart, but she's a professional through and through. She's the reason why Kopolski has success. Not the person named Kopolski."

Don tugs her arm. "Glor, come on. Come on, Alex. Pete got here with Cecelia. Let's go in and have cake. All of us."

As Don and Gloria stumble inside, Alex stays behind. Laughter and talk float from the house. She turns toward the fence on the other side of the property where headlights come and go. Beyond the fence and lights: the road that brought her and leads toward a place she will not stop in. She steps into the box-shaped shadow on the back deck. The clock on the wall ticks away the time left until the season begins—time that charged in and out of her, circling her, wherever she had been, ready to be taken anywhere.

10

Buses, RVs, trucks, and cars honk on their way out of the front gate. Alex focuses on wardrobe storage but turns as the last vehicle—a flatbed hauling a ride like a snake—honks and a clown in full makeup tosses glitter at employees in the field and around the facility. The offices' lights flicker. Chris tips his hat and returns inside.

She rifles through costumes, organizing sections Julie told her needed "freshening up," and runs an inventory on buttons, sashes, belts, and accessories. She tags shirts and pants and leaps around polka dots and vibrant colors and imagines rolling into her prior job wearing any of these and receiving an email from Brooke. She scoots over trunks and reaches one labeled Gorilla-Girl and unzips each bag: a dress; yellow tights; skull necklace; leather and animal-skin bracelets; purple-and-yellow-striped top; headband with purple and yellow flowers. She calls Julie. "Can I go shopping for my show while I'm grounded here?"

Julie stops by and hands a card with her name and KTE on it. "Don't go crazy with it. You can't. It has a limit."

"I wonder who set it?"

"Bless his heart. Get something good."

She types Shopping, Clothes, Consignment, Thrift Store in her phone; results blink on the map but most are big-box stores. She scrolls west. The city and its suburbs appear; a scattershot of results load over the metro area. She snaps off the map and drives northeast toward the result closest to her but doesn't find anything. She drives to an outlet mall and buys socks and a watch. As she heads to the next town, a banner flaps on a corner.

Going Out of Business
All Shoes 40% Off

The salesperson brings her a beat-up box of sneakers—one left in her size but not the color she wants. The salesperson rings up the price.

"How much? You're kidding me."

"They're hot right now."

"But you're closing."

Walls of flats, heels, and prom shoes tower over them.

"If you come back next week, we'll have our buy-one-get-one-half-off sale."

"Will you save these?"

"Are you local?"

"No."

"People have been coming in from all over. If you come back, they may not be here."

Alex slides over the card.

A mother and her daughters sift through shelves. "Get whatever you want," the mother tells them as her blouse puffs. Alex peers at the style, cut, and colors and calls her mother.

"Do you have any of your old clothes? Like when you and Dad were dating?"

"I have my wedding dress."

"That's too fancy."

"So you don't want it if you get married?"

Alex lights a joint. "What about a blouse? Maybe those ones with big shoulder pads."

"I got rid of those."

"What about one of those earthy dresses you wore to protest the war Dad fought in?"

"What's going on?"

"I need a dress. Or something."

"Why don't you buy one?"

"I need something unique. Something that fits my character."

"A gorilla needs a dress?"

"I'm not the gorilla. I turn into the gorilla. My human form needs a dress. A unique one. It has to line up with who I am. Who she is."

"What about all those places you shop at?"

Bags swinging, the mother and her daughters step from the store.

"I got to go, Mom." She starts a text to her father. <Would you see if I left any clothes at your place? If so, can you meet me

halfway and I can get them from you?> She thumbs Julie's card. <I'll pay for your gas.> But she deletes her text and considers sending the same to Brian but deletes that faster. She twists her joint—Damn, Manny, good hits—and turns on her radio. Her car rattles next to the mother as she opens the trunk and blocks her from backing up. Smoke billows out of Alex's car; a guitar solo shreds the air before the singer sings about "sticking and licking it all night."

"I like that top. And I want it. Like I got to have it now."

The woman shields her children.

"Sorry. I didn't mean to scare you. I wanted to ask you where you got your blouse. I want it. Before I get back to work."

The mother herds her children into their seats and, shielding them and herself, shouts, "That's all you want?"

"Yeah."

"Willow Tree in Wayneston."

"Wayneston?" Alex types on her phone. "How do you spell that?"

"If you don't leave, I'll call the cops."

Across the street, a squad car pulls from a drive-through. The woman waves, lays on her horn, flashes her headlights.

Alex flicks out her joint and drives away, punching around for the store name.

• • •

Her car struggles over tracks and, after she parks in the lot, it is the smallest, oldest, and dirtiest among the SUVs, sedans, and hybrids. The crossing arms ding down, the red lights flashing; a train chugs by. She pulls a pretend chain in the air; the train bellows back; the engineer tips his cap. After the train disappears, Alex heads for the door and dodges sorority girls and pampered-up women coming and going from the salon next door. But when the train bellows again somewhere, she steps in the middle of the tracks and turns on her phone's time-lapse video.

In the store she pauses at fliers, events, business cards.

Aileen Comstock, M.A.
"Invite Yourself Back into the Life God Gave You!"

Do you miss the person God wants you to be?
Do you feel everything about yourself has disappeared?
Do you feel you have to build a different life?

Contact me today to find yourself where God wants you to be.

"May I help you?"

"I'm looking for a dress. Or…" Alex scans the employee who asked her; the women coursing the aisles and racks; the clothes; the mimosas. "A T-shirt."

"Anything in mind?" The woman glides to a cubby and displays mesh sparkling under the overhead lights.

"Do you have anything in the price range of a Native American woman kissing a wolf under a full moon?"

"The truck stop is down from the tracks."

Alex holds up the blouse the woman had on.

"Great choice," the employee intones. "It's retro. You can pair it with slacks. Or jeans."

"Not with that number of zeros."

"Anything else?"

"Hold on."

The employee takes the blouse. "I'll meet you at the counter."

Alex dials a number; Julie's voicemail picks up. "I know there's a limit on the card you gave me, but what about a single purchase? Call me back quick." She edits her video of the train—dropping the time lapse; speeding it up; bringing back the time lapse—before fidgeting with her phone and heading to the counter.

"Cash, check, card?"

"Card."

"May I see your ID?" The employee does a double take. "I'm sorry, but these don't match."

Alex checks that her ringer is on full volume. "Let me get my boss. It's her card." She dials again—Julie's voicemail.

A squad car rolls into the lot. The cop speaks into his radio after he stops behind Alex's car. The employee smothers the card and meets the cop halfway. After they talk, the cop approaches Alex.

"Are you owner of that vehicle?"

"Yes, sir."

"We have a complaint that you obstructed a woman trying to leave her parking spot."

"I stopped behind her, but when she asked me to move, I did."

"We also recovered drug paraphernalia off the ground over there."

"Not mine."

"And now I hear you're using a credit card not in your name."

"I can get my boss on the phone. She's not answering now. Let me get someone else." She fumbles her phone.

The employee unwraps the blouse.

"Ma'am, I'm going to ask you to sit in my vehicle until we clear this up."

Alex walks alongside the cop to his car.

"You're not under arrest. But we need to clear this up."

She calls Julie—nothing. She calls Pete then Don—nothing. She hovers over the number for Devon from HR but settles on another number. "Hey. It's Alex. Can you please tell this police officer I was running an errand on Julie's behalf that required using her card? And she knows it." She mutes her phone. "Officer? I got hold of someone from my company."

The officer talks on Alex's phone, to the employee, on his radio.

As minutes go by, the video of the train churns through Alex: a silhouette; smoke and light; wheels spinning—all rolling toward and away from her.

"Everything checks out," the officer says. "You're free to go."

. . .

She runs past the offices, the practice facilities, the animal pens; turns at the motor pool; and enters Logistics.

"Is Manny here?"

"They needed him for the first venue. He won't be back until next week. You need something?"

She slinks off to the corner facing the rides that weren't loaded; their lights click off after the last test run of the day; their empty cars covered; their motors stir through the sunset and the smells of hot grease and plastic. Vehicles vacate lots. The offices remain lit.

She texts Manny. <I stopped by to say thank you in person for helping me out today. I owe you.>

<It's cool. But I can't promise it won't get back to J or the suits. And you better hope it only gets back to J. Not trying to scare you. Just being real with you.>

She flops on the grass and edits the train video—slowing it, speeding it frame by frame; the image going somewhere off the frame or snapping back to it—and texts it.

She heads home and rummages through her clothes and sets aside a stack for the show—"Daisy," she invokes—and ties off the rest of her old clothes in bags for the thrift stores she stopped at earlier.

Clarence calls. "I love that train video. Reminds me of that thing at that arcade by the ocean. The zoetrope."

11

Pete looks over the clothes. "I can see Daisy wearing them. Good job."

"Thank you."

Don returns to props. "I don't feel right asking Julie for new wardrobe funds after we had her rebrand our show. My character is still wearing the clothes I wore the first time I did this. I bought the lab coat and the glasses and all these things you see here. It was my money. Neither Julie nor Chris reimbursed me. I didn't expect them to."

Alex folds a skirt. "These are more me. More Daisy."

"Let's roll with it." Pete's voice fades behind boxes.

"It's not that. Being you is fine. But for crying out loud, it's fantasy. It's a girl who changes into a gorilla." Don grunts. "We're not activists or political theatre trying to shake the middle class. We make families laugh, and we scare them for a little bit in a safe place. It's about illusion." He wipes a microscope and angles it across from tubes leading into beakers. "When we started, we had this chant I said. Ooga bemboppo tippi tippi toomula. And hell if I know what it means. I made it up. It sounded fun and out-of-this-world. Salina would get into the box, and I'd pull out this scroll I picked up in the Amazon. 'An ancient scroll filled with ancient words.' The only way to control the beast inside. I emphasized certain words. Then she'd change."

"You don't need to get new clothes." Alex rolls a chair to the desk. "I think it'd be cool to see Daisy in normal clothes and you in a lab coat. You should keep that. How funny would it be to think Daisy's dad is always in a lab coat?"

"An eccentric scientist experimenting on his daughter," Don says. "Kinda creepy."

"That's right for us," Pete says. "Rumors will spread. Things will get misunderstood. Someone will think we're suggesting Dr. Mandrake is sleeping with his daughter. Someone will get offended and complain about us and the show. It's perfect for us."

"Keep the lab coat, Don," Alex says. "Keep the mustache. Be eccentric. Keep all these things people will complain about. Our show is cheaper than a B movie. Which are all always the fun ones. I'm dressing Daisy this way because she's the normal one in the bunch."

"Now that is true." Pete unzips the gorilla mask and suit. "Which version should we end with for our first performance? Who should be standing over who at the end?" He kneels and rages against the sky. "The man who acts like a beast, or the beast within?"

"Don?"

"As long as the audience reacts."

"Alex, you decide who gets the spotlight. It'll be your first show."

"Which me?" She spreads out a top alongside a makeup kit. "I think we should make it so at the end, if we can get the lights to change, it's me standing over him. But not me the gorilla. Me the girl."

"You change back to Daisy."

"Yeah. I change back to me."

"I don't know. That's another tweak to the show."

"It's her first show, Don. Let's try it. We've stuck with what we've been doing. Alex has got something here. For all of us."

"If it doesn't work out we can go back to Mandrake or the gorilla," Alex says. "But this other way, when she changes back into Daisy, she'll see what she's done. It'll be in front of her."

"I like it," Pete says.

Don sighs. "We can give it a try."

"It'll be all around her," Alex says. "She'll have to live with it."

. . .

She walks from practice and toward trucks lining up—more vehicles than for the first venue; more nuts and bolts; more rides, booths, buildings, tents, games. She stops where clowns test squeakers and water-sprayers and where operators test empty pods and cabs, whipping them around a castle moat and down a helix. Workers clean vending machines and buzzers and bells. She reaches the other sideshows: contortionists warming up their bodies; singers running up and down scales; puppeteers disappearing behind puppets; the Half-Lady alive and dead through mirrors and reflections. Colleagues ask her to leave to "preserve the integrity of the act." Wranglers and handlers keep her away from the animals. Inside a nearby canopy, a man, shirtless and wearing silver briefs, swabs alcohol on his brow and cheeks and shaved head. He stands, and his military boots—anarchy symbols and pentagrams marked on them—drop off the table. Alex and he introduce each other.

"Pierce? Really?"

"Sometimes the universe serves up something too good to miss." He lays out needles, nails, fishhooks. "What do you do?"

"I'm the Gorilla-Girl."

"That's right. Julie put the spotlight on you. You're teacher's pet for now. But the higher you're on that pedestal the harder you'll fall."

"Thanks for the vote of confidence."

"Special K will keep you in check."

"He is."

"Julie used to keep him in check. When he first got his job he said some crazy things to employees. He got away with a lot of stuff. Being a Kopolski helped. Julie knew he was a PR nightmare waiting to happen. Somehow she got him to stop. But now with the moneybags in charge and not his family, he has to watch it.

Hold this would you?" He hands her rubbing alcohol and dips in a safety pin. "Do you like your show?"

"My first performance is coming up."

"It'll be fun to see how long you last. Every girl before was trash and couldn't amount to anything in the real world. Most of them stole from here. Drug addicts. Unemployed artists. They were here to make cash, smoke weed, and get a free ride to another city where they could avoid whatever they were avoiding."

Alex peeks down.

"If Chris had his way, he'd screen everybody who applies. But he doesn't have time. Julie hires these girls who can't fit in anywhere else. She should work for a nonprofit." He feels around his temple. "Stacy didn't work out. Everybody heard about it."

"I don't know much about her other than Don and Pete didn't like her."

"She made it clear this job was her secondary source of income." He forces the pin through. "Somebody said she was blowing the manager at the restaurant she worked at before she came here. Before Julie's bleeding heart hired her." He sinks the pin deeper and does not flinch. "He was, like, forty and married. Had kids. If two people want to bump uglies, they should. Be adults. Marriage is a joke anyway." His long, skinny fingers move up his head but below his green mohawk. "And how about ol' Don and Pete?"

"They're great. Pete brings his acting experience to it, and Don is grumpy about our changes, but he's getting there."

"Old-man Donald. What sixty-something man wants to do this? He's a perv with all those crazy girls around him."

"He's put a lot into the show. He started it from scratch."

"The Amazon? The jungle girl? Totally racist and problematic."

"We threw that out. And made it better."

"Maybe you give them a limp dick." He tugs out his bottom lip. "New job. Freaky workers. Questionable work environment. What more could you want?"

"A steady paycheck. Travel."

"You get all that until they say otherwise." He grabs a nail; swirls it in the glass; spikes his lip. "It's been months since I practiced."

"You didn't go out to the first venue?"

"Last year I did. And the years before that. But I got in hot water. My girlfriend used to help me out with this. We got caught having a three-way with one of the guests. He consented. But it didn't look good. Everyone found out. Which didn't bother me. That's who I am. But it didn't fly with the moneybags when they found out." He taps a cigarette pack. "Before all this, I was a street kid."

"Where?"

"I tell people that. I had all this money. Inherited. Back when I was Michael. My father was a stockbroker. My brother is the

MBA grad, the entrepreneur. I didn't want to be them. You don't know who you are until you start hacking away at what's been put on you."

"Not everyone can do something like that."

"They have to start hacking away. I'm the way I am because I didn't want to be WASP-y." He lights a cigarette and blows smoke through the hole in his lip. "I'm not talking about money anyway. I'm talking about accepting who you are."

"I guess if you want to go back to being who you were you could."

"My girlfriend is always talking about opening a vegan restaurant or bakery." He preps another nail, scrunches his nose, and cocks his head back but focuses on the tip of his nose. "Wanna push it in?"

"Sure."

"Push slowly but consistently. Don't stop. It'll slide."

Alex gags as his nose squishes and crunches.

He twitches. "A little too deep."

"Sorry."

"What do you think?"

"Crazy. But cool."

"You can touch it and jiggle it. I mean the nail. But my girlfriend wouldn't care. We're open. She goes both ways. You're cute, so you never know, but I don't do a lot on the first date."

"Unless you're at a venue." She grips the nail—taut.

"None of that may happen for me if Special K and the moneybags get their way. Pull it out."

She blushes.

"The nail, girl, the nail. Nice, slow, and easy."

"Pete calls Chris Special K."

"We all do. He's just so, so special to us."

"No blood?"

"Nope. The first time, though, you always bleed."

"Funny."

"It's all part of my act. I can pinpoint the squeamish girls in the audience or the jocks who are secretly gay, and I get them up here to do the same thing you did." He dips the nail in alcohol and towels down. "But it's all an act."

"You don't care about any of those people in the seats? They paid. They want to be there."

"You're so new, you're so cute. Did you hear about one of the newbs using a company credit card?"

Shying away, Alex shrugs.

"He tried to buy weed and clothes with it. Scared a lady and her kids. Like, refused to let her leave her parking spot."

"He?"

"Someone said he's in Logistics. But we all thought it'd be one of us. Julie's special cases. Or one of the execs and the skeletons in their closets. Logistics guys are usually straight arrows. They've had their drug problems. One guy was a registered sex offender. Chris lost his mind when he found out.

He was going to bring in his gun and shoot the guy." Pierce flicks out his tongue and rolls over the silver ball pinned to it. "Chris knows about it."

"Knows about what?"

"The person using the company card. Nothing like that gets swept under the rug. Somebody talks to someone who talks to someone else. The money stuff always comes to the surface and goes to Chris who will head it off before it gets to the moneybags. The nitty-gritty stuff stays below for a while. But it comes out too. You can't keep reality at bay." He loads the staple gun. "When we're done here, you wanna go with me to the practice run of The Haunting at Krugel Mansion? It's won all these awards. One of my best friends here dresses up with a butcher knife. There's this room where a corpse is on a bed, and this huge snakehead comes out from behind the curtain. It's all covered in blood and flesh." He pivots his silver briefs toward her. "You can hold onto me if you're scared."

"I should get back."

Hardcore punk floods his canopy as she strolls around a bend leading to the edge of the property elevating her above buses, RVs, trailers, trucks, cranes; coworkers painting rides and inspecting costumes and props; stilt performers striding across the horizon; and in the distance, Pete bounding around outside, kicking up dust. He slumps to the ground, clutches his heart, curses the sky, and thrusts his fist into the air. She imagines him speaking a monologue about fate and its bittersweet irony in the lives of humans. "I was a man trapped inside a beast. Not a beast trapped inside a man!" She slumps to the ground, clutches her heart, curses the sky, and thrusts her fist into the air until she spies Julie and Chris talking—with Pete—before they go inside.

When she wakes and steps off the RV, everything rises from the ground. Everything trucks and trailers brought across miles, through woods and over streams and rivers, across roads and highways; everything her colleagues unloaded like in a mural—leaning on each other and ropes, gears, levers; their bodies pulling something until it emerged and rose. Everything brought to the center that had to be made where everything orbits and where she walks among vests and hard hats checking the big top with its stripes and stars and spines hoisting it toward the sky.

And she enters a labyrinth of smaller tents and buildings and vehicles and stops under racks of black, pod-like cars that will slingshot people; Z-shaped frames; tubes; cutouts of houses; platforms. Great rings assemble, starting like crescent moons on the ground and ending as cables whir like horns pulled together. Behind her, the Ferris wheel near the center unfolds like a fan.

She reaches another circle—her colleagues walking around, stopping to chat, or nodding as they pass; people like her who emerged from RVs and stretched and yawned when a manager handed lists to them. Galley kitchens sizzle; flames from propane tanks pop down the line. Silhouettes with mops and hoses wash booths, rides, and buildings among the arcade flicking on and stuffed animals and toys rolled off dollies.

And on the other side of the midway, she sits among a circle of her colleagues.

"We do this rain or shine. Good weather and bad."

"You get them lights on, and kids'll drag their parents here. That's what we call walk-in-money. You got that and grind-money and no-money. Special K don't want no-money, and we don't want no-money."

"In my twenty years here, I've seen no-money once. It happened up at this county fair, and it was springtime like now. Smack dab in the middle of tornado season. And this storm rolls in out of nowhere. The rain couldn't have been heavier. You couldn't see jack. The platforms for the rides were slick. You lost your footing. Winds were blowing everything around. We shut it down. Called it a day. Made zero money that day. Zero. That hurt. We lost people that day. They bailed on us there or further up the road, getting jobs at who knows where. We were short staffed, but who can blame them? Gotta pay the bills. So when we're on, and the sun is shining, and it's a beautiful day, you grind. You work ten, twelve, fourteen hours on a good grind day."

"Before this, I was working for another company. This little ol' thang out of Mississippi. And we were on our early routes, hitting them still-dates in towns for weeks on end, sitting there until it was time to hit the big stops. Little by little the cash box became depleted. Our manager was an idiot."

"Not like Special K?"

The circle chuckles.

"This manager had no sense handling money. He didn't steal it. I've seen that happen many times. But this guy was flat-out stupid. So the cash box was low, and the show wasn't making enough money for food, let alone gas. At one point, the boss handed out money to our crew supposedly from arcade games. There were thirteen of us. It was all quarters, too, mind you. We sent one of the girls to the store for beer, bread, and cans of beans, and when she came back, we all hunkered down in a trailer parked behind the rides. It was cold and rainy in Kentucky, and we ended up using candles for light because it cost money to run them generators."

"My favorite job is the one no one else likes. The sweep."

The circle moans.

"I've seen it all on the sweeps, usually what you think it'd be. Trash. Vomit. Cigarette butts. But I've found wallets, money, credit cards, kids' retainers, condoms."

"Were they used?"

The circle laughs.

"Did you use the credit cards?"

"I thought about it. Who'd know? But I turned them all in. The best was when I got myself a pedometer. I walked twenty-two miles on one sweep in a day. Look at me now. Ka-plow!"

The circle hollers and claps.

"We get a little lazy in the fall because we're tired and things are starting to wind down. Those last few stops before HallowScream are when we barely check the harnesses on the rides. We're like, 'You in?' The kid drools. 'Cool. Have fun.'"

"This one time I was a show prep for one of the kids' shows, and I walked backstage to check on something, and I saw Speedy the Turtle and Mrs. White the Bunny with their costumes on getting down and dirty on each other."

The crowd howls.

"I was part of the whole Viking Boat disaster."

"I remember that. That was PCK."

"PCK?"

"Pre-Chris-Kopolski."

"It's all about Special K."

"Captain K."

"Captain Kranky."

"Gimme my money!"

The circle laughs.

"So it was PCK, and I liked working it because there was a shelter and a stool, which was perfect for rain or sun. Sit there and operate the ride. Anyway, the Viking Boat gets going, swinging back and forth, when I hear this pop. Black fluid starts spraying through the middle of the ride while it's swinging. I hit the emergency stop button, but the ride doesn't stop. And when the boat comes down, that black fluid hits the passengers. And I'm like cursing and smashing the emergency button. Nothing. I grab the phone and call security, and I'm like, 'Send everybody,' and they're like, 'What's the emergency?' and I was like, 'The Viking Boat won't stop swinging. There's oil or something all over the place. Send everybody. It won't stop.' The ride is at the other end so it takes them forever to show up. And they're all fat. By the time they show up, the boat is still swinging. Here's where it gets gross. You're this passenger enjoying the ride. La-dee-dah, look at me having fun on a Viking boat. When it breaks, you're stuck up there swinging for like fifteen minutes, and you have all this black on you and your clothes, and it stinks, and it's hot out. You've got all this happening, and you want to get off, but you can't. What do you do? What do all of them do? You throw up. You throw up on yourself, on the passenger next to you, on the people in front of you, and they all start throwing up."

The circle hoots and cringes.

"Security finally shows up, and they all look at each other and basically draw straws because no one wants to get under that boat when it's still swinging and the black ink is shooting up and everyone is throwing up. So they call in for more staff. I think half the company showed up for this."

"But not Special K."

"That's way too dirty for him."

"So they get everybody on one side of the platform, and they're going to have everyone grab the boat as it swings by. But the boat is too strong, and it knocks them off the platform. They get back up and decide to push the boat when it swings by, slowing it down. It worked. It took another ten minutes, but it worked. The boat stopped, and people got off the ride. Management was horrified. They tried everything. Full refund. Free admission for life. Paying for cleaning the clothes. I think one of the Kopolski family members arranged to fly in people to hotels and restaurants. All expenses paid. But none of that stopped the lawsuits. I think they all settled out of court. And in came Special K."

"When he took over all the fun went away."

"It took his hair."

"He's got those plugs now."

"That's the wrong thing he needed transplanted."

The circle keeps laughing.

"We have these slushy machines. They're popular during summer, and I was working near one this one day when this shirtless chubby kid walks up to it. The guy who's supposed to be watching the machines isn't paying any attention, and I could tell this kid was waiting for him to go on break. As soon as this guy gets his smokes and leaves, this kid goes up to each nozzle and licks them. Then he sticks his fingers in his armpit and sticks his finger in each nozzle, going down the line, trying to scoop out slushy. He wipes his mouth with his fingers then goes back down the line, in the opposite direction, doing the same thing, mouth to nozzle, sticking his finger up in there. He looks and me and leaves."

"I burned my thighs and stomach cleaning the pizza oven. While it was still on. But my own hell-story was spending hours cleaning years of grease off the fryer hoods. I was there until three in the morning and still had to show up the next day at seven. I told my manager I had zero sleep and couldn't work. She looked at me and said, 'You can take your first break earlier or combine your breaks at once.' I had to get all new clothes after that because they smelled, and I had to get new shoes because the bottoms of my old ones had this grease on them that dried like wax. I was slipping all over the place. My car to this day reeks of fryer grease. And the pedals are slippery."

"You can't smack enough stupid out of the guests. I was working the old roller coaster one summer, and this guy steps off the ride, and his hand is bleeding. Dripping all over the place. He turns to me, and I see this huge chunk missing in his hand. And he says, 'Can I get first aid?' So I call, they come out, stitch him up, and one of them asks him what he did. 'I was trying to touch something.'"

"Remember that ball pit over by the Old West Shooting Gallery?"

Most of the circle hums.

"Kids played in it, but that got shut down."

"Why?"

"Parents would send their kids into it without pants on."

"Speaking of guests, we'd get those Make-a-Wish kids in here. And they are the worst. No, let me take that back. Their parents are the worst because they're all, 'My kid's sick. Dy-ing. Hear me? She got five cancers up in her. She can ride whatever she wants, eat whatever she wants, play whatever games she wants. For free.'"

"The heat and humidity damage those rides after you get 'em going in these parts. Always breaking down."

"And that bottle of soda you bought? We bought it wholesale for way cheaper. Same goes for most of the food in the cafeteria."

"We never say what's wrong with a ride even if we know something is a little off. We never will say, 'This thing, chain, or whatever broke, and we're shutting it down.' And we're never going to tell you when it's going to be up. 'We anticipate a lengthy delay.'"

"The employee RVs could probably double for a brothel."

"That's for sure."

"A whole lot of four-twenty and naughtiness coming out of those late at night."

"Or in the middle of the work day."

"I was nearly raped by one of my coworkers. After I got groped by a supervisor. And I fainted from heat exhaustion."

"Did you say anything about that?"

"To who?"

"Special K would only care if it cut the budget."

"Why are you still here?"

"Who else will hire me?"

The circle agrees.

"I had one of the actors from the shows hit on me big time. I looked at him one day and said, 'I'm not attracted to you.' He was shocked. He's like, 'Why?' Because I've seen you in your spandex, Little Smokie."

"My first day on the job I noticed the Ferris wheel operator would stop the wheel at its top longer for certain guests. It was these guests who were giving him dime bags with their tickets. They were smoking at the top of the ride, and he was getting some too."

"Do you think Special K could stop that?"

"He'd need Raymond."

"Oh, God, Raymond."

"He's before Sherman."

"Have you met Sherman?"

"He got on me about my parking permit. And smoking."

"That's Sherm."

"Raymond was the heavy. Wasn't he security chief or something?"

"Director of Security and Internal Affairs for thirty years. Come on now. Show the man respect. RIP, Chief Ray."

Some in the circle toast.

"He got out of the Navy and joined us. He was the muscle."

"And school principal."

"More like he was a prison guard. He'd write you up for any violation."

"When Special K joined, the employee handbook doubled. Chief was a busy man."

"But some of that is better for the company. I have to wear a harness and hard hat and reflective vest at all times. At first it was tough for an old dog like me, but it's regulations. And since I'm the old dog, I've gotta pass it on to the rest of my crew."

"Chief got too old to do his job. Died while he was still an employee. An intimidating dude."

"Y'all are too young to remember, but back when John Junior Kopolski got us to go on a special tour of California one season Chief flew up there a group of us when this plane he was on had something wrong with its fuel and crash landed in Nevada. Everyone was injured but Chief. I can see him getting out of that wreckage with all that smoke and lighting a cigar."

"You can visit him still to this day when we're at stops."

"Where?"

"On one of the big horses on the carousel there's a name plate on the breast. It says Raymond 'Chief' Lloyd."

"Who's a carny kid here?"

"We don't like the word carnies."

"We prefer show-men and -women and -children."

"We're teasing."

"I'm a carny kid. My parents have been here a long time. There's a tribe of us. It's not too bad having a carnival as your playground. But we had to work too. Most of us stuck together and have a tight bond. I think only other carny kids can appreciate growing up in the business. It makes us certain kinds of adults."

"I remember when we had maybe fifty carny kids and something like thirty or forty families traveling with us."

"Some stick around, some don't. In the old days, you could be like a hobo and join one company, make money, then go find another midway."

"I started working here at age sixteen, and I've been here forty years. It's where we live, and it's what we do. It's our family."

"That's right. We have our downtime. But the seasons, especially spring and summer, all about getting bills paid."

"I'm meant for this job. Nothing else I'd rather do."

"Same here."

"Or could do."

The circle breaks up and heads to their places as the gates open. Alex tosses the rest of her coffee on the grass.

"It's all I've ever known."

13

The backstage clock flashes closer to showtime after Don and Pete tell Alex they're going for a walk and late breakfast. "Everything's ready," they chimed, hugging her. Behind the curtains she peeks at the chairs, stage, and props the three of them set up—the Pepper's Ghost box draped in the corner. She dabs her makeup sponge but can't apply it. She downs her fourth cup of coffee, sugar clumping on top, which shakes her more, and starts lighting a joint but stops when Julie's voice drifts in: "I will talk to her. I will take care of it. Not today. You know better." Alex peeps around the curtains. Julie blocks Chris from walking backstage. Chris relaxes. Julie inspects the stage, emergency exit, and sightlines at the back for handicapped guests. As Chris marches backstage, Alex stuffs the joint under her wardrobe and fumbles for her sponge and makeup.

"Good morning."

"Morning, Chris."

"Just wanted to stop and by, and…" He chews his bottom lip. "Wish you a great first show." He peers around and pauses on the lighter by her wardrobe. "You need to move that. That's a fire hazard."

"I will."

"You can put it in your RV or a locker we can assign you." He lifts her dress off the table but doesn't expose the joint underneath. "Is this what you bought?"

"No. It's mine."

"One of your changes to the show."

"It's who my character is."

"Someone who uses a card at a store but then gets her own clothes?"

"I didn't used the card."

"You were going to."

"Alex." Julie quickly steps in. "It's almost showtime." She takes the dress from Chris. "Is this what you bought helping with Wardrobe?"

"She didn't buy it. You don't know?"

"I like the dress."

"I figured Daisy would look like this."

"It works."

Chris adjusts his ball cap. "Have a great show. Tell Don and Pete I said the same. Let's make smiles today."

Julie looks over the makeup table before leaning on it. Children run by outside; something whooshes, pings, rattles; the children laugh and yell. Alex applies her foundation.

"No more rehearsals," Julie says.

"No."

"No more memorizing lines."

"Nope."

"Don will have to deal."

"We agreed to change things if it doesn't work out."

"And Pete?"

"The professional like Don said."

"Good. I'm happy for you."

Alex notices her joint lying in the open; she stands for her lipstick. "This also means no more figuring out who Daisy is."

"Given what you told me, she sounds brand new." Julie sets down the dress. "Like no longer carrying a secret."

Alex lays a makeup wipe over her joint.

Julie stops her. "You need to dispose of that."

"I will."

Another whoosh and people screaming and laughing as something slings them around.

"Don't make this harder for me. I've told Chris he can count on me with regards to you. But I need to count on you."

"Is this about the card?"

"I know you didn't use it. There's no transaction. But it and other things linger." She nods at the joint. "And word's getting around."

Don and Pete clamber on the stage and test the speakers: doors creaking open; bubbling; electricity. "We got one hour, Alex. You here?"

"I am."

"Hi, boys."

"Hi, Julie. Are you looking to audition for Alex's role?"

"Maybe Pete's."

"You can have it. Yale Drama called me. They want me to teach a masterclass on acting like a man in an ape suit."

"You can't have Alex's because she's gonna knock it out of the park."

"And every show after."

A scream rips through the speakers and into backstage.

Julie touches the dress hiding the joint. "My daughter would love this dress. Break a leg."

. . .

The crowd files into the tent, handing in their tickets. Lights dim, casting the seats and stage in blue-gray. Alex massages her neck while the audience doubles then triples.

Don calls her over. "You look nervous."

"I am."

"Have a glass of water. But not too much. Don't want to have to pee while you're on stage."

"I'm ready to from all my coffee."

"We could talk about making that part of the act." He fogs and wipes his glasses.

An electrician runs onto stage and turns lights and controls.

"It'll be fun," he says.

Her head and shoulders throb.

"Closing the front of the house," the stage manager says. "All cast need to be in place."

Don adjusts his lab coat and tie; smoothes his handlebar mustache; and thumbs-up the stage manager. He and Alex walk behind the wall separating the backstage from the front. She presses against the wall but positions for her cues and watches the audience.

"Green light, Petey."

Pete drops a mouth guard in mouthwash.

"What's that for?" Alex asks.

"You've seen me stomp around. I chipped a tooth once. You ready?"

"Don told me to relax." She rubs her pendant under her costume as the intro music stops and the laboratory bubbles on.

"It's like riding a bike. Listen to Don. He's got all your cue lines. You're gonna do great."

"Did you parents ever imagine you doing this?"

"You mean when they crossed the border?" He waits until she catches on before he continues with an exaggerated Mexican accent. "From Pennsylvania to Illinois?" He raises the gorilla head. "Don's on stage." He slathers black on his eyelids and twists on the head and until his eyes fade into the sockets. He chants before stepping into the box: "The ceremony is about to begin." He disappears, and the gorilla looms over Alex.

She turns toward Don while, briefcase in hand, he bows at the audience.

"Ladies and gentlemen, boys and girls, thank you for coming today to my la-bor-atory. I am your gracious host, Dr. Theodore Henry Mandrake, professor of anthropology, holder of three PhDs." He underscores papers in ornate frames on a wall behind him. "Speaker of fourteen languages, both alive and dead. World-traveler. And collector of the odd, the curious, and the demented. And it is my pleasure to welcome you here, for today you shall experience the wonders of Nature in all its primal form. Throughout my many years researching human nature, I have concluded Nature is but a machine we can pull apart and study. It is more ours than we are its. We can alter and control our reality. There are no mistakes in Nature. We must harness what we assume are abnormalities. Evolution is a circle. Sometimes we move forward like you do on those roller coasters and rides out there."

Heads in the crowd turn behind—toward the midway outside.

"Or we think we're moving forward, but we're moving backward. The two-headed pig down from us or, across from us, the young lady with wings on her back. Or my lovely daughter."

A light shines on him from below.

"My studies and experiments prove we can change our form. That Nature allows us two forms to exist in. Yes, I know it sounds odd and impossible. But think of the caterpillar and the butterfly. The same creature but at different stages. And as a scientist, I have discovered how to bring out these forms and control them. Which you'll see here in this laboratory." He paces the stage and moves notes and equipment. "With proper understanding of genetic structures, it is possible." He underscores a formula before walking to a graphic of a female human on one side and—red, yellow, and blue lines crisscrossing and weaving between—a gorilla on the other. "She will be an accepted member of society. All with my help. And whatever happens, my dear audience, do not panic. I assure you everything is under my control." He smiles at them, tilts his glasses, and turns offstage. "Daisy! Oh, Daisy, my dear. Please come into the laboratory."

She hears her name but forgets who needs to answer. But she recovers and, adjusting her dress, steps into Daisy. "Yes, Father. Coming." Before entering the stage, she glances at the box and the shadow inside. The gorilla head turns toward her from behind the dark glass. "Sorry, Father. I was making cookies when you called."

"Such a sweet dear ever since your mother passed." Mandrake offers a chair. "Would you help me with an experiment?"

"What is it this time? Turning lead into gold? Or controlling all the computers in the world at once?"

"I want to you to show your gift to our guests."

"Remember what happened to Mr. Cribbs? All that blood."

The audience chuckles.

"It was too bad what happened to Cribbs. But he got in the way of progress." He opens a bottle on the table; blue liquid slides from the bottle to a tap where he sets a glass under it. "I've perfected the potion to control your gift." He opens the tap; out pours the blue liquid.

"But all these nice people here, Father. I'd hate for something to go wrong."

"I'll drink some with you. It's harmless. To me."

"I don't want to."

"Come, come. You must listen to your father. Who has more knowledge about these sorts of things?"

She crosses her arms and stomps her feet.

Mandrake grabs the back of Daisy's head until her mouth snaps open; he pours the potion. "There. Isn't that better?"

As Mandrake turns, Daisy spits out the potion and grins at the audience. She wipes her mouth and flashes her teeth.

"Let's get into the box and show everyone your gift."

She slips into the dark, lights fading on her shoulders and hair, and faces the glass that when Mandrake closes the door brings her image to her and seals it.

"Now, ladies and gentlemen, boys and girls, my lovely daughter and assistant Daisy will transform into the thing she is. I must warn you that without the potion she would be dangerous, violent. I have perfected this potion, and it will subdue her so we may witness her true form."

She pounds on the door.

"Please relax, Daisy. We don't want the potion to wear off too early."

The lights lower until a spotlight envelops him and the figure of a girl slouching in a glass box.

"Without further ado, I shall summon the beast from within. Daisy, close your eyes, and see yourself as you were before you met me. Long ago, you were something else. Not a beautiful young woman but something else entirely. Do you see it in your head, Daisy?"

"Yes," she responds under a spell.

"Let that image overtake you. Let it become you."

"I can see it coming closer. I can see it. It's near me now. It's closer."

An image forms over her—a gorilla. The audience oohs and ahhs.

"No, I can't."

The image fades back to her.

"You must, Daisy." Mandrake coaxes her back into the spell.

As she fades again, the gorilla appears in the box. Children and adults stretch and smile.

"No. It's too much. I can't. I…" Her scream fades within her image.

The gorilla overtakes Daisy, its body filling the space she occupied.

Mandrake turns to the audience. "Very good. We must respect what happened here. No sudden movements. No flash photography. No loud noises. The gorilla is completely subdued, I assure you, but we must remain vigilant."

The gorilla's eyes open; dark pupils shine in the spotlight.

"Oh. It's…awake." Mandrake stumbles away from the box. "This wasn't supposed to happen. Uh, hmm. Rest assured, this box is made from impenetrable materials."

The gorilla snarls and pounds on the door, which cracks open.

Mandrake backs away. "I shall get the tranquilizer gun just in case."

But he can't find the gun and scrambles around his lab, bookshelves, furniture. The gorilla bursts out of the box—the audience yells and screams—and lunges after Mandrake and grabs his ankle. The lights click off. More yells and screams and laughter. A strobe light flickers. "Help! Help!" Mandrake gasps. Chairs and tables scuttle about. More pounding. Thumps. A liquid streams into the audience.

The lights slowly come up. Blood on the floor and walls; Mandrake slumped on the table, blood dripping. The audience relaxes. Daisy, no longer a gorilla, stumbles toward her father's body, snarls, and weeps before the lights go out.

. . .

"Dad, I nailed it!" She jiggles in a field near the RVs and buses down from the midway. "I had four performances today. All of them were perfect. The audience had no idea what was coming."

"That's great."

"I was nervous at first, but adrenaline kicked in."

"What's next?"

"We do it again tomorrow. Four a day. Maybe we change them a lil' bit, but I don't want to yet. We go through the end of next week."

"Then where?"

"Louisiana."

"Close to New Orleans?"

She gazes at stars. "I don't know."

"Real proud of you. You rest that voice. You sound like me. But without cigarettes and whiskey." A glass clinks before a long pour. "Any chance you might be coming home?"

Sounds and lights from the midway burst behind her; the smells of hot dogs, burgers, funnel cakes, and popcorn drifts within moonlight. Don and Pete, silhouetted by generators, lift a bottle and food, and yell for her to come over.

"Why?"

"Just wondering. You've been gone a while."

"I have to stay on the road. It's my job."

His glass clinks; another pour. "You should."

"I'll talk to you soon, Dad."

"You better."

She meets Don and Pete and teases they should've ordered double chicken fingers, fries, baked beans, and milkshakes for her. "I earned this."

"You did."

"We all did."

"Congrats."

"To all of us."

Her mother calls; she excuses herself.

"What's the good news?"

"I did my first shows. And they were amazing."

"And you're OK with it all?"

Screams from rides swell. Fireworks pop, signaling the end of the day.

"Yes. I did this awesome thing today."

"Good."

She stops on her way back to Don and Pete and holds up her phone's camera to the midway and its spectrum among wilderness and darkness. She texts the photo to her mother. <A postcard can't do this justice, but I don't know if this picture can either.> She sends the same to her father, waits for him to reply, but shuts off her phone and stays on the perimeter—a half circle—where the midway's lights and flags lead into a kingdom where she no longer guesses which section is hers.

14

A woman sits across from Alex, Don, and Pete and soothes her pregnant belly. She cools her tea and checks her phone when it buzzes. The diner's front door flings open. A man rushes in and shows his phone to the woman.

"They're starting with Accounting."

Alex stops chewing. Don peers over his glasses and newspaper. Pete stirs his coffee.

The woman shows her phone to the man. "I got it too."

"Damn them. They said they'd wait then they'd talk to us. That was it. Just talk. Give us a heads-up to get our things in order. They said no cuts until after the first month. Not this on-the-road crap they pulled last time." He cancels his order and storms out.

The woman sobs while burying her phone in her belly.

"Can I get you something?" Alex asks.

"A job for my girlfriend. They cut her."

"Who?"

"That company that pumped all that money into us. She works in the office. A desk job. Chris says good morning and good night to her every day. He didn't yesterday." She gags in a napkin. "We're not living high on the hog, but it's better money than when we both worked at the factory. And I'm three months out. They're coming for us next."

"All of us?"

"First Accounting then Wardrobe. Maybe the rest." The morning takes her in as she slips out.

"Have we been that bad?"

Don folds his paper. "The last two stops weren't full for all our shows. But better than other years."

"We've seen it worse," Pete adds. "Don, you remember that one season when Julie had to go get an audience?"

"She drove around to schools, telling them about us."

"She was going to go to senior homes, but we didn't want heart attacks on our hands."

"Not that a woman from out of town asking principals and teachers if their students would be interested in seeing a sideshow is any better."

Pete snaps a lid on his coffee. "Our Daisy that year... Excuse me. Our Salina helped Julie put together permission forms on the spot. They stopped at a library and used the computers and printers."

"We were close to where my cousin Alison lived at the time. Up near Chattanooga," Don says. "I told her about us, and she started out but told me she was worried the lights might bring on her epilepsy. 'You stay put,' I told her. I sent her a tape of that day. Back when we used your camera, Petey."

"I hope you didn't see the tape that was in there."

"I transferred it to digital and uploaded it."

"Now maybe I can make real money as a performer."

"Hollywood will finally come calling for you. But not the Hollywood you've been wanting." Don slaps Pete's shoulder.

Their waitress tops off coffee and heads toward the back where a group from the Freak Shows pushes together tables.

Alex stops eating when Pierce flirts with the waitress. "My dad would've come if that happened now and we were nearby. He'd sit front and center. He'd bring popcorn and Milk Duds and mix them. Probably booze too."

"That's a drop in the bucket."

"We've had worse."

"And if you told my mom there'd be an animal in the show, she'd be there. But to chain herself to it while saying it needs to be free."

Manny steps in, picks up a to-go order, and leaves.

"I'll see you two in the RV."

She trails Manny to his truck. He scopes around the parking lot. Buses and vehicles idle. He unlocks his toolbox and opens a case with drill bits and, underneath, fresh-rolled joints.

"You want the same?"

She hands him cash. "Please."

"I may have to make this full time if I get cut."

"I heard about Accounting and Wardrobe. Are they coming for you?"

"The shop said they're getting pressure on going more green. Cleaner energy. He said the company that runs us wants it that way. But less of this…" He slams his truck's gate. "Is less of us."

"You wanna burn one right here in front of them?"

"I don't want my final smoke of anything in front of them. It'll bring it on faster." He scratches the stars and crosses around the script of his neck's tattoo—Stella Maris—and starts his truck. "That's your last one. I can't get caught. I gotta make this last as long as I can." He pulls next to his supervisor and offers a cigarette. The two chat. Manny drives down the highway.

Alex jogs over to a woman who slingshots through rings of fire. The morning sun deepens the woman's mottled cheeks and arms.

"Has anybody on your end heard about getting cut?"

"We've heard it every year for the past seven. But Julie somehow keeps us going."

"Has she ever let you see your numbers?"

"Yeah. You don't have to ask. But she'll only bring it up if she's getting pressure."

"How are you doing?"

The bus next to them rumbles on.

"Don't know. We go out there and do our act. And focus on that. Then we go home and rest up."

Pierce and the waitress step from the side of the diner. He lights a cigarette for them, and they take long, slow drags as he types on his phone and nuzzles her.

"I will say this," the woman continues, "we're the least controversial show here. Besides the petting zoo. Our behavior is A-grade. Our numbers could go to zero, but we'll see through to the next day because of our behavior." She steps onto her bus. "You may hear numbers are everything. But something else counts."

That bus leaves; others trail behind it. Don and Pete start the RV. Before walking over, Alex dials Julie. "Call me when you can."

. . .

After they set up half the stage, Don says he wants to walk around—"Get in my two miles for the day."—and Pete says he wants a nap before the first show and to check in with his ex-wife about Cecelia's year-end field trip.

"Where is her class going?"

"The science center," he answers Alex.

"That's a good way to end the school year. The place I used to live in has a good one. Dinosaur skeletons. Weather. History. Especially the Trail of Tears and the Civil War. They had this thing you stood under. Like a disk. And it had sounds coming from it. Wind. Rain. Thunder. Birds. In front of you was this panorama showing when the city was trees and fields and the river. That image changed to the tribes that lived there. Then the French, Spanish, English. Trains. Robert Taylor buying all the land and selling it. And the Civil War. Reconstruction. The town went bust for decades. By the time the Dust Bowl and Great Depression hit, the damage had been done. They showed the black part of town burning. Where all the descendants of former slaves and freedmen lived. Right next to the poor whites. One of those old newspaper clippings about the race riots rolled across the disk." Alex lays out her costume and makeup. "I went to the library and looked that up. A white girl said a man from the 'Negro side' had fondled her. He owned a grocery store. The first in his family to ever do something like that. The press printed the address on the front page the next day. The KKK showed up and told him to come out with his hands up and turn himself in. He didn't. They stormed in. But across the street, a group of black men had pitchforks, bats, rifles, shotguns. Somebody fired. The whites said it was the blacks. The blacks said it was the whites. The sheriff showed up, but everyone knew he was a member of the KKK. Then it all exploded. Everywhere. There's still a divide. And I remember reading about all that and wanted to go back to that disc and that image and turn it back to the fields and trees and the river. I couldn't crawl into that machine and flip those images back. Like a slideshow in reverse. But I also didn't know how to go forward."

"Because it was blank," Pete says.

"Yeah."

"Because you have what happened. And there's nothing else."

"Yeah. Those images ended in the present. Which now is a long time ago." Her phone rings. "I'd rather go to when that disc played thunder and rain and watch lightning and rain on that panorama."

"I'll see you later." Pete steps out.

"Hi, Julie. Could I get our numbers from you?"

"You've heard about the layoffs."

"Yeah."

"I haven't said anything to you and the boys because from my meetings with Chris the Talent division is not included in this first round."

"First round?"

"We're doing our best to make it only one. And that may mean cutting other departments. But I can't promise anything."

"Could I have our numbers anyway?"

Julie relays them. "I'm pleased. As is Chris. His bosses may not be. But Gorilla-Girl is earning her keep."

"I don't want to earn my keep anywhere else."

Don pulls back the tent and flips up tinted lenses. "The humidity out there is thick as thieves."

"I talked to Julie."

He chugs a bottle of water and pats himself dry. "Are we on the chopping block?"

"She's pleased with our numbers. As is Chris."

"Is he? Haven't heard that in a long time. If ever."

"She said we're at the top of the middle for shows."

"I've never heard of that."

"Have you ever asked?"

"Why would I?"

"We could move up."

"We could." He sets out his makeup and costume. "If we cared about that."

"You don't?"

"I don't. Petey doesn't either."

"What would you do if we got cut?"

"Take up freelance or volunteer IT jobs. There's a church group I know that designs affordable houses for families in need. My grandkids go that church. They talk about the software they use."

"Tech?"

He hums yes as he dusts off his lab coat. "It's still the future. Always will be."

"I've done tech. And I can't do it again."

"You'd find something. Maybe something you loved to do in the past. Or maybe something you've wanted to do. Being let go from here would let you do that."

"I have found something. And right now it says we're doing good enough."

"Then why rock the boat?"

She pushes aside her makeup. "Save me a towel and a water. I'm going for a walk."

Music pumps from speakers by a ride spinning faster, slower, faster as the operator tests it. Alex finds a cool shade between it and the smell of butter melting and dials a number. "Is Chris in?"

His admin connects her.

"I want to talk with you about our numbers. I asked Julie for them. She said you know."

"I do. I'm pleased with them."

"Me too. What I understand of them."

The popcorn vendor sets aside a test batch, which Alex grabs and steps from the shadow and into the sun coming on.

"And I'll see if we can keep them that way," she continues. "Or build off them."

"That's what I like to hear. Anything else?"

Manny and his crew lower beams onto a forklift. He jigs with his colleagues like when he sold her a joint loaded with "herb that'll take you to the happiest place on Earth. Deep, deep inside you. The rest of the world will melt away."

"I'm focused on doing this."

"Good."

"My first show of the day is soon. I need to finish getting ready."

"I appreciate you calling me about all this. Have a great show, Alex."

⋆ ⋆ ⋆

They break down the stage and props, Don and Pete don't say much to Alex, but the two men talk to each other in shadows and half lights of the midway and moon when they step out and load gear. The tent, rides, and crowds muffle their words; they talk louder through the noise but whisper in the quiet. She drops Mandrake's clipboard, but neither Don nor Pete look her way; she kicks over a trash can, but no one checks on her. They come in after closing a trailer.

"Don, I'm sorry about getting ahead of one of your lines," she says.

"Which one?"

"Which line or…?"

"Which line. And which show. You were jumpy all day."

She shrugs.

Don and Pete glance at each other. Beakers and cylinders chime in boxes.

"We want to talk you about this numbers thing you brought up with Don."

"Did he tell you it's good?"

"What about Julie?"

"Chris is happy."

Don zips up his costume. "We've never considered ourselves working for Chris. We know who he is and what he does. He's the boss at the end of the day except for this Wall Street group they got holding us. We work for Julie."

Pete sits in the chair Daisy sat in. "She's the one who lets us do this. It's never been about numbers. We're not naive. We know they play a role. But that love we get from doing this and sharing it matters the most to us."

"Without Chris," Alex says, "we can't share anything."

The two men guffaw.

Don stops folding up a table. "Are you telling us we need to perform for Chris?"

"We should've been from the start. We have good numbers."

"You keep saying that."

She fiddles with a hair that fell from Pete's mask.

"We could tell him the Skee-Ball machines have more players whenever we're in town. Or more chili-cheese dogs are sold when we let Don have the last line."

"Julie told me the numbers, Pete, and I didn't have to tell them to Chris because he knew."

"You spoke to Chris about us?" Pete crosses his arms.

She snaps the hair. "Before out first show."

"Had you talked to him when you brought this up with me?"

"No," she answers Don.

Pete snickers. "Are you sleeping with him?"

"Are you serious?"

"People here scratch itches however they can."

"OK, Petey, lets's calm…"

"We don't care what Chris says. We care about Julie. Not Chris. Tell her, Don."

Alex tosses the hairs onto the ground. "But you care what he does. Because it's either more stops for us while the rest of them go back. Or we go back. Which I don't on plan on doing."

"You can't stay on the road forever." Pete digs in his backpack for a beer. He grabs two and shares one with Don.

"That's not what he'll do."

"You don't know that, Alex."

"You don't either, Pete. Julie backs him up on that."

"This talk from you... Putting him before Julie. Man, he is Special K with you."

"Alex..." Don flicks his beer's tab. "Just listen to us. They do this. They start with the workers, justifying fuel or food expenses. They pass the duties like that onto us."

Pete interrupts, "We're already doing that work because of cuts from years ago."

"They won't cut our show."

"Have you talked to anyone this evening from the Freak Shows?" Don asks.

"I've been working."

"And we haven't?" Pete snaps.

"They've asked some of Logistics and the Freak Shows to come back," Don continues. "That's code for something else. The watchlist."

"More like the blacklist." Pete sips his beer.

"But we could change it for the better."

"He's not going to change it, Alex. We go where we go based on what they gave us."

"And I don't want him to change that. I don't want more."

Alex snaps at Pete. "You don't want more? You don't want to go anywhere else?"

He crushes his can. "Nope."

"You don't want to see if we could get more from them? If they could give us more?"

"I've never wanted that. Like Don said, they give, we go."

"They're doing what they said they wouldn't do. And they'll end up pitting us against each other. All because of numbers." Don hands his unopened beer to Pete before leaving.

"Is that what the two of you were talking about out there?"

"We don't need to focus on the numbers." Pete offers the beer to Alex. "We never had to."

"Maybe we should now. Especially if we got momentum with them. Julie can't do everything."

"But neither can we."

She spins the can but won't open it. "I asked Don what he would you do if they cut us."

"I bet he said IT or something about his grandkids' church."

"Yeah."

"That's what I love about him. The guy's an atheist. Went from Methodist to not. I love he can do that." Pete opens a second beer. "Do you how many times I see my daughter?"

"No."

"Legally it's supposed to be every other weekend. Holidays mixed in. Swapped. But not with this."

The PA announces one hour until closing.

"If I lost this? I'd go back to being a full-time dad. Wouldn't have to deal with Jess's lawyers or mine or the court about me being on the road. Maybe I'd teach drama somewhere. Maybe an acting coach. Carpentry too." He swaps out his sneakers for sandals and stands. "My daughter sent me this photo she looked up. That silver ball thing you touch, and electricity goes through, and your hair goes everywhere. She can't wait to do that at the science place. And I won't be there to see that. Unless they cut me. Or I quit."

"My physics class in high school had that silver ball. I fainted touching it."

"Did it shock you?"

"No. My dad and I had moved. New school. New faces."

"You lived with your dad?"

"Yeah."

"That's not usually the case. You're an outlier. I wish I could've been." He crushes his second can, slings on his backpack, and leaves.

She opens her beer and gazes into the can as golden as the light from the camera that blocked her locker. THIS IS IT, SENIORS! said the banner on the wall next to the lockers alongside doodles, in-jokes, well wishes, smiling faces, and names of people she had heard. She slumped against another row of lockers and waited until the interview with the football coach ended.

"Most of these seniors are pretty good, and they have a bright future," the coach said while his players jostled for camera time in front of him and tapped each other's butts and groins. "But some of them had better get used to saying, 'Would you like fries with that?' I think it'll be the first time we'll have a surplus of fry cooks."

The girl wearing a jersey and pink bandana dropped the microphone and asked the acne-ridden beanpole holding the camera to reset it for another take.

Charlotte asked, "Can I jump into my locker?"

"I don't think we've ever met."

"We're in Econ. You sat next to me."

"Don't you remember, Lindsey?" The camera operator scooted over his tripod. "She fainted in Mr. Glass's class."

"That's right. How's everything now?"

"Given that that was in September, great. Thanks for asking."

"Would you like to be interviewed?"

"For what?"

"The senior video *Looking Back*. We ask you questions. Like your favorite moment, favorite class, what you'll miss."

"I guess. Sure."

"It's Sharla, right?"

"Charlotte."

The tripod jiggled. The camera and microphone lowered, rose, lowered.

"Are you ready?"

The red light blinked above the lens. A gold tint glowed around the skylight. No one answered her when she asked how much longer this would take. She wanted to leave but had nowhere to be, but she was ready to slip out as quietly and namelessly as she had slipped in.

. . .

Clouds cover the moon, the air cooling, as she walks in drizzle through the midway. She pauses under the canopy of a game where kids behind the yellow line throw a baseball into the mitt of a cut-out catcher; the speed gun above its head flashes. One of the dads asks the attendant if there's an adult version of this where a cop is dressed as a catcher and has a breathalyzer. "I'd win all those tickets right there." He unrolls some; the attendant rolls them back. The drizzle picks up, but Alex leaves when the dad wonders why his son misses the mitt and flings the ball into a nearby game. Alex tells the attendant she's got it and reaches into a game with carrots at the finish line and polka-dot bunnies at the start. She ignores the dad asking to see the ball—"This game is a cheat. That ball is loaded. I want a refund."—and places the ball at the boy's feet.

The drizzle accelerates into a downpour. The crowds scramble. Rides halt. But the games and shows continue. She follows a crowd heading into tents stitched together behind the sign Freak Shows, Grotesqueries, Curiosities & Oddities.

"Welcome, latecomers" says the bearded lady in a purple top hat on stage. "Don't be shy. You're not violating any rules here. We have no rules. We've got one last show for you before the rain scares everyone away. Or we do." She opens her plate-sized pocket watch. "And our bosses say we've got this much time left before we close for the day." She shows the audience her watch: silhouettes of devils poking a pitchfork into a person running. "We did sign a lifelong contract."

Performers yell offstage, "We can't get out until the end!"

The mortician sitting at an organ plays a funeral march. Flowers and gravestones pop up from the top of his organ.

Alex keeps to the shadows where behind the stage Pierce wipes down, wiggles his silver briefs, and offers the towel to someone. Alex leans his way. The waitress from the diner takes Pierce's towel. A lithe woman and man, dressed in black and whipping open black umbrellas topped by skulls, slide through. A man covered in tumors trails behind them, rolling out an organ grinder and looping a snake around his shoulder. Little people dressed like dead movie stars march onstage. Pierce has the waitress adjust his briefs and joins the ensemble. Rain falls harder —no thunder. The crowds outside dissipate. Alex moves over when drops plop on her from a leak in the tent.

After the finale, the houselights come up, the crowd leaves, the midway quiets except for workers closing for the night, and Alex walks through odors of chainsaws and barking from the two-headed stuffed dog and flame-smothered swords and hooks and finds Pierce placing his props in a trunk.

"Good show."

"Gorilla-Girl. What's up?"

"I missed your part, but I caught the end."

"The climax." His pink fingernails explode in the air.

"I'll come back next time to catch you. Without the rain."

"The rain drives them here when they're wet."

One of the little persons tells Pierce she'll see him tomorrow.

"Have you heard about the cuts?"

"To Wardrobe?"

"And Accounting."

"Hadn't heard about Accounting." He slips on a crop top. "Is that why you're over on my side of our world?"

"I wanted to see if you were still here."

"Why wouldn't I be?"

"Don said the Freak Shows were getting cuts."

He rolls on rainbow-colored socks. "Did he say this to you while you were taking a shower in your RV? And he was gonna jump in there a sec to grab something he forgot?"

"I told you he's not like that. Don't talk that way about him."

"Got a thing for him now? Daddy issues?"

"Is it true?"

"He's wrong. We're not going anywhere." He calls over the bearded lady who removes her top hat and cools off her bald head. "What did you Julie tell you the other day about our show?"

"She said we're doing great. She said Chris was pleased. Why?"

"Gorilla-Girl here heard cuts are headed our way."

"My name is Alex."

"I don't believe it based on what she told me."

"Did she mention your numbers?"

"She did. I talk with her after every stop."

"Every stop?"

"I run this. It's mine to make or break. We got rents to pay and mouths to feed."

Pierce opens his and rolls around his tongue's silver ball.

"Who told you we were headed for cuts?"

Pierce jumps in. "You remember that pervy old guy who plays the weird scientist in her show?"

"Don is his name. He heard."

"I don't know Don, and I don't know nothing about no rumors of cuts for us. If we get cut, it won't be because of receipts. Or our merch sales."

"You have merch?"

The bearded lady nods at tables coming down: shirts, posters, trinkets, bobbleheads.

"You have one merch, right?" Pierce asks Alex. "A poster?"

"We do."

"But it's not sold at your show. I've seen it in the gifts area."

"That's something we can work on," Alex says. "We also have good receipts. We're in the top of the middle. Julie said so."

"We are too."

"And Chris knows that."

"We're not focused on making Chris happy. We're at the top because of what we do and because of Julie. She's helped us with our numbers. Not Chris."

Pierce answers a text. "Anya, what can I do to speed up calling it a night?"

"Help Xian fold the buntings," the bearded lady answers. "And make sure Logistics knows we need them on Thursday for loading."

"Let me give you my number if you want to talk some more about merch or how our show's doing," Pierce says to Alex.

"I'm good. Thanks."

Pierce leaves, and as Anya readies to, Alex confirms with her no one from the Freak Shows was sent back.

"Raquel was. But only because she had a reaction from something she ate." Anya sets her top hat in a box and covers it with a purple cloth that matches her hat and Pierce's mohawk. "You're new, right?"

"Not anymore."

"Rumors swirl around here. And someone'll get cut or leave. Julie works with this. She always has. She works with us. She wants to. She knows numbers. She knows they have a place. But she knows we do too. She's been around long enough to blend the two. She's better at that than Chris. Be thankful you got her. I am."

As Alex turns for the exit, she overhears Pierce on his phone: "Just calling to make sure we're scheduled for a pickup. Thursday. I'll check with Anya."

The rain scales back, but clouds thicken in patches across the sky, and sections of the midway darken while she heads for the area on the fringe where Logistics parks their vehicles. Two trucks and an ATV with a trailer dip across softer ground; drizzle fuzzes their red taillights.

Alex dials a number. "You around?"

"I gotta go replace a pen for one of the goats." An engine in Manny's background cranks on. "What's up?"

"I heard they were maybe cutting y'all."

"I don't know if it's a full-on cut, but they sent some of us back. They say it's budget, but it's not. Something else is being talked about." His engine whines into neutral.

Over a small hill in front of Alex headlights flicker while a vehicle pauses. The silhouette sitting inside holds a phone glowing like a blue cube. Another silhouette jogs from the lights of Logistics, chucks ropes in the back of the vehicle, and gets in.

Manny's tone turns serious. "Do you need assistance with any loading or unloading during our closing processes?"

"No."

"Has your show or division manager requested you to contact Logistics about any concerns during our time on the road?"

"I'm sorry if I messed up with you earlier." She hangs up.

The blue cube dies out. The engine turns over. The vehicle crawls across fields and slopes and alongside trees halfway between dark ground and hidden stars.

Her RV brightens when she enters the performers' area. Don reads by a window and sips his evening tea. Pete video-chats while he meanders under the awning: "Daddy loves you. I'll talk to you later. From our next stop. Goodnight." Alex wrings out her shirt and hair but turns back deeper into the field.

A car alarm squawks; headlights flash. The couple next to it snicker. "They'll find me now," the man says. The woman clicks off the alarm and opens the door. As clouds break, moonlight shines on the purple mohawk of Pierce running his hands over the waitress.

Alex dives behind a stump. She checks her phone's bars—low. She sneaks closer—lower—then to the right—two more bars. She zooms in, but the waitress gets into her car while Pierce turns from Alex's camera. A branch snaps under her. Pierce checks around but can't get away from the waitress when her headlights flick on. He jumps in before they drive off.

Rain falls harder. Alex shields her phone as she runs from spot to spot, stopping for better bars on her phone. She jogs back to her RV: dark; Don and Pete asleep; her other colleagues saying goodnight. She grabs her toiletries bag and slips into the bathroom where she composes a text.

I saw one of the performers from the Freak Shows leave grounds with a guest before curfew. He was all over her. Just thought you should know.

She hovers over Julie's number but removes it and inserts Chris's.

15

The pump's gallons tick away, and Alex asks Don and Pete if they want anything from inside. She sprints for the store through a downpour, but before she's halfway Don yells at her that she needs the food card. Thunder claps; wind swirls rain and trash off the highway. She sprints back and dodges a motorcycle pulling under the station's overhang.

Don reminds her to keep the purchase under a certain amount or the difference will come out of their pockets. "But that may change if we're told we have to go back."

"We should ask if we can go over the limit."

"We don't ask. We're told."

"Maybe that should change." She wipes water off the cards.

"Don't mix those up. Pete and I can't pay for gas again until we're paid."

"I can cover it."

The convoy honks as it exits the pumps.

"Coffee. Black for you," she says. "Beef jerky for Pete."

"And snack mix, muscle rub, ibuprofen." He looks her over. "Do you need to write all that down?"

"Why?"

"Because you also left the pump in."

She clicks it back in place. "I'll be back."

"We'll be here."

While Alex cruises the aisles, a woman and her kids approach.

"You with that circus that came through?"

"I am."

"You became a gorilla."

All three kids wiggle around their mother's legs, snotty noses wiping her jeans.

Alex hunches over, grunting and panting. The kids chase her, laughing.

"They loved it." The mother picks up the smallest—a boy who sucks his thumb through his cleft lip. "It was a little pricey for us. But what more could we do on a rainy weekend?"

The boy buries his face in his mother's shoulder.

"I'm glad to hear that. Thank you for seeing my show."

"We didn't get to ride many rides, but we saw all them shows y'all got. Yours was our favorite."

They walk toward the counter. Alex's phone buzzes.

"Just you and that other man do it?"

"I have help for changing into the gorilla." She ooh-oohs and snarls at the kids. She says to the employee, "I'll get hers too."

"You don't need to do that."

"Let me, please. It's a treat to meet fans." Alex puts away the food card and uses hers.

"Declined," the employee says. "Do you have another one?"

She slides it to him.

"Also declined."

She cringes at the total—over the allotted amount—and hands the food card to him. "You can keep following us to our next stop and see another show."

"We got to get home," the mother says. "Rain's heavy now."

The kids wave and grunt and bound toward their car. The small boy beats his chest and flares his teeth.

She slows her sprint to the RV when she listens to her voicemail: Alex, it's Chris. Call me back when you can.

Don steps out. "Took you long enough."

"I got to make a call."

"It's your turn to drive."

"Can I do it down the road?"

"Pete's crashed. And I'm not far behind him."

"I got your coffee." She shoves the bag at Don. "That should help."

He struggles opening the ibuprofen bottle. "I need to stretch my legs. They're cramping. And I want to relax in the back. Read. Drink my coffee there. And it's your turn to drive."

After Chris doesn't answer, she hangs up. "I can take us to the next rest stop."

"We should get at least fifty miles before stopping again."

She yanks herself into the driver's seat and positions her phone on the dashboard.

"You know where we're going?"

"GPS will tell me. It told you and Pete."

He empties the bag. "Do you have the receipt for this?"

"I'll take care of it." She cranks on the engine.

Don pulls up the stepladder. "Keep an eye on that blue cloud." He moves her phone and taps the screen. "That's hail. We don't want to get caught in that."

She sets her phone back.

He pops open the muscle rub and shuffles toward the back, passing Pete snoring. Alex draws the curtains between them and turns up her phone's volume. The RV careens onto the onramp.

. . .

Under darker clouds, her phone rings: Incoming Call – Dad. Heavy rain smacks the RV and concrete, lets up, smacks again; traffic slows. She pushes on the hazards and drifts. Clarence calls again; Alex silences it and accelerates into the other lane but slams on the brakes when red lights burst from wind and rain. Pete jolts awake; Don topples off his bed. They rip open the curtain separating the cab. Orange and red tubes glow on sections of the highway.

"Why don't you pull under that underpass," Don suggests.

Clouds break off to the southeast on the map while the RV's arrow blinks northwest.

"We'll keep going."

"Alex, pull off."

"I got it, Don."

"Let me call and see how far ahead they are." Don heads to his bed.

Pete flops into the passenger seat and, kicking his feet on the dashboard, yawns. "I needed that."

"Sounds like you could use more."

"Thunder woke me up. Or maybe it was your driving."

"Feel free to take over if you don't like my driving."

"I already did mine."

Her phone rings.

Don returns. "Some of them pulled off at the exit for the caverns."

"You want to answer that?" Pete points at Alex's phone. "Chris is calling. Maybe he wants to tell us something."

Don leans in. "Why is Chris calling you?" He checks his phone. "Did he call you?"

Pete digs out his phone. "Nope. Did Julie?"

Don checks again. "No."

The blinker click-clicks as they exit, but Alex stops the RV short of a steep decline winding down to the visitor center. Hail plinks around them. Alex's phone rings.

"Is that Julie?" Pete slips on his boots.

Alex hides her phone.

"Who is it?"

"It's none of your business."

"If it's someone from work, you should answer it."

She flings open the door, jumps down, slides on the wet road, and jogs past the line for tickets inside the visitor center. A tram arrives, its headlights emerging from the dark, and slows for passengers. Alex meanders around them and cuts off her father's voicemail before she reaches a map and the years someone discovered fissures—a Cherokee princess and her Spanish lover; a slave on the run; a boy searching for his dog; a woman whose vision of Christ told her not to jump—and the vein-like tunnels leading into pockets. A sound recording of bats flutters over her while she calls Chris near an exhibition about the things living below and the sign reminding visitors not to touch anything while they're there and never bring anything back into the light: it all must stay behind in the dark where it was found.

"How's that weather?" Chris asks.

"We're taking a break."

"About your message...thanks for letting me know."

Children in the gift shop poke stuffed animals.

"I also want to talk about your assignment."

<The hail is letting up.> Don texts.

"I don't want to come back, Chris. I want to stay out. And if there's a town that doesn't want us, I'll change our show so they will. Or I'll work on something else. Wardrobe again. Anything."

"You're not coming back. I'm promoting you and your show to full capacity."

"Yeah?"

"You've impressed me. More than I expected. And I like being wrong about something like this."

<We're ready to go.>

"All our shows had strong numbers even with the rain. The rides took a hit. But that happens. But we have our shows. And yours was among the top. Keep it up."

"I will."

<Where are you?>

She selects a hoodie—the cave printed on it like a portal to another dimension—and slides the food card to the employee behind the counter.

Pete steps aside in the RV. "I was about to come find you. Did you talk to Chris?"

"I had to pee and...call my dad."

"And you bought something."

"I was cold."

"Did you go all the way into the cave do that?"

She sits in the driver's seat but doesn't set her phone out. Pete returns to the recliner. Don asks Alex if she has the food and gas cards. She hands both to him and pinches her nose at the amount of muscle rub oozing off him.

"If you bought something that's not food or gas..."

"I know, Don. I'll make sure it's resolved."

"Julie is who you contact."

Her phone buzzes: Incoming Call – Dad. But she grinds the RV into drive.

Don hobbles to bed; his light clicks off.

Alex accelerates onto the highway amid scattered rain and sunshine.

. . .

Her father calls again, but she hits Silence. In the passenger seat, Pete drops down his sunglasses and, zooming in and out on the map, notes the stop for the convoy up ahead. Alex tells him she'll keep going.

"It's a planned stop. We need to stick with them."

"We can get there before them."

"It's not a race, Alex. We get there around the same time."

"The Welty County Fair will be the first to greet us." She white-knuckles the wheel. "We'll be the first they see."

"That matters to you?"

"They'll see us rolling in, and they'll know we'll bring them one smile at a time."

"Are you with Marketing now?"

"We should market ourselves. And have merchandise to sell before and after our shows."

"We already have that."

"We have a poster. Nothing else."

"What else do we need?"

"Mugs. Shirts. Bobbleheads."

"Bobbleheads?" The road rushes by in Pete's sunglasses like white bolts across black squares. "Last time I checked we don't have anything about the show on the side of the RV."

"Maybe it's time we did."

"What would you want it to say? Come See Alex the Gorilla-Girl and No One Else?"

"Daisy, not Alex."

"Aren't they the same?"

Don's alarm beeps. He yawns and asks if they're close.

"About fifteen miles away."

"Did we pass the next rest stop?"

"Alex did."

"I could've used it. Petey, can you give me a hand?"

Alex glimpses the rearview mirror: Don swings his legs over the edge of his bed and points at his toes and calves; Pete massages them and slides Don forward and offers his shoulder, which Don staggers onto and rubs his back. The RV jolts to the side and rocks the two men. Pete lowers Don into the recliner and returns alongside Alex.

"Do we need to call Gloria?" she asks.

"Why?"

"Have her come pick him up. Or maybe one of their kids could come get him."

"He's stiff. Like I get sometimes. After we perform as much as we do."

"Well, being on the road together has paid off. We've been promoted to full capacity. We're all in with it."

"How do you know?"

"We've got great numbers."

Pete snaps off his sunglasses. "That again."

"Chris let me know."

Don chugs a water bottle. "Is my ibuprofen up there?"

"I'll get it for you." Pete wobbles out of his seat while Alex maintains high speed through a turn.

"You got something to wash it down with? Something other than water?"

"An ale or an IPA?" Pete asks.

Alex snaps, "No drinks like that on the RV."

The two men stare at each other before glaring at her.

"Which one do you want?" Pete continues.

"The IPA."

"Great choice, mi amigo." Pete's voice rises, his tone slicing. "It's a clean, crisp mouthfeel with water from a spring in California and hops from Colorado."

"Don't take it with alcohol, Don. Please. We need you fresh for our shows."

"I won't be fresh for any of them if I don't hit this now."

"That's why it's called Skybridge IPA," Pete continues. "And if you look closely on the label…" He hands the bottle to Don. "You'll see a bridge linking mountains in the middle of a beautiful blue sky." He opens a second. "Which is where I'd rather be right now."

"Are you sore too?"

"No, Alex. I just want to enjoy a beer with my friend who's roughed up."

"It's not that bad. I get this way. I'm past retirement."

Alex glances at them and at wildflowers pushing yellow, orange, and purple on slopes and around signs.

DO NOT MOW

LET THEM BE

AND LET THEM BE WILD

"I can open a third one," Pete says to her. "If you want to pull over and partake with us. Like you have before."

"We have somewhere to be. Unless you want to drive."

"Would you let me?"

She accelerates and clamps down on the wheel.

"That's what I thought." Pete smacks the galley's counter and toasts Don and Alex. "Then onward, my trusty steed. Onward into the unknown under a sky that is all our own."

Alex follows the GPS's directions at a junction.

Don scrolls through his phone and shows something to Pete. "We're full capacity now. I have an email."

"I heard."

"How did you hear?"

Pete swills. "Alex told me."

"How's this?"

"Chris told me."

"Not Julie?"

"He said the show has done so well he's promoting us. When all that bad weather happened back there we got a boost."

"I'll have to get hold of Gloria and change plans."

"I'll have to rearrange my schedule for Cecelia." Pete flings open a magazine. "But we got numbers."

Alex hears Don whisper to Pete before she turns for the fairgrounds. She registers at the gate where the guard wonders why there's no line of trucks and cars. "They're behind us," Alex replies. The RV rumbles down a road for a large field where it's the only vehicle. The cab, galley, and beds thrum after Alex kills the engine; the chassis croaks while the brake latches down and support legs smash into the grass. Alex snatches her phone and pops out. Don flings open the side door and struggles down the stairs, asking her when she planned on telling Pete and him. "My dad has called a lot since the gas station. I need to find out what's going on." She vacates a spot a truck from Logistics wants. "You made it," she says to them but withdraws from Manny's stare while he waits for her to move.

The rest of the convoy pulls in and sets down. Cranes unfold. Tractors fire up. Trailers jangle over the grounds. Alex stops under an A-frame shelter and leaves a voicemail for her father. "I know you've been calling. I've been working. On the road. Going to the next stop." Vans and cars related to the Freak Shows sidewind into the field. As she walks toward them, her father calls back, but she hits Silence.

"Anya? It's Alex. The Gorilla-Girl."

The bearded lady charges up an e-cigarette before opening a trailer.

"One of my cast is not feeling well," Alex says. "Do you have someone you could loan?"

"Not for free. I'll have to charge you for that."

"You couldn't do it as a favor?"

"We're down a person. And if we weren't, I'd still charge your account."

"Is that something Julie handles?"

"She does."

"I can say something to Chris about it."

"It's Julie's concern. Not Chris's." Anya pulls over a wagon and loads two-headed creatures sloshing in jars. She adjusts a baby shark; amber liquid drizzles the ground; she checks the stitches holding the two heads and reseals the jar. "You can't take time away from an act or a department without compensation. We each have a budget. Don knows this."

"Don's the one who's not feeling well."

"Like I said we're short now. We've got our hands tied being down a performer."

"Who's out?"

"I got stuff to finish before we get going."

Alex spies the rest of the freak-show cast and crew dragging out gear—no Pierce. She runs back to the RV. "Let's put on a show right now."

"What?"

"Alex, my back is worse. I need the rest before tomorrow."

"Pete and I can do it."

"You're assuming I want to," Pete says.

"Then I'll do it." She jumps out and flings open the RV's storage.

Pete follows her. "What's going on?"

"We have an opportunity to get ahead."

"With what?"

"Attendance. Ticket sales." Her wardrobe box scrapes as she tugs. "Plus this gets us out of the RV."

"No one is coming until tomorrow morning. That's on all the fliers. Our website. And the fairgrounds."

"Then we'll post things around town. Like they used to do in the old days. We can tell the big wigs we did it. They'll love it. Like old Kopolski days."

"The town is miles away. We're in the county."

"How far is it, Pete?"

An ATV and its trailer rattle by.

"We'll take one of those. Grab an extra gas can. And you hold on. Unless you want to drive it. And I can stand on the back and hand out fliers. You can dress up as Dr. Mandrake. And I'll wear the gorilla mask."

"Why would I dress up as Don's part?"

"Because you can play any role."

"What does that mean?"

"You're talented. I've seen it firsthand."

"We're not doing that. Get out for a while, Alex. Go walk around. Get a feel for the place. It's a big fairgrounds. Don needs to rest. I need to figure out my schedule. If you want to eat with us, be back by six. We're all going into town. Barbecue contestants will be serving their grub."

Her phone rings; she hits Silence.

"If that's your dad, you can answer it. You said you've been playing phone tag with him."

"If I'm not back by six, go on without me." She looks over the fairgrounds' map, outlined like a wagon wheel, and the flyer taped near the hub labeled Exposition Hall.

Welty County Fair

Thurs. – Sun.

BBQ, Woodworking, and Quilting Festival + Rides,

Sideshows, a Midway & More from Kopolski Traveling

Amusement

She walks through the other campgrounds and areas trucks and trailers fill in and where people unload smokers, grills, chairs, tables, meats, crafts. Fresh-cut mesquite and hickory drift around her. On one truck's logo, a cartoon pig wearing a chef's hat and wielding a fork and knife chases another pig. She samples sauces and rubs, teases the vendors she's not a judge but would place a blue ribbon on them, and mentions her show. "Be sure to check it out. We're the best show. And if you mention Daisy the Gorilla-Girl sent you, I'll get you in for half off."

Her father answers her call before she finds a bench inside Exposition Hall.

"I know you've been calling."

"You been busy with work?"

"It's so much right now, Dad."

"That's good."

"You'd like this stop. They got all kinds of barbecue."

"I'll be there as soon as I can."

"And Mom would like it too."

"It's not barbecue tofu, is it?"

"Quilts."

The custodian at the other end spins his buffer over the concrete of empty stalls.

"She loved doing that. Your Grams did too. You'll get all her sewing stuff and machine. Unless your cousin Rachel commandeers them."

"Which she will," they say together.

"You'll get your Mom's too, I reckon."

"I hope so."

A man enters from the side, asks the custodian something, and sets up a rack in a stall. Following him, a teenage girl carries a tub.

"I was calling you because I got tests my doctor wants me to do," Clarence says. "Checking some things."

"I'm sorry I can't be there."

"It'd be nice if you could."

"I'm so busy with all this. By the time I get back, you'll be done."

"I will. I'll be in and out like a wildfire. Not worth your time."

"My boss promoted me."

"Congratulations."

"He's the family who owns the company."

"You're rubbing the right shoulders." He coughs up something; spits it out.

"Which means I've got so much going on. It's good. But it also means I'm on tour more. That's part of the promotion. I won't be back for a while."

"You stay out as long as you need."

The teenage girl unpacks the tub and hands objects to the man.

"Who's this guy's boss?" Clarence asks. "Maybe you should let him or her know you're on your way up."

"The next boss is invisible. We've never seen them. They control the money."

"They're ghosts."

"Yes."

"Ghosts never go away until they get what they need." He coughs again. "They're in the right place but at the wrong time, but they don't know that. And they think they're after a thing, but it's never a thing. It's something else."

The girl spreads out the objects on a table. The custodian and his buffer glide down the other wing. The clock above ticks closer to six. The girl and man lay a sheet over the display then exit through the side door.

"I got to go, Dad."

"I go in next week. Like I said a few tests. Won't be nothing on my end."

"I'll call when I can."

"Love you, Charlie Girl. I'm proud of you."

The swirls of water and suds evaporate the closer Alex walks toward the table. The custodian finishes the rest of the wing, the sound of a wheel spinning as it spirals out. Alex peeks under the sheet: woodcarvings of turtles, whales, eagles, and galloping horses. A trunk slams shut; the girl and man slip back in with more boxes. Alex wipes her cheeks on her way out.

· · ·

The employee area bustles when she reaches its edge. She pulls off the trail while her colleagues clamber into vehicles. Pete jumps into the back of a truck; Don grimaces pulling himself into the cab before the truck heads for the gate.

She rummages through the RV's galley and gags after she sniffs a milk carton but cobbles together stale crackers, one string cheese, a quarter-pound of deli meat that is not gray, and a sticky bun Don bought for her when she improvised on a line he flubbed. She rereads his note: *Thanks for *sticking* with me when I got stuck.* She opens the beer and rubs the label of the bridge between mountains and thinks the silhouette is not a bridge but the remains of a mountain that had to be hollowed out for a bridge to appear in its place. As she eats, she leaves a message for her mother. An email from Chris pings. She skims the first part—*a warm welcome to our family of entertainers and crew on the road;* changes to policies; an update of facilities and motor-pool concerns; *a challenging first half to the season including weather and reducing overhead in departments*—but slows when he highlights the season's tour to date.

> But after we consolidated cash flow and trimmed expenses, overall, we've had a great month—one that we can build on as the tour goes into summer, which is when our gate receipts, rides' in- and outflow, shows' margins, and merchandise revenue take off. The rebound is brought to us by our sideshows, such as the Gorilla-Girl show helmed by Alex Long and her cast mates, which have exceeded ticket sales and attendance records for the

first time in three years. Those sales and the number of guests in seats are more than those three years combined! And if we look back five years, sales and attendance for shows are four seats and mere dollars off those numbers. What a great thing to share with you all, and I look forward to our quarter-end newsletter when I know, thanks to every one of you who have put in the hard work because of our challenges, we'll have more great news to share. Until then, keep giving our guests One Smile at a Time.

The sunset hovers over the road to the fairgrounds' main gate, and Alex imagines the convoy that went into town for dinner will read Chris's email and storm over the hills, tear down trees, maul dirt and grass, circle the RV, and ask her to step out; but she won't know if they'll throw food at her or clap for her. "Go on," her father's voice says from a corner in the RV. She turns toward it. "Find out."

"Where're we going?" she asked him when they stopped at a store. The road split green and gold grasses; trees dotted the road.

"I thought we'd go for a drive. I have a birthday surprise for you." He told her to sit tight while he paid for gas.

The road smoothed into a straight shot—no cars on either side. Clarence fished around the bottom of his slushy and peeled open a pack of cigarettes. He pushed in the lighter but looked at

Charlotte staring at him. He nixed the lighter and stuffed the pack in his pocket.

"Did your mom like your Mother's Day gift?"

"She said she already had that book. I told her you said you were certain she didn't have it. She said you wouldn't have known."

He smirked as his truck idled at a corner. "I'm sure she did."

"But she liked the box I made her."

"She still with what's his name?"

"Trav. Travis. They broke up."

"Your mom needs to get her act together." He wiped his mouth across his jacket. "Sorry. I'm trying not to talk like that. I liked the box you made for her. You're creative."

"I like art class. It's my favorite."

"Here we are."

She thought he was joking—the two of them in the middle of nowhere.

He pulled his truck off the road and onto dirt scattered along a grassy hill. "I know it's no ocean like a couple of years ago." He took her hand and led them into a ditch and up to the hill's fence where rust sparkled on barbs across a vast field and new buds on trees while insects snapped around the blue sky. In the field at the crest of a hill, horses whinnied and dipped into grass and wildflowers.

"Do you want to pet one?" He clicked his tongue.

None of them were interested.

"Oh, come on, you goddamned horses. I've got my daughter with me." He opened a bag of peppermints.

The ears twitched on the brown horse with white bands around its legs.

Clarence crackled the wrapper.

The horse trotted closer.

"There we go."

The horse pulled up weeds and dandelions near the fence.

"Go on, Charlie."

"What if it bites me?"

"Go on."

She offered wildflowers through the fence.

"Use these." He unrolled another peppermint.

The horse drifted closer.

"See."

"How do you know?"

"I found out."

The horse snorted.

Clarence handed the mint to her. "Go on. Find out if he'll take it."

The horse started for her shaking palm. She shut her eyes when whiskers and hot breath touched her hand. As soon as she felt the lips, she flinched and dropped the mint in the grass. The horse grunted and stomped its hooves.

"Do you want me to find it?" he asked.

"We don't want to make him sick. Who knows what he does?"

"True. He may be a show horse or work the fields here."

The horse tossed its head and swayed its tail before lumbering into the middle of the field.

Before bed, she said to him, "I wasn't scared."

"I know you weren't. But you had to find out."

That night, she dreamed of a never-ending field where storm clouds gathered over a horse cutting toward her through the gray-green landscape. The horse stopped, and Charlotte froze. It backed up and snapped its legs, its ears rigid. Thunder crackled. The horse backed up again. The wind picked up and tousled her hair and the horse's. The Charlotte in bed watched this happen and told the Charlotte in her dream to move toward the horse. And as they moved closer, the horse swayed away from her, tucking its tail. "Don't be afraid," she said in her sleep and in her dream. Her arm lifted off the mattress while her arm in the dream reached for the horse. The horse's black eyes shone in scattered light. "Go on," the Charlotte in bed said. "Find out." The other Charlotte reached for the horse's chest, but before she touched it, water burst out and up to her ankles; both Charlottes flinched. She woke, believing water was in her bed and up to her ankles, and checked around her mattress and sheets. She felt lighter but empty as if something had been jettisoned but remained nearby if it had to return.

· · ·

Headlights and the sounds of engines cut through the RV. She washes her dish and finishes her beer while the convoy files in. She steps out. Her colleagues chat, walk toward Exhibition Hall or around the fairgrounds, and mingle with vendors; but no one notices her. She looks around—no Don or Pete—and cruises through the lots—no truck like the one they left in—and readies for bed. Lights and lanterns dim or click off. Guitars and a banjo strike up. Silhouettes snuggle, dance, drink, roast s'mores around a campfire, but as the hours deepen, neither Don nor Pete appear. She checks her phone—no texts or voicemails from them or staff—and reads in bed until she falls asleep.

Two voices outside her open window wake her. She peers out: moonlight shines on Don and Pete.

"According to that email it's her show now."

"The hell it is."

"Keep your voice down, Petey."

"I don't care if she hears me. At this point, she can have the show."

"I'm not there yet. It's just an email. We're still under Julie. And she knows that."

"She who? Julie or our Daisy?"

"We have a contract stipulating how we're organized. We can show that to both of them."

"Julie needs to know more."

"She does."

"If she does know or if she doesn't, either way this is getting out of hand. I can't keep changing my schedule with Jess. Her lawyer will run with this. I could lose my visitations with Cecelia."

Don rubs the back of his neck. "Gloria wants me to take it easy. She's afraid she'll be picking me up at a hospital."

"Maybe we can get our Daisy to sweet talk Chris about that."

"If that doesn't work, she can turn into a gorilla and threaten him."

They chuckle.

"Lord knows my time as the gorilla is short. She'll want to charge tickets for everyone to see her. Or make bobbleheads out of it."

"She can stick them on the RV."

Alex ducks when they glance behind them.

"She can do anything now."

"Maybe we should find out if she can without us."

16

Before the first show, Alex skips breakfast and heads for the tent where backstage she keeps an eye on the opening while creating social-media accounts for the show and encouraging posts, hashtags, and photos. She opens the wardrobe trunk, lays out her dress and makeup, and flips her script to the middle; she sets her phone's timer, poses, and writes.

> Buy a ticket, join us this weekend at any of our shows throughout the day, and see what happens after.

She holds up the gorilla mask in front of the Pepper's Ghost box, angling her reflection through the mask's. She snaps photos of the set, audience area, outside of the tent, the poster, and the midway and edits and saves each in a folder on her phone she labels Marketing. She sends the accounts' logins to her email and starts another, copying Pete and Don and Julie on it, but replaces them with Chris.

> I started social media accounts for my Gorilla-Girl show. I know the Freak Show and some of our Mighty Midway

post rides, games, and special events, and I know we have a topnotch marketing team that handles a lot of this, but these new accounts are all free except for me putting in "elbow grease" as my dad would say. I'm looking forward to keeping it up to date with where we are, where we'll be next, and tease what my show's about. And we can also use what our guests photograph and video (we can't stop them from doing that anyway). Why not put all that to good use and have them help us get the word out?

She sends this before Don and Pete shuffle into the tent.

"Morning, Alex."

"Morning."

Pete doesn't say anything and strides to his wardrobe. "Were you in here?" He holds up his gorilla mask. "Did you wear it?"

"I put it on the table next to my stuff and took a photo of it. I got it out for marketing."

"Marketing?" He waves away her phone.

Don buffs Dr. Mandrake's loafers. "Why do you need that for marketing?"

"We can use it."

"Are we doing that now?"

"No, Don, you mean, is she doing that now?"

"Did Julie ask you?"

"I'm doing it." Grabbing her clothes, she heads for the dressing area where she disrobes slowly while Don and Pete whisper; one of them storms off. She slides on her dress and shoes and reads Chris's reply.

Thanks for this. We need this initiative and effort. Exactly who we are.

She switches to social media: three likes and a comment from someone saying they'll be at the afternoon show and a marketing company offering "twenty times the impressions your posts get," which she screenshots and adds to her folder.

Don lowers Mandrake's clipboard when she steps out. "There's my Daisy."

She curtsies.

"Got a minute? As Alex?"

"Where's Pete?"

"Cecelia's sick."

"I'm sorry to hear that."

"You should tell him that. He also wants to talk to Julie."

"About what?"

"Making this more than what it is. What I started. And what Petey and I built."

She strolls to the other side of the laboratory. "You two 'built'?"

"I said I'd talk to you first."

"Here I am. As Alex."

A technician enters the front of the stage and cycles through lights; one brightens over the Pepper's Ghost box like a spotlight on a black ocean.

"Petey and I are pleased this is taking off. But it's taxing us. Him with his daughter. Me physically."

She reaches for her script, unclips a pen from it, and strikes out or rewrites sections. "We can move you offstage faster. We can cut your lines here and here." She flips backward. "That monologue you have early on could be cut down. We should've done that earlier anyway. We could scale back Pete's grunts. How many times does he need the audience to feel what he's about?"

The light over the box flicks off.

"We're asking you to bring this back down to art rather than making it a business," Don says. "The joy we had."

"You've seen the audiences?"

"I have."

"Packed, Don. When was the last time you saw it that way?"

"I'm not focused on that. I'm an amateur. In the original sense. The love of it all."

"Do you want more than Pete?" She flips through her script. "If he needs to leave because of Cecelia, I can figure this out. We'll give you more lines. Or move these. Which'll give me time to put on the suit."

"That's not the trick."

"We can adjust that." She opens the box. "We could borrow tools from… I don't know. Logistics?" She grimaces. "Maybe not.

Maybe the guys in Rides. They have all those tools. Then we get in one of our electricians. Like the one who was here. He knows our show. Speaking of, I want to be standing over you…Dr. Mandrake…at the end. And keep it that way. Maybe until the summer is over."

"You mean you as Daisy? Or you as the gorilla?"

"Whichever."

He takes her script. "Is that why you ate breakfast by yourself this morning?"

"I didn't eat breakfast. I came here."

"Starving for art?"

People file into the tent.

"We need Pete to get back," she says. "Or else we're doing it without him. And I'll be standing over you for the first show."

The audience swells and stands in the wings.

She strides onto the stage. "Ladies and gentlemen, thank you for coming to our first show of the day. We have a great show in store. Let's make sure we give room to everyone."

A person in a wheelchair rolls in but can't find a spot.

"Especially for those who need help seeing a girl transform into a gorilla." She motions to a spot near the front for the wheelchair. "But I would't sit too close." She hops around and grunts like a primate before returning backstage.

Pete gnaws his mouthpiece. "What was that?"

"I welcomed them to the first show of the day."

"We've never done that."

"I did. And Don and I talked. I'm standing over Mandrake at the end. Me as Daisy. Not a gorilla. You know what to do with that." She writes on Don's clipboard and tears off the paper and skips onto stage and toward the technician.

Pete thrusts on his mask, lumbers into the box, and slams his fist on the door.

The audience quiets then murmurs.

"We got our gorilla into place." Alex skips back to the stage. "Did you hear him? He's ready."

They clap.

"Are you ready?"

They cheer.

The houselights fade; stage lights come up. While the show unfolds Alex changes lines; improvises; jumps into the audience; delays entering the box. And at the end of the show, as a plain girl, Pete and Don alongside her onstage, she thanks the audience for coming; reminds them about future stops and "keeping up with the show on our social-media channels"; and calls out "Don Haskett as Dr. Theodore Henry Mandrake, the brains behind all this" and "Peter Arrojas as the gorilla I became." She motions for them to bow; they do cooly. "And I'm Daisy. An average girl who transformed into something amazing before your eyes. Thank you. I know I'll see you soon."

Pete rips off his mask and charges offstage.

Don waves to audience members hanging around. "That was a lot, Alex."

"Did you see the third row, stage left? The group with the all those kids? They covered their eyes but peeked out and giggled."

"You got lucky with what you did."

"What do you mean?"

"We kept up."

"I knew you could. But I wasn't sure about Pete."

"He's the professional actor. He could. And did."

"He didn't want to. I could see it in his eyes. Even with that mask on. But we did it. And we'll do it again the rest of today. Tomorrow. More." She slides off the stage and mingles with the audience, showing them where she can be found on the internet.

The tent opens. Morning light pours in. Shadows stroll by. Screams and wheels rush over tracks and echo all around.

· · ·

Her phone rings, and when she checks the ID, she glances at Pete, beer in hand, on his phone strolling toward a car with Don and others on their way to dinner.

"Don and Pete are concerned about the show," Julie says. "And you."

Alex scoots over a plate of barbecue pork, baked beans, and slaw she bought from a vendor before the family packed up. "What'd they say?"

"Don was diplomatic. He understands your ambition but feels it's misplaced."

"And Pete?"

"The PG version is he's going to quit because of you. He was hot when he called me. And he let me know."

The sunset blurs the car with Don and Pete as it turns for the main gate.

"But I want to hear from you. Your side. What's going on?"

She pulls back her plate and devours a forkful. "They don't want to work like I do. I'm out here doing this all on my own."

"They're not team players?"

"Don is more than Pete. But not by much. I have avenues I want us to pursue. I see potential in spots where they're blind. They're focusing on the wrong things."

"Which is what?"

"Julie, you know our numbers, right?"

"I do."

"Chris wants this to go."

"Go where?"

"Wherever the tour goes. And beyond."

"He went over my head on that. Which he can. But he shouldn't have."

"But I can't get to where I need us to be."

"Which is where?"

The second line on her phone buzzes—her mother; Alex silences it.

Julie presses on, "No one in your show has been assigned a leadership role. It's not in the contract you signed. It's not in

Don's or Pete's. No one is the manager. But I'm the manager of all our shows. And while I appreciate you taking charge, it's not your show. The show belongs to all three of you. Don and Pete have the experience you will get if you let them. And I believe you are, based on the numbers you and Chris are high about."

"But they want to go back to what it was before." Alex silences her mother calling back. "I don't know, Julie, but maybe this is a good thing for Pete. If he left the show he could pursue a bigger stage. He's a big talent. He showed me his acting résumé. He has TV and movie credits."

"But you're not his manager."

"Aren't you pleased with what you're hearing about our show? We've helped bring the other shows up."

"The other shows are doing fine without you. They have their audiences. You have yours. Focus on yours."

Janet calls a third time; leaves a voicemail.

"Focus on your team. You've accomplished this because of them. The three of you. You're not the only one in the show."

<Charlotte call me ASAP.> Janet texts.

"You can push the show and Don and Pete. But push in the right direction. And know when to push and when to stop."

Alex deletes the text. "Did you talk Don off the ledge?"

"Don will never walk to the ledge. Pete will. And that's why I called you. I'm here for all of you. You're all doing good work. Goodnight, Alex."

Janet calls again.

"Mom, what is it?"

"It's your father, Charlotte. He's in the hospital."

"What happened?"

"He never changed his emergency contact after we divorced. But I'm in California. You'll need to go."

"I can't. I'm days away."

"Ask for time off."

"I can't miss them. I'm on the road. I have shows coming up."

"You can't find a way back? For your father?"

"How bad is he?"

"He's in the hospital, Charlotte."

"But he's OK otherwise?"

"Let me give you the number to his room and the nurse on duty. And the doctor who called."

"Just tell me what's going on with him, and I can google it and see how bad it is."

"He was coughing up blood when they left a message."

Janet relays the number, but Alex doesn't write down anything and, her stomach knotting, throws away her plate.

"Charlotte? Are you there?"

"Hold on." Crying, she rummages through the trashcan and pulls out the plate and scrapes off crimson-colored sauces and chunks. She clicks a pen but can't write. Her voice quivers, "Text it to me." After it comes in, Janet asks for updates: "Please. I want to know what's going on with him."

Alex calls the hospital and speaks to the nurse who confirms Clarence coughed up blood, slipped in the shower, but called 911 before he passed out. The car from earlier pulls in and drops off Don and Pete who pass the RV and stroll the fairgrounds. The nurse tells Alex they've stabilized Clarence and will know more as the night progresses.

"I can't get there. I can't come."

"You can leave a message for him," the nurse says. "I'll make sure he gets it."

"Tell him I'll call him when I can. But I don't know when. Tell him I'm sorry. Please tell him that. Please tell him I'm sorry." She pushes out of the RV and gasps as a ride swings across the sunset and spins every shadow strapped inside toward the ground.

17

At the next stop, she follows the smell of pot toward a ride being tested. The young woman at the controls snaps toward Alex and smashes a joint under her palm pressing a button. The flying-saucer-shaped cars stop and rattle the arms suspending them; the lights around the domes and laser guns flicker; the voice from the speakers says *Welcome back, Earthlings. Please stay inside your ships until we release your safety belts.* The young woman snatches her inspection list and flashlight and starts toward the cars.

"It's cool." Alex stops her. "I don't care. I smelled it from over there. But you should watch out who can. It may not be me the next time."

"I thought I was alone. I usually am when I do this."

"Where'd you get it?"

"It's mine." She sets down her flashlight on the panel. "My uncle and aunt grow it."

"Where?"

"Outside Texarkana."

"I'm Alex."

"Bryn." She pushes back her black stocking cap. "You're the Gorilla-Girl. I've seen your photos on one of the accounts I follow."

"Good."

"It's cool what you do. Your show."

"We're in a good place right now."

Bryn rubs her forearms' tattoos and reaches into her pocket. "I wish I could say the same. People are complaining about head trauma with some of these rides."

"Ours?"

"Ones like ours. They're making the rounds on the internet."

"How much do you want?" Alex nods at the other woman's fist.

"On the house." Bryn hands over a joint. "I'll stock up when we get close. Jaymon will drive me to my uncle and aunt's. I'll bring back a lot for the crew. I used to bring back some for Logistics, but they've gone quiet with it."

Metal clanks behind them in the distance. Another ride rises; another spreads across the ground.

Bryn offers her lighter. "Need to blow off work stress?"

"No."

"I can't imagine you'd have stress. Your show is super popular. Not that you can't have stress."

Alex rolls over the lighter: a Japanese woodcut of fishermen in a boat at the base of a wave ascending over them. "My dad is sick in the hospital."

"I'm sorry."

Alex inhales deeply and holds in the smoke until the image of her father lying in a bed and asking for "my Charlie Girl" dissipates. "It's not that I can't get away. I won't."

"You don't like him?"

"I love him."

Bryn relights her joint. "I'd go back to my daddy if he were in the hospital. He's never left his hometown. He played football there, married my mom, raised us."

"Are they still married?"

"Forty years. They did it when they were eighteen."

"And they still love each other?"

"They'll be buried next to each other. They got one plot. That's all they could afford. My daddy says that's all they need."

"My dad would say something like that. Everything nowadays is about money, not who you were or could become."

"He said that?"

Alex demurs.

"You like the people you work with?"

"When they see what I'm doing here."

"You like your boss?"

"When she sees what I'm doing here."

"Who's your boss?"

"Julie Herndon."

"I thought maybe Chris shut you down from going to see your dad." Bryn takes a drag. "We had a guy at the one of the last stops request time off for his son's military graduation, but somebody up top told him no. It's Chris."

"You don't know that."

"Who else would've it been? Screw him until the end of time."

"Don't say that." Alex snuffs and pockets her joint. "He's doing his job. Those who don't work hard will feel that way about someone like that."

"Are you saying I don't work hard?"

"Thanks for the hit. Like I said, watch out for who can smell it." Alex struts back to her side of the circus where she finishes her joint outside a provisions tent for sideshow crews and performers. Her high eases everything inside her. She asks the attendant if anything in the tent is "better than hospital food." The man shrugs. She spins a package of donuts but flings them back onto the shelf. The man moves down to help one of the trainers. Alex says goodbye to the air and verifies her alarm labeled First Show is turned up.

· · ·

"Ladies and gentlemen, boys and girls, thank you for coming today to…" Don crumples over the desk, clutching his hand.

Alex wobbles onstage but doesn't move toward him. Don hides from the audience and nods away Alex. He dusts off his lab coat, adjusts his glasses, and picks up where he dropped his lines, but as he reaches for the blackboard depicting Daisy transforming into a gorilla, he breaks chalk, his hand spasming. Alex, her eyes bloodshot, her head like a balloon, bursts out laughing. Don glares at her. The audience chuckles; their phones lock on the stage.

Alex staggers to the front. "Ladies and gentlemen, boys and girls, what my dear old father is trying to say is you are about to witness science and nature to converge in one point. Are you ready to experience something you will never experience again?"

The audience cheers.

"That's why you came here, yes?"

"Yes!"

The crowd blurs in front of Alex, but she focuses on a teen boy at the back wearing a red baseball hat. Don shuffles to the side of the table.

"You may see blood. You may see terror. You may hear sounds that belong in a nightmare. But I assure you what will be in front of you is something you can't run from." She whimpers but composes herself and, snatching the chalk from Don, lunges for the blackboard where she X's out sections, circles others, and underlines the phrase It Was Within Her the Whole Time. "Now my father, shall I enter the box and become what you made me?"

Cradling his hand, Don clears his throat. "Yes."

"Louder, father. So the back can hear you."

"Step into the box, my lovely daughter. And show our guests your true self."

She teeters while she curtsies, and after she enters the box, she whispers to Pete, "You end this. Not me today. It's all you."

"No Daisy at the end?"

"No. All you. And…" She swallows—her tongue swollen. "Red baseball hat at the back. Knock yourself out."

The gorilla head turns toward the door. Daisy fades in and out. The gorilla bursts out. The audience jumps on their phones, squealing out of the tent.

· · ·

Backstage after the show, Alex scrolls through likes and comments adding up—the most she's seen. One video shows Pete slinging chairs while the audience scrambled away from him. Another post captures Pete snatching the teen boy's red baseball hat, wearing it, and dancing around.

Don switches the bag of ice from his hand to his knee; he keeps his back toward Alex and Pete who asks Don what happened. "My arthritis flared at the wrong time."

"Can you do the rest of the day?"

"It's a flare up. They come and go."

"Did it start before today, and you didn't tell us?"

"I'm old, Alex. It'll happen to you some day."

"Maybe you should sit out the next one."

"Petey, no."

"I think Pete's right. You should."

"I'm not going to. What is this? Is this about my performance?"

Pete towels off his neck.

"When the two of you flubbed a line we kept going. No big deal. Alex, you missed a cue. No big deal. Petey got off his mark. No big deal. But me? Why?"

"I'm OK with it if you want to keep going," Pete says. "It happens to the best of us."

"And you out of all of us here should understand that."

Alex flops down her shoes. "What's that mean? I'm still not up to your standards?"

Don rips open his bag and chomps ice.

"I guess if you mess up like that again I'll have to step in," she says. "Again."

"Were you drunk or high out there, Alex?"

"Don…"

"She was off, Petey. I could smell something the minute she showed up for wardrobe."

"Were you Alex?

"No, Pete. I was tired from dealing with my dad. God, Don, where's this coming from?"

"Where did all that come from?" He motions at the stage.

"I did what I had to do. Like a professional would." She scrolls through more likes and comments while Pete leaves for coffee and Don heads to the RV to rest until the next showtime that Alex reminds her followers.

. . .

The three of them dress backstage, no one talking, while crowds line outside the tent. The next two shows—midday and afternoon—go on without any hitches, but halfway through the last show, Don's hand locks up, and Alex improvises and repeats to Pete, snarling and huffing in the box, he needs to finish the show "again because Don can't. He's worse."

After Don heads to Medical, Alex and Pete eat in the RV. She thanks Pete when he offers a beer.

"We got a two-day break coming up," he says. "We could ask him to take advantage of that."

She sips. "I could use those two days to rewrite his part. Combine Daisy and him."

"Dr. Daisy Mandrake?"

"Dr. Daisy."

"You don't need to do that."

"You didn't see what he did. He dropped a beaker."

"I didn't hear that. But I saw the crowd react to something."

"The crowd was on their feet. The biggest I've seen. They couldn't tell if it was real or an act. But it shattered everywhere and could've hit someone."

"We don't want that. Julie and Chris would be all over us. Not even our numbers will bail out something like that."

"I don't think I could say anything to them to make it better if that happened."

He smirks at her. "And you of all people here should be the one to make that happen. What did you do when he dropped it?"

"I told myself to be like in a play. It's an accident, but you use it."

He toasts her. "That's what you do."

"I learned it from you. But it could be one of us the next time."

"We're all prone to dropping stuff."

"He could drop something near us. And injure you or me. Cecelia wouldn't want you hurt."

He gets up for another beer; Alex says no. "So what's going on with your dad?"

"He's in the hospital. I need to call him. I haven't yet."

"Why?"

She rubs her pendant. "I can't go there, Pete."

"Where? The hospital?"

"The city where he is."

He swirls his beer. "You know those posts you've been doing?"

"You hate them."

"No. A talent rep reached out to me. He handles stage and screen actors. He saw one of your posts, did some digging around, and sent me an email."

"That's good, Pete."

"Nothing may come of it. But yeah… Thanks."

She finishes her beer and pulls out a joint. Pete pops in the RV's lighter. They pass the joint between them and head out for the night sky.

"He could go away for those two days we have a break. Or more," Alex says. "I could rewrite it so it's the two of us. We could do it that way. Prove to Julie and Chris we can do it."

"That's a direction I'm not sure about."

"If it ends up being the two of us we could get someone from the audience onstage, and that person could be in the box."

"We could do that now. With Don."

"It'd be better if it's you and me. Daisy and the gorilla."

Stars shine through smoke they blow upward.

Notifications light up Alex's phone. "We don't need him if he were to come back."

18

A car stuffed with cast and crew heading to the lake idles outside the RV while Alex finishes her lunch and coffee near open windows and the side door where she overhears Don and Pete: Don saying he could use the rest; Pete agreeing and saying he'll catch up with home and see Don later. Don starts for the RV, saying he forgot his wallet and muscle rub. Slurping down soup, Alex turns away but doesn't close a new document labeled Rewrite or hide the marked-up script.

Don stops alongside her. "What are you changing now?"

"I have an idea I want to get out."

"Based on all my ideas?"

"Have fun at the lake, Don."

He pauses on the last step down. "I don't know who you want to be, but it's not who Petey and I and Julie wanted."

The car door opens for Don and drives down the road and onto the highway.

Pete stuffs away his phone and pulls himself into the RV. "I'm off. I've got some things I need to take care of today."

"Not going to the lake with them?"

"I will later. You want to come?"

"I'm gonna stay here."

He nudges the script and looks over the rewrite under the blinking cursor. "I'm going to reach out to another agent. Show her what we've been doing."

"Good."

"Don't cut him out, Alex. Let him leave when he wants. If he ever wants."

"Either way we need to be prepared. Or I do. After you leave me for Hollywood or Broadway. Or both."

"Text or call me if you can't get a ride to the lake."

After Pete leaves, she reviews her edits, starting with the title: Daisy the Gorilla-Girl. She types Dr. before Daisy and Mandrake after it; nixes Daisy and stares at Dr. Mandrake the Gorilla-Girl; adds Her Brilliant Scientific Mind Cannot Save Her or You! She comments in the margin: Could I do this without Pete? Could I get in the box and change without him? Her laptop sputters as a video of the Pepper's Ghost trick loads. You'll lose the effect, she reminds herself. She rewinds the video. You'll be a kids' show where you make the audience wait while you have a costume change. She plays and slows the video. You can't see it coming no matter where you are. Her phone rings.

"Why haven't you called your father?" Janet demands. "He's been in that hospital bed for days, and you haven't said anything to him."

She puts away the script and closes her laptop paused on a man gazing out a window while ghosts of his long-dead family walk toward him. "This is our first break. I'm been swamped with work. I haven't had time."

"You make time for something like this."

"You're one to talk."

"I beg your pardon?"

"For years you dumped on him."

"I still care for him. But you need to call him. I saw him yesterday."

"You were there?"

"I changed my return flight. I got a rental car and a hotel. I would've stayed with him had there been space in that room."

"Oh God… You went into his room."

"He's conscious. His color's back. They moved him up from critical to stable. They don't know what's going on yet. More tests down the road."

"When can he get out?"

"Why don't you call him and ask?"

She fidgets with her laptop. "Are you there now?"

"I was. I stopped by to see if he wanted me to stay longer."

"I can imagine his answer."

"He said, 'That would be like being married again. And we both know how that worked out the first time.' We laughed."

A PA announces something in the background.

"My flight is boarding. Call him, Charlotte. Today."

She grabs her things and walks down the road and follows a sign for exits to the lake. A car honks at her; the couple waving she's seen working the children's section of the midway where the rides float over clouds, rainbows, suns and moons, and fairytale animals. They U-turn and ask if she wants a ride; she declines but asks about the lake.

"Lots of boats and people out," the woman answers. "Can't beat this weather."

The man adds, "A lot of us are down here today. It's like everyone needed to blow off steam."

His thin mustache reminds Alex of a boyfriend her mother had after she was divorced and moved away. They all look up at the blue sky.

"Be sure to stop in at this place called Randall's. That was some of the best buttermilk biscuits and chicken-fried steak we've had."

"I will."

The woman leans over. "We saw Don down there. But no Pete. And no you until now."

"We're each doing our own thing today."

"I guess y'all gotta do whatever to keep that energy alive. You earned it, but y'all making the rest of us look bad. We work hard too. Give some of that mojo to us, Gorilla-Girl."

The radio blasts as they drive off.

Richard, Alex recalls, seeing the thin mustache on the man who picked her up at the airport. He followed her after she stepped off the plane and asked her if she was Charlotte. "Your mom sent me." She wanted to scream "Pervert!" until he handed a handwritten note to her.

Charlotte,

Richard here is picking you up at the airport. I'm tied up with some things I have to do before you get here.

Hugs and kisses.

Mom

While they drove to Janet's new place he explained he traded futures. "It's a risk-to-reward ratio. Betting on the future. Everyone bets on the past or present."

"My dad is way bigger than you."

"But he did he take her to a five-star resort in the Bahamas? He doesn't have the means. That's what your mom says in bed." His smile spread his mustache.

Charlotte turned up her headphones' music.

They walked into the house, and from a side bedroom Janet yelled she'd be out soon. Richard poured a glass of wine and told Charlotte she could have one.

"I'm fourteen."

"Not in here." He drifted to the living room where a TV clicked on.

The bedroom door opened, and out came Janet dressed in tight jeans and a sheer blouse. "You made it."

Charlotte couldn't tell if her mother was talking to her or Richard.

"But you look pale. Did your father feed you before the airport?"

"No."

"He didn't feed you?"

"I didn't eat anything because I don't feel good."

"What's going on?"

"Allergies. I guess."

"I'll start brewing chamomile." She pinched Charlotte's arm. "You could use fewer calories anyway."

Richard stepped in, kissed Janet who offered her cheek, and showed a brochure to her. "What do you say?"

"Give me a couple of minutes. I want to show Charlotte my studio."

She followed her mother into a room where shelves held stretcher bars, paints, paintbrushes. She lifted a sheet and spun around a canvas.

Janet closed the door. "I'm breaking up with him tonight. I can't stand him. All his dribbling on about money. Your father and I were poor, but at least he has a heart. Something I could feel inside me. Something I could want underneath everything else."

Charlotte glimpsed the painting. A woman—blanket covering her face and legs; her breasts exposed—reclined in a chair on a circle suspended in darkness. Lights arranged around a dome shone down. Photographs were taped to the canvas: patients undergoing implants; Mary holding Jesus beneath the cross.

"Do you still love Dad?"

"I'll always love him. And care for him. But from a distance."

. . .

When Alex reaches restaurants, shops, and boat rentals near the lake's edge, she calls her father's room, but he doesn't answer. She stops by Randall's but, after seeing Don and cast and crew from Freak Shows in there, bypasses it and roams until she ends up under lights strung across a patio behind a bar. She orders a tequila flight, downs the first three, and orders food before she finishes the glasses. The barkeep recommends the flan for dessert, and she agrees to it as long as he promises the kitchen can add ice cream. "Two scoops," she mumbles. Her fingers blur when she lifts them. Speakers pump out more grooves; she dances and pretends shimmying out of her clothes. She stumbles calling her father and swears the line sends her to the hospital's gift shop where she argues with an employee about cancer. The woman at the next table calls Alex a slut while the man she's with holds up his phone and rotates around Alex. She grinds on a man's lap; he pushes her off and tells her to "knock that crap off." She passes out, and when she comes to, sits against a wall, her legs flat on the ground, across from fireworks exploding over the lake and boats zooming under them. She dials a number.

"Where are you?"

"I'm down here."

"It's almost curfew."

"Can you come get me?"

"I can't. I'm on my way back."

"Pete, please."

"I'm on other side of town."

A shadow walks toward her. "Alex?" A blast of red fireworks brightens the face.

"Don. You're still down here."

He helps her up. "You need a lift?"

"As long as you don't say anything."

He checks his phone. "We need to go, or we'll be late for curfew."

"It's all good. It doesn't matter when. I'll take care of it if we're late. I want to go back."

"Back to where?"

"A time. Not a place."

"They're the same, Alex."

They stagger toward a car idling under colors exploding and splintering the dark.

19

I'M FIXIN TO GET THIS HERE FIXINS! says the speech bubble coming out of the sign's hillbilly, hound dog, and crawfish while they drool over a massive cinnamon roll. The family in front of Alex orders a baker's dozen. The next line opens—the crowd merging with crowds by gifts and beers. Alex drifts toward the open line, but her phone rings: Incoming Call – Chris K. She slides into a corner near the statue of a life-size armadillo wearing a hat and vest and holding a fishing pole and cooler.

"You got back after curfew the other night."

She scans the crowd. "It was only ten minutes later."

"But that's still ten minutes past when we told you to get back."

"Don's ride picked us up late."

"I haven't spoken to Don yet. I wanted to talk to you first. You were with Don the whole time at the lake?"

"No."

"He was there on his own?"

"Yes."

"And Pete?"

"He went off on his own too."

"One of you needs to manage the show's cast according to our expectations. I'm asking you to do that. You need to take more of the leadership, Alex."

"That's what I've wanted to talk to you about. I don't think Don can do it anymore. None of it. And Pete doesn't want to."

"Pete's never been a leader. And that's fine. Not everyone can."

"Don's health is a concern for me. And for Pete."

Customers film themselves devouring cinnamon rolls.

"We've noticed he's had trouble with lines and props. He dropped one at a recent performance. I didn't know if you knew."

"That usually doesn't come my way unless a guest is injured or irritated."

"That could've happened. I kept the show going. I pretended it was part of the act."

"Good for you. Thank you for doing that."

A woman and children waddle over to the armadillo, and posing, she tells her husband to photograph them.

"Don is close to retirement," Chris says. "Past it arguably."

"I've started writing a script without Don in it. Pete and I can make it work." Her stomach growls. "Until he leaves too."

"Is he talking about that?"

"He's reaching out. But it's good, Chris. A talent rep found him because of the videos I posted on our social media."

"If we can help him reach the next level he wants, by all means, let's do it. That's what my grandfather believed in."

"And like I said, if he leaves, I have another script I can do without Pete."

"So you didn't have much of a break."

"I got out to the lake. But only after I worked." Alex relaxes. "I may have embarrassed myself loving it so much."

"Your numbers are great. Your followers on social media are the highest I've seen. Keep it up. And be a leader for whoever's in the show with you."

The woman and kids walk away while the husband hooks the fishing pole in his belt and pretends the armadillo snagged him. Alex hangs up and, while the man flops, hands a flyer to him—"Stop by and see my show."—and orders cinnamon rolls for her, Don, and Pete. She eats hers, returns to the RV, and tells them she "picked these for you two. Enjoy. They say they're out of this world." Pete devours his and starts the RV. Don sets his aside and teeters for the recliner. Alex receives a voicemail from Julie asking her to call after they arrive at the next stop. The RV rumbles away from the visitor center and, catching up with the caravan, onto the highway.

. . .

They set up for the first performance, but Alex stalls calling back Julie while triple-checking wardrobe, the set, lights, sounds, the tent, chairs, and audience viewing angles. Don grumbles about which script he should use. Pete keeps quiet as they move gear and prep. Julie calls again. Alex lets her voicemail pick up.

> I know you're busy, and I know your first show is about an hour away, but you need to call me. We need to talk.

"I'm stepping out for a bit." She calls Julie.

"Are you're cutting Don out of the show?"

"What did he say to you?"

"You can't cut him out, Alex. He's a part of the show. He has an important role. The roles require each other. It's a three-person show."

"The audience is part of the show too."

"You need to use the script given to you when you started."

"So I can't make changes? Or suggest improvements?"

"You have, and you did, but those first improvements were within the bounds of what we wanted."

"You told me you hired me because I could freshen the show up. And I have. Audiences are coming to us, Julie."

"I'm happy to hear that. I am, Alex. Because we're all doing our best here to feed mouths, pay for our homes, and take care of whatever's going on. But you're going too far. You can't cut Don out of the show. It's his as much as yours."

"His health is a problem. Pete and I are worried he'll injure someone."

"He's taking care of that."

"Did he tell you that? I don't think ibuprofen and ointment will help."

"He stays in the show, Alex. No more about that."

"I want him in, but he needs to get it together."

"No more, Alex. All three of you are in charge. Not one." Julie pauses. "The other issue I want to talk with you about is your behavior at the lake."

"The curfew? Christ, Julie, if you want to discipline me over ten minutes…"

"You were drunk."

"Says who?"

"I don't allow that behavior in my department."

"Did Don tell you this? He was late asking his ride to come get us."

"Don would've made it back on time had he not helped you. After he found you drunk against a wall. You should be thanking Don, not throwing him under the bus."

The PA announces *Welcome to Kopolski Traveling Amusement. Our gates are now open for you to enjoy your day with us.*

"I need to finish getting ready for the show."

"I'm writing you up. Putting a warning in your file."

"For what? Both?"

"Yes."

"Go talk to Chris about all this."

"I'm not going to talk to Chris about any of this. You're my employee. I'm your manager. You start and end with me."

Lines form outside rides and games. Don sets out the sandwich board with showtimes and audience reviews and social-media icons.

"I've got a show to do, Julie."

．　．　．

After the performance, Pete watches the audience file out, which packed the front, sides, and back, and before the last person leaves, spins toward Alex and Don, beaming. "Hot damn. ¡Vamos! That was the most we've seen."

"It was the best we've put on." Alex checks social-media accounts. "Out of everything we've done so far. The best."

"You got that right. All of us were on. We started strong and finished stronger." Pete struts around backstage, a headless gorilla. "Did you feel that energy?"

"If we could've bottled it, we could've sold it with tickets."

"Don?"

He mumbles, massaging his joints. "Good stuff from all of us." He drops a bag of ice on his knees and another on his knuckles.

"Listen to this." Alex scrolls. "'I was supposed to drive back home tonight but stayed to see the next two shows because the first one was awesome. The next two were even better.'" She reads more praises. "We have a ton of comments and likes. And the videos. Someone captured Pete in the audience doing his improv dance. They're all cracking up."

"That came to me out of nowhere."

"I'll see y'all back at the RV." Don shuffles for the exit.

"Don."

"Yeah?"

"Thank you." Alex opens her arms for a hug.

Don shakes her hand. "'Night, Daisy."

"Lemme see." Pete takes Alex's phone and screenshots comments and images. "Send me those. I want to pass them on to Nicole."

"New girlfriend?"

"My agent. I hope." His phone pings after Alex sends the screenshots.

"How could she say no?"

"I'm doing everything I can to show her she can't." He strips off his costume and stuffs his backpack. "I'll see you at the RV. I got one bottle of that ale I picked up in Shreveport. Want some?"

"Yeah. Be sure to share it with Don."

"I will."

She walks toward the Pepper's Ghost box and plays hide and seek with her image in the black glass and, closing in on it, tells the two of them standing there, "We did it." She steps into the night, and the vigor that swelled during performances rolls around her, lifts her off the ground, and charges into everything around her.

Her phone rings: Incoming Call – Dad. She pushes Mute. He leaves a message.

Charlie Girl. They're letting me get out of the hospital this week. I'm up to snuff. At least enough to be let go. I was wondering if you could come back and help. If you can. I know you're swamped with work. I've been following your tour on the website. I understand if you can't make it back. Plus I reckon you don't got much vacation. You gotta stay at work to get the hours to leave work. Your mom came and visited me. That was real nice of her. It's amazing what you've done with your show. I saw a video of you turning in a gorilla. How'd you do that? But a magician never reveals her secret. You've done good, Charlie. Er... I mean, Alex. Or Daisy, right? You're a bonafide star. The first in the family.

She deletes his voicemail but recovers it and, replaying it, drops to the ground while the vigor releases her and electricity pulls out like a tide before coming back in.

20

Alex wakes up before Don and Pete and, slipping out of the RV, calls her father. While his line rings, she picks scabs where the door on the Pepper's Ghost box broke open her knuckles.

"Mornin', Charlie."

She presses bloody her knuckles into her shirt. "I'm glad you answered."

"They're bringing me my last breakfast. And, I swear to God's wisest angels, I can't wait to be done with it. It's no better than a military hospital."

"What are you having?"

"Cardboard eggs with last year's syrup. And a piece of sausage so small that hog must've been penned up in a shoebox."

"I've had some pretty good breakfasts on the road."

"What's been your favorite?"

"A couple stops back in Texas I had the best breakfast burrito. Eggs, sausage, gooey cheese, potatoes. Salsa. And guacamole. And it was like a baseball bat on my plate."

"Are you calling me from Heaven? Because that sounds too good to be true."

Blood seeps through her shirt. "I know it's been a while since we talked."

"You've been busy. It would've been nice to see you here. But it'd be tough to get you back." He coughs. "And why would you? You don't want to see me like this."

"What's next?"

"More tests. A specialist. Maybe two. Lungs and stomach. They think all my years of smoking and drinking have worn those down. Cancer is still a possibility."

"I'm sorry, Dad."

"If it is, it is." His voice weakens. "The other thing is, I'm thinking of moving back to Virginia."

"You're not going back to the valley, are you?"

"Why not?"

"Don't do that, Dad. That's all in the past. Remember the photos you gave me for my birthday? It's all gone. Or what's left soon will be."

"There's still something there."

"You have to keep moving on." She tightens the shirt over her knuckles; the blood deepens. "Past what you know."

"What I know is the past. And that's a better thing to know than the future. Or the present." He hacks up phlegm. "They're bringing in my breakfast."

"I'll let you go."

"No. Stay. I haven't talked to you in so long. Where're you headed next?"

"The Ouachita Mountains Festival. The Oklahoma-Arkansas border."

"They've got a Bigfoot festival there every year. They got TV shows talk about it."

"Of course you would know that."

"They love that area. All those forests. And rivers. And mountains. Deer to eat. Food campers leave behind. They use passes through the mountains and caves to get from point to point. The whole thing connects. It's one big web."

"I don't think all the caves in the South connect, Dad."

"They do. It's required of the region. If it gets broken or overlooked, we have to secede again. The Midwest has to take us. The coasts won't." He chuckles. "You can go from eastern Oklahoma through Arkansas. Up into southern Missouri where you'll want to say hi to Huck and Tom. Touch the tops of Alabama and Georgia. Then into Tennessee. Cut across Kentucky. And end up smack dab in Virginia. And you got good food the whole way. Barbecue. Steaks. Okra. Cornbread. Slaw. Moonshine. And if ever get stuck, why, you stick your thumb out for a hitchhike on a UFO that's in the area whenever Bigfoot is seen."

"And ghosts?"

"Ghosts are everywhere, Charlie. Wherever the dead and living are. The land never lets them go." He slurps a drink, coughs. "You come see me before I leave for Virginia."

"I thought you said you were thinking about it."

"I am."

"So you're leaving."

"Keep up that show of yours. I don't know if you heard my message the other night, but it looks great. I'm proud of you. Daisy."

His voice lingers after he hangs up, and she unwraps her shirt and clenches her fist while gazing over her knuckles and dried blood. She searches for his voice but, closing her eyes, loses it among cave paintings she read about when she had chicken pox, and her father, on the phone, asked her what she read while she was sick visiting her mother, and he told her everything with weight comes from the earth and everything without weight drifts into the sky. "Like souls?" she asked. "Yes," he answered. "And if we want to say they were here among us, we put them on things with weight." And he told her to spread a hand, and she did, pulling one from under her sheet, and he said, "Show me, Charlie." And she said, "Dad, I can't. You can't see. You're on the phone." And he giggled, and she giggled. And he said, "They painted horses on those cave walls, and we measure horses with hands because things like that have to be touched, and things like that want us to touch them. And they left them there on those walls to remind us we're not from the sky but out of the earth." And her mother came into the bedroom, while snow fell outside the window, and said it was time for bed, but Clarence convinced Janet to hold on—"for our daughter"—and Janet cradled the phone between Charlotte and her, and Clarence and Janet said goodnight together while Charlotte drifted asleep.

And as Alex slides into sleep, she punches the cave walls and chips away paintings until horses land at her feet, and she arranges them in a circle—head to tail—ready to run but frozen on the ground. She runs inside the circle, but they stay flat; she spreads her arms, circling them as she runs, but the horses do not move. She glances into the darker dark where the paintings stood and her father's voice called, and she asks for anything to step into the light—a sound, an end, a beginning—but nothing answers, and she reaches in but pulls nothing out and reaches in again and pulls back blood on her hand. She slathers the blood on the back of the chipped horses and glues them to where they were, but she arranges them as a large horse looming over her and measures the height starting from the head and ending in the dark beneath her where she crawls toward frames spinning around a light.

She jolts awake facedown on the grass while the caravan starts its engines. Pete steps out of the RV, yawns, and stretches. Don adjusts the driver's seat and steering wheel. Alex inspects her knuckles—oozing, red, swollen—and the flattened grass and dirt beside her. Thunder rumbles; dark clouds gray out the morning's blue horizon and hang low over woods. One of the games' managers checks a tarp covering stuffed animals dangling off a trailer; he inspects down the line pink bunnies and tie-dyed turtles and waves to Alex who waves back before he jumps into his truck.

Pete offers a cup of coffee to her when she reaches the RV. "It's Don's. He cracked open a bag." He whispers, "His mood brightened when he did." He shows her the bag: a drawing of a black horse wearing a monocle and reading a book while standing on a mound of cash under the handwritten phrase Bet on the Dark Horse – Don's Dark Blend.

She sips. "Don, this is good."

"That was the last one I mixed together with the new roaster Gloria gave me before we got on tour. I'd been saving it." He starts the engine. "I figured we could all enjoy our recent uplift. And home-roasted coffee is one of the best ways. Petey gave us his beer. I'd like to share my coffee." He turns down the radio as it fades into static—the song about shelter being a shout away—and they head deeper into woodlands thickening along slopes and crags and shadows of the Ouachitas.

· · ·

The RV jerking wakes Alex. Don massages his elbow while a man stands outside his window and yells at Don he's "gotta watch it, man. I got kids and a dog in there with me." He points toward his truck towing a boat—hazards flashing; angled toward the ditch wound against rock, dirt, and trees. "It's a tight road for everybody on here, but you gotta keep it in line."

"I will." Don buries his elbow into his ribs. "I'm sorry."

The man hikes up his shorts and waddles to his truck.

Alex asks, "What happened?"

"My elbow locked up. And I swerved into the other lane. He honked at me. I motioned for him to pass me. And as he did, my elbow locked up again, and I swerved and almost nudged him. Then he slammed on his brakes and read me the riot act."

The truck rumbles away.

Don checks the side mirrors and waves around vehicles blinking their high beams. A car slows by his window; a group from Wardrobe asks if everything's all right. He answers yes. "See you at the gate," they yell, chugging up the road. Pete snores from his bed.

"Do you want me to drive?" Alex asks.

"I'll be fine."

The road drops off into browns, blacks, and greens and fog pooling in pockets.

"Just get us there in one piece."

"What makes you think I won't?"

"I didn't mean anything else by it, Don."

"But you said it."

"Let me know when you want me to take over."

He pops off the parking brake and sets the RV in drive. "It's Petey's turn next."

"We don't have to go in order."

"Your shift is after him. That's how we've done it."

"Except when your hands hurt back there. And I had to jump the line."

He pulls out but hits the brakes when two trucks loaded with camping gear and kayaks roll by. "Had to?" He accelerates up the road.

Pete snores awake and staggers into the front. "Are we standing in for one of our roller coasters?"

"Mountain roads, Petey. We had to take them."

"I can take over if you want, Don."

"You catch up on your sleep back there. I got this."

"I'm next, Pete. I'll take over when Don's done."

"If I let you."

Pete crawls back into bed.

"Be sure to let everyone know too if you don't like my behavior," she says.

"What's that mean?"

"You tattled to Julie about the lake. You could've come to me."

"You were as drunk as a skunk."

"My feet were tired after walking from our campsite to the lake. I needed to rest. And I fell asleep."

"Is that what they call that nowadays?"

"I didn't drive down there like you did."

Pete stirs in his bed.

"Did you say something to Julie because of the show? Because you think you won't be in it?"

"You've been taking out my stuff since day one."

"I've built off your stuff. It worked for all those years. But Julie wanted a change."

"Julie?"

Motorcycles zooms around the RV.

"That's why she hired me. She said it all needed a change."

"She wouldn't do that. She's not like that."

"She did."

"She knows how Petey and I were doing that show."

"She's got the pressure of money on her too."

"It's not."

"But it is, Don. It's not only us or Chris or anyone here. She took a chance. Like I did."

"Changing my ideas is your chance?"

"Leaving what I knew and taking this job."

"Do you think you're the only one who did that?" He slams on the horn when a sign ahead says Sharp Turn Ahead – Honk Horn for Oncoming Traffic. "We all did that. Get over yourself, Alex."

"It's not about what you and Pete did years ago."

The horn blares.

"Julie wanted something fresh. I had my ideas."

"After you saw mine."

Pete shuffles toward the cab. "What's going on? Is someone honking at us?"

The RV coasts toward a bridge.

"Do you want me to drive, Don?"

"No. But thank you, Petey."

"You should, Pete," Alex says. "It's your turn."

"I thought we were taking turns whenever we wanted because…"

Don slams on the brakes. "Because why? Of me?"

The horn fizzles out.

"Because I'm the old man keeping the younguns down?"

Traffic builds up behind the RV.

"I didn't know old men like to tattle like they're in grade school," Alex says.

A park ranger's SUV rolls alongside the RV. "Need any help?"

"No, sir." Don massages his elbow. "I apologize for this."

"Let's keep traffic moving." The ranger pulls on ahead.

"Petey, would you mind? Help an old friend."

"Sure."

Alex stands. "Take my seat, Don." As she walks toward her bed at the back, she hears Don say, "We've put all those years in. Now they're gone." He snaps his fingers. "The love of doing it is all gone. And it only took months."

The RV dips, crests, dips, curves through gray light and clouds moving in, and on a gravel road heads for the entrance, but Pete slows, pulls onto a grass field, and says he knows most of the vehicles waiting outside. "They're all with us." He kills the engine. Alex steps out. Protestors block the gate, holding signs.

> Circuses Kill Animals
>
> Animal Rights Is Climate Justice
>
> Fair Wages for Wranglers Now
>
> The Days of Circuses Are Numbered

Protestors dressed as a horse, an elephant, and a tiger—bloody bandages wrapped around their snouts, legs, and tails—raise their signs when Alex comes closer.

"We don't have elephants or tigers," she tells them. "We're not a circus."

"But you have animals."

"We have a petting zoo. And a dog-trick show and pig races. Could you move? We're here to work. We want to put on shows for families."

The three animals fall in line; the blockade tightens.

More of the caravan pulls in. Trucks beep backing up beneath the overcast. Someone from Logistics directs them. Alex jogs over.

"Is Manny here?"

"He's on strike with the rest."

"On strike?"

"Look at this crap we have to put up with." He thumbs at the protestors. "We haul this equipment up here, on those roads, and get to here. We made it. But this is waiting for us. Plus corporate is tightening down. More cuts back home."

"But the office side, right?"

"More cuts are headed out here. They love to do it on the road after we've put in the work." She jogs after him between two cranes arriving. "Some of the bigger gear had to go interstate and sit there while we got our vehicles to them and brought it in. It's never been like this. Two of our guys got injured. Then they get cut. They got mouths to feed, but now they can't." He crosses his arms in the air, signaling *Good stop. All clear.* "And it's happening more and more."

Protestors handcuff themselves to the gate.

"I heard they missed us at the last stop," he says. "But they beat us here. I appreciate them talking about workers' comp and stuff like that, but not like this. This ain't worth it no more for me."

"Hey, Alex, I just now got this. Dated early this morning."

She turns toward Pete showing an email on his phone:

Do not engage with the protestors. We are working with the grounds administration to make sure our contract is fulfilled. Your department manager will contact you when you may proceed.

"Julie sent a followup."

Their phones buzz: emails and voicemails arrive through the mountains.

"She says to sit until further notice."

"No," says Alex. "We put on our show." She runs through the field, checking each trailer, until she stops at one and asks the driver to open it.

Don steps out of the RV and asks Pete if he's seen these messages about the venue. "What're you doing?" He dodges a tub Alex slings out from the trailer.

"We're putting on our show."

"Julie and Chris asked us to suspend performances until they say otherwise."

"Think of this like tailgating before a game. Chris will understand." She drags their wardrobe bins toward the RV. "Give me a minute to change. Then you two can."

"I'm not doing it."

"Don, we have a chance here. This is an opportunity."

"For what?"

"To show them what we'll do."

"I'm not doing it." He walks for a trail winding into the woods.

She steps into her dress and sticks her head out the window and tells Pete it's his turn. She throws on Don's lab coat over her dress.

Pete starts for Don but turns for the RV. "I'm not putting on the whole thing."

"You could mingle with them." She nods at the protestors dressed as animals. "How funny would it be to see that? I turn into the gorilla, and you stomp around them. I'll set my phone on the fender and record it."

He unpacks his gorilla head and gloves. "I don't know, Alex."

"A gorilla in cargo shorts and a Hawaiian shirt will be hilarious. And let your hair down so it sticks out under the head." She pops out the sandwich board and scrawls *Today's Show Is Right Here + Now!* "Your agent will love seeing you do this. It'll show you can adapt on the fly. She'll love it. Stay in here until your cue."

"Ladies and gentlemen. Boys and girls," she begins. "Please direct your attention to this humble RV I drove up here on our way to my lab-or-atory hidden within these mountains. A secret lair where I perform experiments humanity is not ready to see but must accept."

People get out of their cars. Protestors quiet. Campers and hikers slow down.

"I am your host for this afternoon's revelation of what we can learn if we don't work with nature and if we don't harness who we are." She bows. "I am Dr. Daisy. Holder of many, many degrees. Interpreter of languages ancient and modern. And I am more than pleased to show you my latest finding. And I will assure you as long as you stay in your place, I will not harm you. Much." She winks. "Let us begin."

Phones in the crowd come out.

"Something was inside me that had to express itself. I wasn't sure what it was. A memory? A dream? Something else? Maybe all of that. But I knew if I pushed myself my answer would appear. Out of me. Where it was the whole time."

Pete opens the RV door; he takes off his head and gloves.

She glances over. "What're you doing?"

"I can't, Alex. This isn't right."

"Pete... Run with me on this."

He drops his head and gloves on the step and walks toward the trail.

The crowd holds their phones aloft. The protestors return to the gate. More of the caravan pulls in; their loads wait to be assembled.

"Wait until we're inside this majestic campground," Alex continues, her voice rising. "I promise you you will not be disappointed at our show."

"If it's anything like that, no way!"

Breaking up, the crowd laughs at the man.

"I'm happy to give tickets to anyone who'd like them. While we wait to be let in. We put on three shows a day. This is a preview."

The crowd dwindles. The caravan's engines pop and hiss as clouds grow and gray overtakes the sliver of blue sky.

"And if you give me your email, I'll put you on my mailing list for upcoming shows, merchandise, behind-the-scenes videos.

Check out my social media." She pulls them up. "I'll have T-shirts and bobbleheads down the road. Posters."

Security arrives and talks with the protestors who move from the gate, which opens. Campers and vehicles file in and leave Alex standing in the middle of the grass field surrounded by woods, drizzle, silhouettes.

The drizzle falls harder into rain; the silhouettes scatter for cars, trucks, shelters, and tents. Alex slips into the woods while Don and Pete return to the RV. Lights inside come on, the generator humming in the graying day, as Alex considers returning her wardrobe and Don's lab coat but walks deeper among trees and rain.

Bigfoot Big Run – Mile 3 says a sign nailed on a red-blazed tree. She drapes the lab coat like a hood and jogs until she reaches the next marker where she sprints around shrubs and lightning-blacked trunks and slows in a field alongside a church and graveyard. Halfway There says a sign drooping on a string buried in mud where she walks through chipped and sunken gravestones. Nothing calls to her—not the stones, names, dates, wars they fought in, their kin; not the paint weathered and flecked off the church or the cross on the roof or the busted-out stained glass or the doors sagging off their hinges; nor the woods and whatever within crawls or flies to; no signal that she is where she needs to be or that she is close but needs to stay or move there or there or over those next three humps of land where rain and thunder will relent. But she waits among the dead and the hidden and wishes something would emerge from the woods, not to scare her or defend its territory but to show her it can come to her without her asking.

Rain falls harder. She tightens the lab coat over her head and retraces her path, checking over her shoulder that the red-blazed trees are behind her.

She walks to Pete smoking against the RV.

He tells her everything is canceled. "No shows. No rides. Not enough people. The protestors didn't help. Neither is the rain."

"I don't want to sit here."

He flicks off ashes. "You're not the only one."

"What about tomorrow?"

"It sounds like the whole thing is off."

She strides for the RV, but Pete doesn't move. "Let me in."

"Let him cool off. We all don't need to be in there on top of each other. And take off his lab coat. Please. You'll ruin it."

"What am I supposed to do?"

"Go for a walk. Check this place out. We may not be here again."

"I went for a walk and checked it out."

"Then make something up." He snuffs his cigarette under his boot. "Like you do."

· · ·

That night, as sounds of the forest swell and fade and rain patters, Alex eats in her bed, facing away from Pete and Don eating and talking in the front. Don swivels around and asks Alex if she can come up. She flicks her spoon into her mush and zips up her hoodie and, crossing her arms, posts between the seats. Pete finishes his beer but doesn't look at Don or Alex.

"This is my last stop," Don says. "I'm leaving at the next one."

"Are you coming back on tour?"

"I'm retiring."

"You said all you needed was a rest."

He grimaces. "It's your show now, Alex. All of it. Every line. Every entrance and exit. Every flub and glory. Every second you're out there."

She asks Pete if he's sticking around.

"Yeah."

"That sounds like 'Yeah. For now.'"

"That's fair."

"Is that it?"

Don and Pete glance at each other.

"That's it."

Alex returns to her bed and nibbles her food until Julie's voice from her interview echoes through her: "They're great guys. They started the show." She chucks her plate in the trash, opens her laptop, but can't update her scripts.

21

Pete pulls into a parking lot near the airport while the rest of the caravan heads up the highway. Don double-checks storage and his bed; he offers a magazine to Pete who takes it, telling him about an article in there about George Washington's dentures. "I'd take them over the modern ones I've got." Pete tells him he'll ship anything back if he comes across it.

"I've got photos from over the years. I only want my lab coat back." Don glances at Alex lounging in her bed. "I can watch videos of the latest version of the show whenever I feel like it. If I ever do."

"I hope you do."

"It was a great ride with you. I hope something good comes your way because of all this."

Don and Pete hug.

Phone to her ear, Alex steps out of the RV and shields her eyes. "I'm calling about the T-shirts I ordered. Can I get those delivered to a post office? Or maybe a delivery service can get them to me? I'm on the road with my work."

"Have a safe flight," Pete says.

"Have a safe drive." Avoiding where Alex stepped out, Don slips out the driver's door.

Pete honks twice. Don waves and heads for check-in. The customer-service rep confirms the T-shirts with an outline of Alex inside a gorilla on the front and the outline of the gorilla inside her on the back are the ones they will ship, not the previous order showing three characters. She checks her phone's map for hotels in the area and climbs into the passenger's seat. Pete puts the RV in drive.

"Let's go to a hotel. We can get a room. I don't want to be in here."

"We don't have that in the budget."

"I'll let Chris know."

"Run it by Julie."

"It's just down the road. We'll be close to the venue." She shows him the dots on her map. "This one has two single rooms. And it's cheaper by the highway. Unless you want a double. But we don't have to tell Chris that."

"I'm not going to stay in a double or single with you. We're sticking to the RV. Like Julie said. If that changes, it'll come from her."

"Let me call Chris and see if he can get it to come from her. It's the best cell connection I've had in a while."

He puts the RV in park. "Get out."

"What?"

"You got a ride-share app?"

"What are you doing, Pete?"

"You can go to a hotel. On your own. I'm taking this to our venue and sleeping in it like I've been doing."

She calls a ride-share and gathers her things. "First performance tomorrow is…"

"Christ, Alex, I know what time."

After he drives away, she turns on her Daisy persona and videos herself strolling around. "Hi folks. I'm excited for the next stop where I can't wait to put on another great performance for you and you and you. Come see me transform before your eyes." She rambles off showtimes and how to get discount tickets. A plane descends for the runway. She pauses her video and records the plane landing and sends it to her father. Her phone pings, but it's her ride-share pulling in. She uploads her video to her social-media accounts and, as the ride-share heads down the road, refreshes each: fewer likes and comments. She refreshes again: nothing different. The ride-share exits for the hotel where Alex connects to the wifi and checks her accounts: no changes. She unlocks her room and collapses on the bed.

<They putting you on first class now?> her father texts. <Next you'll be sending me a video of you going to the moon. Don't forget us little people down here when you leave us for the stars.>

<I just wanted to say hi. I thought you might like to see it land.>

A plane outside her window ascends. Tracking the plane's direction, she turns on her phone's compass and compares it to her map. The plane drifts toward where she's come from.

. . .

Julie calls the next morning. "I told you not to cut Don out."

"He left on his own. Pete dropped him off at the airport. He got on a plane and left. That's what he wanted."

"That's not what I wanted. And that's not what I told you to do. That's not how I told you to handle him."

"The other night he told us he was leaving at the next stop. Which is this. I asked him if this was a break for him. For his health. He said no."

"Did you try to stop him?"

"He wanted to leave."

"Did you ask him to stay? Work something out?"

"For the umpteenth time, Julie, he wanted to leave." She rubs her eyes. "This was all Don."

"I asked you to consider him, Alex. And I asked you to behave in a way that would show Pete and him that one person does not run the show. The three of you were supposed to work together."

"I can't control when he's going to retire. He could've waited until the season was over. Which would've been nice. That could've been something for him to consider. But he didn't." A plane ascends outside her room's window. "I hope he got home safe and sound. I'm sure Gloria's happy to have him back."

"What about this show you put on at the Ouachita Festival?"

"Putting on my show is a problem?"

"It wasn't scheduled."

"Who told you about it?"

"I'm writing you up for that."

"For putting on my show?"

"You're not the girl who changes into a gorilla and plays Dr. Mandrake."

"I wasn't." She flips through the hotel's breakfast menu. "I was Dr. Daisy."

"There are three distinct characters in that show."

"I did what I did, Julie, because I wanted to give those people there a reason to stay. It was raining. We were delayed. We avoided those protestors like Chris asked."

"I asked for that too."

"It was like when Don or Pete flubbed lines or something like that during a show and I had to cover for them. Make up something on the spot. It's a good pressure. I can do that."

"Pete doesn't say any lines. He can't flub those. Unless you've changed that too."

"He's missed cues. He's bored. He wants out. He thinks he can break into Hollywood or the big stage now because of my posts."

"I don't want anymore of these conversations with you. I don't want to call you while you're on the road. And I don't want to write you up again. But I am. You're not the only one involved in all this. You used to know this. You acted like you did."

Alex closes the menu. "Anything else?"

Julie says no, reminds Alex about what will go in her file and to HR, and hangs up. Alex orders her food and schedules the time for her ride-share pickup.

.   .   .

The police officer at the gate directs the ride-share to the side, but Alex tells him she's in the show. "I'm an employee." But the officer restates his request. On its way off the main road, the ride-share passes Pete, his feet propped on the RV's dashboard; ambulance and firetrucks' lights flash across the windshield. Alex tells the driver to drop her off.

"What's going on?"

Pete doesn't look at Alex. "A car fell off its track. Landed on its side. The riders were banged up."

"Why were rides going before we opened?"

"They were given the green light to open up early today and make up sales. I rolled up and was told to sit out there."

"Why weren't we told?"

"About the accident?"

"About opening early. We could've got here when the rides started."

Pete snaps toward her. "And done what?"

"Get our show going. The first of the day. Of many. A preview. Discounted tickets. We could put on five or six shows now."

"By yourself?"

"If it comes to it." She glances at the long line of vehicles waiting to go through the gate. "They could let the shows go on. We don't have anything dangerous like that. Not ours anyway. The animal shows could cause trouble. Or that science show. The Freak Shows would be lots of trouble."

"We had someone complain about the strobe lights we use."

"That was with Don."

"It's a comment I saw on one of the posts."

"I block those."

He scrolls his phone. "Someone said they're concerned about the 'intensity and violence.'"

"It's a gorilla bursting out. What do they want?"

"'I felt unsafe,'" he reads. "'It was triggering. I don't want to relive trauma.' That one got lots of replies."

Two EMTs load a stretcher in the back of the ambulance.

"'Now's not the time for this literal violence. We live in a dangerous country and uncertain times right now. Do better, Kopolski.' This user directed that at the main account."

"That's a fake user."

"How do you know?"

"How do you know it's not our competitors talking trash about us?"

The ambulance and firetruck roll out.

"There aren't many left now, Alex." He shows her an article titled "Eight Ways Traveling Carnivals and Circuses Can Be Concerned about Social Issues—Or Be Left Behind." "'I remember going to a circus when I was a kid. I was amazed at the acrobats, clowns, animals, and pageantry. But the time has changed...'"

"You don't need to read it to me, Pete."

"People will follow the herd. Off the cliff without thinking. And this herd right now says places like ours need to change or else."

The police officer at the gate stands aside; vehicles go in.

Alex climbs into the RV. "Let's go. We can set up. Help Logistics out. And our sound and light guys."

"Do you know their names?"

"Rico."

"Rico was at the start of the tour. His wife had twins. He had to leave when they got sick. Then he got cut."

"We got new guys. Fine."

"Ben and Demetrius."

"Ben and Demetrius. Got it."

Cars pull ahead of the RV.

"They might get cut too."

"If we don't get in there and put on a show, they will."

He turns on the engine but keeps it idling.

She slides toward his seat. "I'll drive."

"You sit down. I'm scheduled to get an audition. I won't be here for much longer."

"When?"

"You'll be the first to know."

The RV crawls through the gate and heads for a lot, but before Pete parks it, Alex jumps out and calls Chris and tells him Pete is thinking about leaving. "But that's OK," she continues. "It can be a one-person show. I can make it that way. I've been working on that."

"You're prepared."

"Yes."

"And this is after you ran off Don. That's what I'm hearing."

"He retired."

"It was time for him to retire."

Pete grabs his backpack and walks toward the tent.

"I wish he could've done it back here," Chris continues. "But you spurred him into retirement."

"His health would've caught up with him. And the show. It already was."

A truck from Logistics backs up between tents and vendors.

"And you can do this by yourself when that day comes?"

"I have all my notes and ideas. I can reduce the show's expenses."

"I like the sound of that."

"I'm OK with Pete onboard until the end of the season. Or at least through the summer. During the break we get between summer and fall I can work on blocking out the show with just me."

"We may have to shift our focus to more shows," he says. "Fewer rides for a while."

"I heard about the accident this morning."

"Our numbers have softened. And this won't help."

"But I'm still a top draw."

"You're near the top. But not what you were. This morning won't help anyone. But onward we go."

She starts for the tent until Pete and the others unload the truck, and she turns for the rides where silence overwhelms her and she could count on one hand the number of people waiting. It'll pick up, she tells herself, checking behind her: the gates open; her colleagues lean on their stations, waiting for anyone; music echoing. Before her: rides, games, and shows stilled like an abandoned amusement park. In the distance: a calliope, which she follows. Around the corner, in the middle of the park near the vacant big top, a carousel turns, and one child rides it while a man standing near the handrail waves and blows kisses whenever the little girl and the horses come around.

· · ·

That evening, after the last show, Pete rummages through their wardrobe and pulls out Don's lab coat and folds it in a box. Alex wipes off her makeup and checks a message on her phone: New Voicemail – Dad.

"Thanks for shipping that to him."

Humming yes, Pete writes Don's address on the box. "Nobody out there today. Rides and games were dead too. We should've asked someone from another department to drop in. We could've helped them out and played games or ride something. Made it all look like things were picking up."

"I don't need their help."

"All your hype didn't bring them in." He snaps a photo of the box.

"This is my fault? We had..." She scrolls through a note on her phone. "Seven people. Five in the afternoon show. And two tonight."

"One of them left in the middle of it."

"You don't think I saw that?"

"I don't know what you see anymore." He cradles the box and exits.

She restarts her father's voicemail asking her to call him. "Dad, whatcha need?"

"Good evening to you too, Charlie."

"Sorry. It's been a long day."

"What happened?"

"Things have been rough. Poor attendance. Low sales. People are either going on strike or quitting. And we had an accident on a ride."

"Sorry to hear that."

"What's going on?"

"I'm leaving for Virginia."

"To visit?"

"For good."

"When?"

"As soon as I can. And I was hoping you'd come back to help me."

"I can't, Dad."

"I'm willing to hold off until you get a break or can come back for a weekend. Help me gather up my stuff. You might come across something you want to keep."

"I can't, Dad."

"I was looking over your schedule. I know you're headed to Tulsa next, but I'd pay for your flight back here."

Her brow burns. "I can't."

He wheezes. "OK."

"How are you feeling?"

"That's the other thing I wanted to talk to you about. The doctor says I'm not in good shape. He recommended changes. But I'm not taking the drugs."

"What did he recommend?"

"I bet you can guess."

"Have you done anything?"

"I haven't had a drink in two days."

"Good."

"But I don't think it's gonna last. So…" He coughs. "I'm making my changes and moving to Virginia."

Lights clank off outside the tent.

"I'm sorry I can't help you move. Work is more demanding than ever."

"I understand. You've got to keep it going if it keeps you going."

"Let me know when you're settled."

"I will. You'll have to come visit."

She puts away her makeup and wardrobe and pulls out her pendant. A silence descends around her: no crowds taking their time; no last-minute calls for food or rides or games; no final sales. A colleague calls out, "We got everything packed away for the night. Alex? Pete? Hello?" But she flicks off the lamp on the table she uses to become someone else, from somewhere else, and sits in the dark.

22

Into the big top they go, finding seats or standing while workers finish up—metal clanging and scraping; structures lowered and put in place; dust in the afternoon light—but Alex and Pete sit in different rows. Julie and Chris emerge from a crowd near trucks and gear. Alex shifts in her seat and rubs her pendant. A microphone squelches when Chris announces he's ready.

"Julie and I felt we needed to stop in at this tour after the last few weeks. Our numbers have not been great. They've gone down since peaking in May. Attendance is down. Sales on all fronts are down. Those two go hand in hand. And the recent events of the rainout, concerns from our workers…"

"They're called strikes!" someone yells from the crowd.

"And the protestors and an unfortunate accident have compounded these down-numbers. By the way, the injured riders have checked out of the hospital. Only one of them needs long-term physical therapy."

"What about the operator?"

"I heard she was fired."

Chris scans the crowd for those voices. "She was not fired. She was placed on probation."

"And then she was fired."

"Was she, Chris?"

A woman flanking Julie whispers to Chris who hands off the mic. "She was placed on furlough until investigations are complete. If those investigations show she's not at fault, and our economics improve, she will return to her duties."

"So she'll be let go," a voice says.

Alex looks around, convinced the speaker is Pete.

The crowd swells.

Chris snatches back the mic. "We don't want that. But our guests are not rewarding us the way they had. And we need to return to that. We're seeing declines across the board as well as challenges." He thumbs down his phone's screen before speaking. "But we're confident our well-established business model coupled with a leaner balance sheet and long-range plan and our partners at Avé Asset Management will drive us back to success. But in the near term, we're taking action to navigate these concerns."

"Layoffs here we come!" A man bolts up and exits.

"More layoffs. They're already doing it back at HQ."

"Wait until lawsuits from the families of those riders come in."

The crowd breaks up. The mic bumps off. Pete walks out with the people who shouted.

Alex marches toward Chris and Julie but speaks only to him. "What can I do to help?"

Julie crosses her arms then responds to someone asking her for a signature.

Chris pulls Alex aside. "Be on your A-game this weekend. B-game won't cut it. We have guests coming in. They're from Avé."

Alex promises she will.

○   ○   ○

As the sun sets, Alex double-checks her list, script, angles from audience to stage, marks on the stage, props, and the Pepper's Ghost box. She asks Pete to double-check his part of the show. He toes over his bins, speaks one cue from the new script Alex rewrote, and storms forward, swinging his arms and legs, bounding about, grunting. "I think I got it." He tosses in his water bottle, slings on his backpack, and doesn't tell her goodnight.

She hovers over the script and considers chopping out his role but turns off the light. "Hope Hollywood is better for you." Before she exits backstage, she turns toward the box—a silent rectangle blacker than the shadows around it and across its glass a single streak of light from somewhere.

The ride-share picks her up outside the gates and, leaving fields and farmland and trees, crosses the river and heads into the city. Alex rereads Julie's email to her department:

I wanted to follow up on what Chris said at our meeting today. We have a lot to navigate, but I know we will come out on top because of our business model and our long history of success. Some of you expressed your dissatisfaction with where we are, and please know none of us in management want you to leave. I will do everything I can to make sure your employment is my top priority.

In the meantime, enjoy yourselves this evening. Get out. Relax and be renewed for tomorrow when we open the gates and start fresh. Remember to represent our company with nothing but the highest integrity while you're here. I know you will. And don't forget our earlier curfew tonight. We want to be ready and well rested for our guests tomorrow.

The ride-share drops Alex off at a diner her father would love. "I bet they'll call you Hon or Shugga," she hears her father say about the waitresses. She tips her driver extra and heads in.

Bells chime over the front door. A jukebox glows in the corner. Countertops and stools sparkle. She looks around like she's in a box in a dream that night surrounds, blacking out the windows, and the light within bounces off chrome and the seafoam-green Cadillac at the back. The hostess ushers her to the counter where she perches her feet on the rail. A man greets her, offers a menu, and tells her to take her time.

"No, sir." She doesn't open the menu. "I'm ready." After she orders, her phone rings.

"Why aren't you helping your father move?"

"I'm busy with work."

"I can't help him."

"Did he ask you?"

"One of us should. I'm headed to Flagstaff."

"He's nostalgic, Mom." She stabs her straw in her drink.

"He had a health scare, Charlotte. He's the last one. He's outlived his family. The universe wants him to be in Virginia."

"You sound like him." She thanks the man after he serves her order.

"I wish you would help him. You're closer."

"I can't. I have a big day tomorrow. I have top management coming to my shows. I have to be at my best." She sets down her burger and sucks at the shake, which doesn't soothe her throat or stomach. "Besides, he said he'll be fine without me. I'll get in the way."

"Where are you now?"

"Tulsa."

"Clarence used to sing 'Tulsa Time' to me. Among other songs. And he would sing it to you when you were in my womb."

The front chimes, but no one comes in.

"At least check in with him. Visit him when you can."

"Bye, Mom." She finishes her meal and tips the staff fifty percent. She checks the big clock behind the counter and requests a ride-share. But the first one doesn't arrive, and the next two won't arrive in time. She steps out of the diner, under the sign glowing pink neon, and heads to a nearby bus stop, but none of the timetables or routes line up with where she needs to go. She glances at the ride-share app—nothing better—and scrolls through her contacts, past Pete, Julie, Manny, and pauses on Chris but closes her phone. The diner's sign rotates over the bus stop's map, fading it and her reflection in and out against a black background. She photographs the map and compares the routes to her phone's suggested routes. The driver icons on her ride-share app jostle farther away.

"Forget something?" the man behind the counter asks after she steps back in.

"Would you walk to here?"

The man looks over her map. "No. Not me. Do you need a ride down there?"

"I'll call a cab." But after checking the time, she bolts.

. . .

She takes a break at a boarded-up movie theater and reviews the map and her location: miles from the diner. Her current path is the shortest and most direct toward the fairgrounds. She jerks when glass breaks behind her. Silhouettes and cars scuttle on the street and in and out of shadows. Tires screech. Cars slow passing her; one circles the lot before turning around. Her other option is longer and farther from the fairgrounds, miles away, but the path loops and branches off major roads, restaurants, gas stations, and traffic. <I'll be late coming back for curfew.> she starts a text to Chris but deletes it and continues in the dark, thinking there's bound to be a Good Samaritan along the way.

She stumbles upon motorcycles and trucks outside a dive: no name attached to it; beer signs missing letters and blinking in windows; curtains drawn tight; roots breaking up the street; rusted roof. Her map freezes; her phone can't locate her. She slowly opens the door. Shadows and screens flicker.

"We're closed." A barkeep with mutton chops and tattoos wipes a glass.

Men and women in the corner booth grab helmets and saddlebags.

"I need directions. Please. I want to make sure I'm headed the right way." She touches the bar top—wet and sticky—and jolts when motorcycles out front rumble on.

"Where you headed?"

She turns toward the man leaning back in his chair, which lightens his dishwater-blond ponytail and short-sleeved shirt, while he nurses a shot. "The fairgrounds," she forces out.

"What's down there for you?"

"I need to get down there."

"Now that's pretty loose. What's a girl like you need to get down there at this time of night?" He lifts his glass. His chair creaks under his tall, broad frame and boots slung on the bottom rung.

The barkeep sneers.

"I need a ride down there. It's dark and…"

"Oh, it's dark out there. That's for sure. Ain't no doubt about that." He motions for a top off.

"I'm here with my company, and we're staying down there."

"Well shee-it. Now your story's done changed on me."

"It's true. I was eating at Lou's Diner…"

"Lou's is a mighty fine joint. Great burgers. I usually get the double patty." He leers at her hips and backside. "Thick and juicy."

"If you can help me…"

"Your company brought you here, you go out walking by yourself, but you don't know how to get back?"

"Yes."

"You got a hotel?"

"No."

"Where're you staying?"

"In a RV."

"Meth," the barkeep says.

"What's the company? Maybe you know that."

"It's a traveling amusement company."

"That's not a name."

"Bowling Brothers Amusement."

"Bowling Brothers? Never heard of them. Bowling's an amusement now?"

"My ex-wife would say that." The barkeep slides his dirty finger in and out of a hole his other hand shapes.

"Not bowling. Amusement."

"Like clowns?"

"Yes," she exasperates, trying not to cry and laugh.

"You a clown?"

"I'm in a show."

"Now we're getting somewhere. What kind of show?"

"It's this stage show."

"I've been to some good stage shows before but never at a circus."

"I turn into a gorilla."

"How do you do that? You're not as hairy as Gibby over there."

The barkeep snickers back.

"It's all lights and mirrors."

"No, see, I don't like smoke and mirrors from women. I kick all that to the curb." His boots drop to the floor.

"If you're going to do something to me, then…"

"Hon, if I wanted to do something to you, it'd be happening right now. You waltzed in here. Know what I'm sayin'?"

The barkeep flips off the TV. "Cops don't bother coming over here."

"Got unsavory individuals around here. Some of them don't like whitey. You got meth rednecks around here too. And then you got plain ol' Stars-and-Bars rednecks like me and Gibby. But I'll give you a lift." He raises his right hand. "I promise my parole officer won't mind."

Between the bar and flag of an eagle snatching a snake, the clock ticks forward. She follows him to his truck, jokes to herself it's not a windowless van, and is surprised seeing only RIDE THE MOTHER ROAD and IT'S SOUTHERN PRIDE, NOT HATE as bumper stickers. She notes his gun rack—empty—and climbs in, shaking, after he opens the door for her. The smells of old beer, leather, and cigarettes crawl out. She leaves her door unlocked and grips the handle.

"What's your name?" He leans across and pulls out a joint and lighter.

"Andi."

"With a y?"

"No. I."

"Short for something?"

"My name."

"I knew a guy named Andy. With a y. You sure don't look like him. You can call me Coke. Like the drink. I may quench your thirst."

The truck grinds them forward into night.

"I'm messin' with you, girl." He rolls down his window and lets out a long drag and passes her the joint.

"No thanks."

"Now, look, I'm giving you a ride and offering you a gift. It's rude to accept one but not the other."

She takes a short toke then a longer one before handing it back to him.

"Good Lord, your hands are shaky. Is this your first time?" He cranks the wheel. "We may have to go the long way. It's such a nice night out for cruising."

"I need to be back as soon as possible. Please."

He takes a long drag; his pockmarks deepen. "You're right. What was I thinking? I didn't see you're the one driving."

The truck pulls to an isolated four-way stop. A car arrives, and Alex turns, pressing against the window, hoping the driver will remember a woman in the truck. The car disappears in the dark when the truck grates forward. The cab and bed rattle and clang—heavy, loose things somewhere—and Alex's legs tighten at the next corner where she could fling herself out and hide behind the shop with bars on its windows. Turn the handle, lean into the door, roll onto the street, she coaches herself. Bruises and cuts will be worth it, and I can find the street name or crisscross until I'm on one. But the truck turns into the countryside and thick copses. No street signs. Dark, abstract shapes. Bugs smack the headlights. Houses and neighborhoods thin. How long has it been? she wonders. The truck has no clock. A stream and a bridge roll under her. Oh God, he's taking me to the woods.

"Just 'bout there."

Please. She rubs her pendant. Please don't.

The stream and moonlight disappear—all black.

She closes her eyes; she opens them; closes; opens.

The truck slows until it stops; gears underneath scrunch. He shifts in his seat. The gears grind again. The truck turns and heads back into moonlight and toward shapes of cranes and blockades.

Please, please, no.

Barrels and signs for new patterns blink ahead.

"All that highway construction makes it hard for a straight shot to that part of town. Had to go all the way around pretty much." He takes another long hit; stains on his shirt glow under the blaze. "You should see what they're doing to downtown. Tore that place up like a fresh one." He blows smoke out one side of his mouth toward her.

She takes a longer hit. "Right," she stammers. Her legs relax; her grip on the handle eases; her color returns. "Construction. Didn't know about that."

"If you had walked this way, you would've fallen smack down a hole in the road. We can't have that, now can we, sunshine?"

She laughs and cries. "That'd be pretty bad."

On the horizon the city appears, its colors crisper and clearer as the truck moves toward them.

"All the way around." His burning joint circles the air. "I got a cousin who lives out here. They want to build an outlet mall right next to his place and drag the interstate closer."

The roads become more complex—multi-lane and single-lanes weaving in and out—and city blocks and neighborhoods return. Restaurants. Shops. Parks. Pruned trees and lawns. Roads with streetlights and names. And when the truck crosses the river and turns for the dark shapes of roller-coaster rails, towers, booths, the big top like a black cloth, she exhales.

"Where do you want me to drop you off?"

"Here's fine."

"I could walk you to your RV. Make sure no one does anything to you."

"You've done so much already." She staggers out of the truck before it stops at the gates; she staggers back. "Thanks again, Coke."

"My pleasure, sunshine."

She runs to the gates but slows when a cop car blocks it. An officer, a security guard, Julie, and Chris stand inside.

Chris spots her, gestures to the others, and marches her way. "What the hell, Alex?"

"Are you OK?" Julie slips between him and Alex.

"I'm fine. I went to out to eat and couldn't get back. I had to hitch."

"Why didn't you call Pete?"

She glances over Julie's shoulder. Pete tells the security guard goodnight and strolls back to the RV. "I thought it wouldn't be a big deal."

"Did you authorize this?"

"No," Chris answers Julie. "She's your employee." He hovers over Alex. "You reek of pot."

"That man who drove me here had some."

"You didn't smoke it?"

Alex grimaces.

"Which credit card did you use for dinner?"

"I used my own."

"We'll talk about all this later." He strides away.

"Alex…"

"I don't want to hear it now, Julie. I'm tired."

Pete rolls over when she enters the RV. She sneaks into the bathroom where her adrenaline dwindles but her high does not and something compresses her. She splashes on cold water and slips into bed where she imagines leaving her body. And this out-of-body Alex floats through the RV and over the fairgrounds and the road the truck rumbled over—all glowing under a sunrise that darkens toward the stars.

Higher this other Alex floats until this part of town patches blacks, greens, browns, and the trees around the river spell out Be Who You Want To Be, and she sings the beginning to a poem she read years ago, "Little Lamb, Little Lamb," while ghosts of her rise. And these Charlottes and Alexes rise higher, filling the sky, into images of an ocean churning and horses galloping, frame by frame. The sleeping Alex twists in bed when all this bobs in the sky and the other, out-of-body Alex asks, "Who made thee?"

23

A woman sitting at the back scrolls her phone while speakers inside the tent play Alex's new soundtrack and voiceover.

Welcome to the show Daisy the Gorilla-Girl. I hope you enjoy your time here being part of mystery and magic. After the show, stick around to meet the cast and check out souvenirs. Feel free to photograph and video. But please no flash. And remember to tag the show with…

Peering from backstage, Alex thinks, One. I'll take it. That's more than zero. She pops open a third can of espresso and forces a yawn away while pacing around Pete's gear. "With or without you," she chants, passing the shadow of the Pepper's Ghost box separating her from the stage. She peeks into the audience again: the woman photographs herself. Alex motions *Stop the house* to the man who volunteered from Food & Beverages. The soundtrack and voiceover stop. Alex signals *One more minute* and cracks her knuckles at Pete's spot. "Damn you." Her laptop sputters opening files, but she pulls up her one-woman show, and jogging to the front of the tent, trips on a cord in the middle. Her laptop smacks the ground and blacks out.

"Did you put that cord there?"

The man behind the control panel shrugs. "Where else does it go? The generator's on the other side."

The woman looks up from her phone.

"It's never gone there before."

"That's not what this says." He rotates a diagram.

Alex dusts off, her knee and elbow oozing, and hobbles backstage.

"You ready?" The man at the control panel pushes a button: Don's music and voiceover start.

Scowling, Alex storms out of the tent and scans the morning: no lines; one ride near her running but not full; coworkers shooting water pistols at each other; no Pete. She drags Pete's gear onto the stage and waits for Don's voice to fade out and bubbles and laboratory beeps and bloops to fade in. She scrawls a circle taking up one half of the blackboard, arrows pointing out of it, and on the other half underlines her scribbles before grabbing the gorilla mask and leaping into the box but can't rock it like Pete could and can't slam it onto the ground and emerge from it like a coffin. *Salina,* Don's voiceover cuts in, *the Amazon princess who harbors a dark secret.* Alex spins and bursts out of the box—blood on her dress; the gorilla mask crooked. But the woman is gone, and the man from the control panel is onstage and tells her he's "gotta jet. A corndog machine isn't working."

"Can't someone else fix it?"

"There's not many of us left."

"Is there anyone here today to eat them?"

She pursues him out the tent but eases when he turns a corner near an empty ride. Down rows of similar rides she bolts toward the RV, pausing at the Freak Shows where cast and crew inside lounge, chat, or scroll their phones among empty seats. When Pete—sunglasses on; backpack slung over his shoulder—steps out of the RV, she rushes at him.

"Coward." She wipes off spittle. "You left me in a lurch."

"I spoke to Julie and Chris this morning."

"You could've told me."

"It's not what you'd want to hear."

"A text. A call. A note backstage. On a prop. Anywhere."

"Like the empty seats?"

"You'll play in front of zero crowds too."

"I've done that. Before this. During this. Long before I met you. I'm done, Alex. But I'm not leaving because I got an acting gig." Pete waves to a taxi after it pulls up outside the gate. He hands the RV keys to Alex. "I hope you find what you want when this is over. It won't last forever. And I won't be the first to tell you that."

"You could've told me before the show."

"It wouldn't have changed anything."

"Get your things and run. You have no honor or courage."

"Like when your dad was in the hospital?"

She slams open the RV's door and climbs into bed.

* * *

She wakes to her alarm beeping, her head throbbing, and flops onto the floor, which splays her knee and elbow wounds. She disinfects and bandages them and limps for her show's tent. More people on rides and walking around and eating, laughing, and playing games rally her. The four people sitting inside turn when she yells from the back she's made it "from my lab at the other end where my father… My experiments could make their way here. I'm the only scientist and researcher over there. I'm the experiment. I do this to myself." She gestures toward the stage lit only by sunlight. The audience half chuckles, half demurs while she scrambles around the control panel. Don's media starts. Fine, she says to herself, leaping onto the stage.

"Welcome, my weary travelers to my show. I'm your gracious host…"

"Where's the scientist guy?"

"I'm sorry?" She squints at the audience.

"Your posts had a crazy-looking scientist guy in them. Like in the movies."

"We dropped him. This is better than those movies."

"I brought my mom for that. She loves that stuff."

"It's just me."

"Whatever. Come on, Mom."

Two silhouettes leave.

"Those of you who stayed will be amazed beyond your wildest imaginations." She pauses midway on the stage and can't recall what she wrote for her one-woman version. Her ears ring.

The boy in the front row bobs, his pudge wiggling about.

"Would you like to see me become who I really am?" She snarls.

But as Alex closes in on the boy, the light brightens her wounds, bandages, tired and spit-crusted face, and disheveled and blood-stained dress. The boy screams and scrambles for his mother who cradles him as they flee.

"Wait!" She chases them but halts when Chris and, from the morning show, the woman on her phone turn toward her.

Chris quickly shields the woman and points out features along the way before he shepherds her into the Freak Shows.

. . .

No one sits in on the next shows, and before the last show of the day, Alex paces through rows and scoots a chair to the side and another and another, all stacked on the same side, until the grass underneath appears like a green circle. Her caffeine crash drags her down, and a comment posted from earlier snips at her:

Terrifying, traumatic, problematic. My son has been bothered all day. I would give this show negative stars if I could. Where was the warning? Movies and books do it. I'll be notifying this company of this. They won't be getting my money again if they come through here again. I'll report them to government agencies too. If you've experienced something similar, DM me.

She moves more chairs and steps on stage, looks over what she's made, turns off the control panel, writes *Canceled* underneath the showtime on the sandwich board, and closes off the tent. She expands the circle and lies in the middle and extends her arms and legs and says to herself, Twenty-hundred o'clock as Dad would say. She slides out her arms and legs, both V-shaped, while the rest of the day and the start of the night halve her. Feet and silhouettes meander outside the tent. She shuffles the chairs about and steps on stage and spins inside her maze but can't find the entrance or exit. She lumbers toward a section, crying like an ape, and smashes through—again and again. And on the piles of what she's broken she sits but can't comprehend the time it took to break it all down.

24

The caravan lumbers east without her as she drives toward the hotel Julie and Chris asked her to come to. The RV pops and sputters after she parks. The hotel's front glass doors slide open for a group of softball girls exiting, and she wonders what would've happened had she stuck with sports when she was their age rather than crying when nothing went her way. The vehicles the softball girls climb into head in the same direction as the caravan. Chris texts they're in the lobby. She switches to the website. Her show remains listed, but the changes she requested have not appeared.

"Have a seat." Chris motions to the chair across from Julie and him—a tight triangle in the lobby's corner. Dishes, cups, saucers clang. More softball girls and their families stand in line for breakfast. Two envelopes lay across Julie's lap. "Your recent performance and behavior requires us to let you go," he continues. "The show is not what it was. And your behavior is not who we are."

"Is this because of Don?"

"Don retired."

"So this is because of Pete?"

"Among other concerns," Julie intervenes.

"You kept Pete from me yesterday morning. On purpose."

A father and the softball girls in line glance at Alex.

"We did not."

"You told us you could do it on our own."

"That's not fair, Julie. Not on a day like that."

"A rep from Avé was there yesterday. At the morning show. And you canceled the last show without consent from Julie. Among other changes and issues you've gone through without her consent."

"That's now a problem? Chris, are you serious?"

"You've been going over me, Alex. I'm your department supervisor. I am *the* Shows and Talent director."

"This is effective immediately," Chris says. "We need your keys to the RV and other access points and all materials related to the show and the company."

Over the table Julie slides the larger envelope stamped and addressed to corporate.

"We're allowing you one business day to return to headquarters and clean out items you have there. If you do not obtain these items, they will be considered property of Avé Asset Management and disposed of."

"Property of the hedge fund? Not Kopolski? So that's where we are."

Julie hands over the smaller envelope.

"Inside that you'll find funds to purchase a ticket back to wherever you need to go."

"How? Bus? Plane?"

"However you need."

"What if I go to overseas? You paying for that?"

"If you go over the allowance, the difference is on you."

Girls dance by the table, using their bags as partners. Moms and dads kiss their heads and hats. The woman from the morning show and the one Chris ushered away stops in the lobby.

Chris rises. "Thank you for time here."

Alex charges for the RV where she rummages through drawers and her clothes and charges back into the hotel and finds Chris and the woman at a table in the dining room. She butts in front of Julie loading her plate.

"I have something for you in the RV."

"I don't want to talk about any of this. It's over, Alex. What's done is done."

"It's not that. It's something I don't want. Please."

They reach the RV. Alex steps in while Julie stands outside.

"It needs to be cleaned. Sorry about that." She hands over her dress. "You said your daughter would love to wear something like this."

Under the hotel's canopy Chris steps out and scans the lot.

"I'm sorry this didn't work out," Julie says. "I hope you get to wherever you need to." She walks in with Chris.

Alex waits until they're gone and walks into the long shadow along the side of the hotel and calls for a ride to the airport. <Where are you now?> she texts her father.

<Made it to Louisville. You still in Tulsa?>

<Not much longer.> She pauses. <Ft. Smith is next. Then Fayetteville.>

<If you keep going east you'll be in Virginia in no time.>

<How are you feeling?>

<Had a spell yesterday but feeling OK today. Not 100%. Dr. says I'll never be. I have to have to my stops. Or else it catches up with me.>

<Let me know when you arrive.>

Her ride-share pulls up, and she assumes her father will reply, but when he doesn't, she doesn't look at the hotel or the RV or toward the fairgrounds or the road the caravan took and doesn't care if she's left anything behind.

25

Now boarding... People drag their luggage toward the gate. Alex checks times and destinations flashing on screens and reviews Early Termination by Tenant in her apartment's lease. She's locked in unless she pays an amount that buckles her legs and crunches her forward. The boy and girl across from her mimic her and squirm off their seats. The Departures row updates. She calculates the months left on her lease, the money in her checking and savings accounts, and balances on her credit cards and student loans and convinces herself to hunker down until her lease expires and accept she'll run into her former coworkers. The row switches to Boarding; the PA follows.

She stands in a line growing behind her. The agent announces the next group. The line shuffles forward. A woman pants, slinging her backpack to her other shoulder, and starts for the end of the line. "You can have my spot," Alex tells her, stepping out and heading to the ticket counter.

・ ・ ・

The front door opens.

"Charlotte." Music, talking, and glasses and plates clinking drift behind Janet. "Did you drive here?"

"I flew in late this afternoon and got a ride." She waves off the driver who reverses into the street under moonlight.

"Put your bag in that room. After everyone's gone we can set you up in there." Janet nudges over purses, hats, jackets and helps a man searching for the trash bin. She whispers, "Are you in trouble?"

"No."

"Thanks, Janet. Lovely evening."

"Goodnight, Carl. Bring Tom next time."

"Will do." The balding man with a ponytail steps out.

"Are you pregnant?"

"Mom, no."

"You have the right to end that."

"I also have the right to keep my legs closed."

"You sound like your father." Janet crosses the hallway and into the kitchen where she dodges a salt-and-pepper-haired woman gathering fliers.

"I have time off."

"I read the other day about those circuses you work for. They're all being exposed and going under. Abuse. Tax evasion. Workers' rights. Race and gender discrimination. The animals. And those rides. All those poor souls with head trauma."

"We don't have those kinds of animals."

Janet ties off the bag inside the bin.

"And it's traveling amusement. Not a circus." She smashes cheese and meats. "Not the way you mean."

The salt-and-pepper-haired woman offers a flier. "Are you Charlotte, Janet's daughter she talks about?"

"I'm Alex."

"I'm sorry?" Her head turns—a hearing aid.

"Yes. I'm Janet's daughter."

"She said you handle a gorilla for the circus. And you get into a box with it."

Janet swoops back into the kitchen. "My one and only."

"Your mom was sweet enough to host us. We switch locations so everyone can feel comfortable."

"Oh, God, are you a swingers' club? Mom, are you still doing that?"

"No, Charlotte." Janet cleans up a table. "We're a book club."

"And we picked this bookstore to patronize." The woman presses the flier into Alex's hand.

Bodhi Tree Books & Imports

There is only one you for all eternity. You're more than matter. Fearlessly be your true self. Let our books and imports find your true self. Because you matter.

"Night, Janet."

"Night, Deb."

"I don't want this, Mom."

"Keep it. They have remedies. Could be good for the stress you're carrying."

Alex stuffs the flier in her pocket and flops in a chair.

The rest of Janet's party tell her goodnight.

"So a book club."

Janet hums yes, scooting out the other chair. "Last month we read about pharmaceutical companies keeping their drugs addictive. They and the FDA claim that's not the case, but if it were, no one would keep taking them. And these companies would be out of business."

"Or they move on with their solution to the next problem. Because they're a business."

"But that does't require drugs, Charlotte."

"What does it require?"

"A village watching out for each other."

"Like Salem did with the witches?"

Janet slices an orange. "Want some?"

She takes one. "I can stay at a hotel."

"I don't mind you staying here. But I'm surprised you came here. You could've picked any place but here."

"I changed my flight at the last minute."

"Is that part of your stress?"

"Flying is stressful."

"Let me show you where things are before I go to bed." Janet scoops up the remaining oranges but misses a rind on the table.

"I changed my flight at the last minute. That's all." She spins the rind. "I picked a place where I knew someone would be when I got there."

⋅ ⋅ ⋅

The next morning she reads her mother's note.

Help yourself to whatever food I have in the cabinets and fridge. Will be in and out for the day. Drinks and dinner later?

She starts her laptop, but it cycles through blacking out and glowing with missing pixels. She jumps on her phone and sends an email to the utilities company asking if she can turn them off for a span of an uncertain time without incurring fees. She logs into her job-search account and starts with her mother's town and towns around it; bypasses those results; scrolls over states near Minnesota—opportunities popping up; and ends over Virginia but closes her account before results appear.

⋅ ⋅ ⋅

The ride-share drops her off in front of a house.
"This is it?"
The driver reviews his map and address on the flier she gave to him. "That's what you got here."

She slowly opens the door and, stepping into a parlor, expects someone to tell her she's trespassing on private property. A sign hangs on a balustrade.

Bodhi Tree Books & Imports Upstairs
<u>All</u> Are Welcome

She follows incense wafting downstairs and, at the top, checks out business cards, events, and announcements covering the bulletin board. Journeys into spiritual realms, dream-analysis workshops, yoga, holistic psychology, energy healing. One guarantees "unearthing the vision of you that you've needed but never knew waited for you."

She steps into rainbow light flooding the second-floor room where rows of crystals and stones shimmer. She rubs her pendant while walking behind the rows and among pottery, baskets, blankets, bracelets, necklaces, and paintings and posters of angels, Buddha, Jesus, the history of medicinal marijuana, the history of LSD, ghosts, UFOs, and a woman in a headdress kissing a wolf under a full moon. She winds her way toward bookshelves and in the center of the room desks forming a square. The cash register sits atop one; catalogues, papers, office supplies, boxes on the others.

A man in round glasses rolls back his chair. "May I help you?"

She does a double take: he reminds her of Don. "Just looking."

"Let me know otherwise."

She drifts from aisle to aisle—Philosophy; Dreams; UFOs and Aliens; Taoism; Buddhism and Hinduism; Christianity; Judaism; Islam; Occult and Wiccan; Health and Exercise; Clearance and Poetry—and picks up a copy of *Jesus Was a Red Man* by Reverend Tony Seeking Eagle.

"Charlotte."

She looks over at Deb from Janet's party. "Hi."

"I have a copy of that. He's red for his spirituality, his connection to the earth, his rebirth, and his economy. The last chapter is all about sharing our resources. Like Jesus encouraged."

"Unless you're forced to do that."

"But you have to be on the right side of history."

"How do you know you are?"

Deb turns her head; her hearing aid angles out. "How do you know who you are?"

"It was nice to see you again."

"You too, Charlotte." Deb hobbles off.

She cruises the UFOs and Aliens aisle and, stopping in the Bigfoot section, unfolds a map at the back of a book highlighting sightings across the country and runs her finger east into Virginia. The line from end to end runs through hotspots. She flips to the back cover.

I spent decades in the military, and now in my second half of life, I'm taking my love of the Unknown and being in the woods and putting them together. Join me in my quest to find out if any of what we know is true.

The man at the front desks rings her up and suggests a book he wrote: the face on the cover shifts from Buddha to Krishna to Christ.

"You write and own this store?"

"Me and my wife." He taps the back of the Bigfoot book. "Unlike him, I dodged the draft. I wasn't going to serve."

"My father served."

"They served someone else. Your father might like my book. I deal with living behind a mask."

"Which is what?"

"Any and all. I'm much happier now. Not as heavy."

"No mask?"

"None."

"I guess self-knowledge is power."

"You got that right."

She folds her receipt. "But it's never free."

. . .

Outside the bookstore she walks streets where people mill about restaurants, bars, and shops and pauses under a marquee attached to a faded-brick building: The Lomax – Est. 1923. She reads each movie's synopsis and approaches the woman inside the ticket booth.

"Which one do you recommend?"

"What kind of mood are you in?"

"I'm unemployed and visiting my mother. But I shouldn't be."

"Unemployed or visiting your mother?"

"Yes."

"I've seen all of them. You can't go wrong. They're all beautiful and speak to the human condition. There's magic in each one. The processions of souls across space and time into eternity." Clouds move across the glass as the woman inside the booth gestures to something inside reflections.

"I'll take this one." She points to the series of vignettes and slides her card under the glass. "You're a showman."

The woman bows and slides back a ticket. "And you are our welcomed moviegoer. Transcendence awaits inside on our screens. Enjoy. And we have popcorn with butter from local cows. And five local beers on tap."

She finds a seat front and center and looking around—alone—props her feet in the seat on front of her and sets the book in the vacant seat next to her. She chews slower, realizing she mixed popcorn and candy and sat where her father would. The first vignette starts; subtitles flash on the screen. *I can finally put my high-school French to use*, she thinks. *I'll be sure to add that to my résumé.* A man balances on a ledge where he brushes off snow and taps a window. Traffic below zips and zags; horns bellow. The man swallows hard, his breath curling in the night, and forces himself to concentrate on the figure in bed. He taps again on the glass—no response. A neighbor opens a window and dangles out a cigarette. Sweating through his stocking cap, the man flattens against the wall and asks God for guidance. A raven snags the neighbor's cigarette and disappears in the night. Crouching, the man wags his arms and legs, but the figure inside rolls away from the window. The man sings until nearby windows light up. He peeks down. Cop cars, with their lights on, roll up to the building but drive off. The man fogs the glass, draws a heart, and around it writes *J'taime*. The figure rises from the bed and leaves the room—and leaves the door open, light pouring in. The man waits on the ledge while the square of light brightens.

Alex weeps, spits out her food, and exits the theater, but she runs back in, shielding herself from the screen, and retrieves the book.

. . .

"You're back," the man behind the desk says to her.

"Do you have something for stress?"

"We got books. Meditation CDs back when those were a thing. We got herbs and vitamins. And that crystal over there worked wonders for my wife's breast cancer."

"Something like that. But herbal. Stronger."

"We don't sell that here."

"What about that woman in here earlier? Deb. The one with the hearing aid."

"What about her?"

"She seems like she would have something like that."

"I beg your pardon, missy, but this is a store of metaphysical inquiries and introspection. I don't know if you're with the law, but don't I appreciate this harassment. And if this is about my taxes, I am paid up."

Heat creeps down her forehead and neck. "Sorry." Alex steps outside and calls her mother. "Do you have something for stress?"

"There should be aspirin in the hall closet."

"Do you have weed?"

"Is it only weed you want?"

"Yes."

"And you're at my place?"

She hails a ride-share. "I will be."

"Cabinet over the kitchen sink. There's a carved chest. You'll find everything you need in there."

When she returns to Janet's house, she chucks the book on her bed and stretches for the cabinet over the kitchen sink. She rolls and lights a joint and drops onto the rug in the middle of the living room—the design under her like a sun in stained-glass —and scrolls through her phone. She reads about "big hits to the big tops and the financial cliff traveling-entertainment companies are falling over." She takes a long drag and opens Kopolski's website and chokes after seeing stops cancelled. She staggers into the kitchen and opens a bottle of wine but stops pouring when she notices initials on the chest: CL. "Did Dad carve the chest you told me to use?" Janet's voicemail clicks on while Alex continues rambling. "Why would I want to see that?" She dumps the wine. "And why do you still have it? It's been decades since he did that." She snuffs her joint. "What's done is done. But what hasn't been done yet?" She unclasps her pendant and sets it in the chest and falls asleep.

• • •

The garage door rumbles up. Alex clutches her neck and runs into the kitchen while Janet steps in. She dumps over the chest and, wrapping the pendant around her palm, sinks against the cabinet.

"Is that my jade I gave you?"

"I thought I lost it again."

"How much did you smoke?"

"It didn't help."

Janet tops off a glass of water and pops out aspirin. She rummages through her cabinets and baskets and jots down a list. "I'll make us soup tonight. Something hearty. Girls' night in. Will you be OK until I get back from the store?"

"I'll go with you."

When they pull into the lot Alex's phone buzzes: Incoming Call – Dad. "I should take this. I'll see you inside." But she lets it go to voicemail and catches up to her mother who weighs leeks and carrots while on her phone.

"That was your father. He said he tried calling you."

"I couldn't get to my phone."

"You answered it when I left. Who did you talk to?"

She shies away.

"What's going on, Charlotte?"

A clerk restocks a pyramid of potatoes.

"It's Alex, first of all."

"You're Charlotte to me. I'm not changing it all now for you. What's going on? Did you talk to your father or not?"

"I'm not ready to talk to him."

"Why?"

"Can we eat? I'm starving."

The clerk rolls away his cart and restocks tomatoes. Janet thanks him for getting two for her.

"You had a bigger hit than you should've."

"You're right, Mom. As usual. Do you and your book club take hits like that?"

"We know when to pace ourselves. We're old. And we do it for aches and pains."

"I want to relax tonight. I love that you'll make us something. Like you used to. You're a great cook. And it's a treat to have my mom cook for me."

"Would you get four of those red potatoes?"

Alex heads to the pyramid.

"He called to let me know he made it," Janet says. "He wanted you to know too."

"You told him I was here?"

"Yes. But you need to tell him."

"What else did you tell him?"

"Nothing."

She pulls. Potatoes spill over the bin and scatter across the floor. Customers stare. The clerk starts for the mess.

"I can't go now, Mom." She fumbles a potato. "Remember when you helped me make a stamp with this? And I sent a letter."

Janet picks up handfuls alongside the clerk who thanks her.

"I mailed it from... Where did I mail it from?"

"You sent me the letter. Clarence helped you make the stamp out of a potato. You wrote that to me."

"What were the stamps?"

"Stars and a smiley face. And circles."

Alex returns the potato and apologizes to the clerk.

"Pick out dessert for us. Ice cream. Rocky Road. Or mint chip." Janet continues down the aisles.

Alex heads for the frozen section where she hovers over lids with giraffes and elephants balancing on balls. She props the door open and presses her palm against the door and her image behind fog.

• • •

They set up Janet's table on her back porch: plates, dishes, silverware, napkins, glasses. Alex brushes off a bottle of wine—"Better not. I need to keep coming down."—and gulps water. Janet flicks on the string of lights tethered to the pergola with flowers and ivy.

"Thank you for coming." She toasts Alex.

"Thank you for letting me stay without notice."

"Surprises keep life interesting."

They dish out roasted veggies, rice, grilled chicken.

Janet dashes ginger in a sauce she offers to Alex. "You're welcome to stay through next week. Then you need to find your own place."

"I don't plan on staying here."

"Are you going back?"

"I have my apartment I need to resolve. Near the circus."

"I thought you said it wasn't a circus."

Her fork clangs on her plate. "It's not, Mom. I use that as shorthand."

"They're not doing well."

"You said that. And I'm sure your book club knows that while they chant about their intentions to start another day of their retirement."

"Why aren't you with them now?"

"My coworkers weren't on board with me. Management had control issues." She pauses. "It was me."

"Money and egos?"

Her food loses flavor; she scoots away her plate.

"We can look at apartments around here this weekend."

"Thank you. But I'm not staying here." Alex walks into the house and, while she preps dessert, spies the book on her bed. "Is there a post office nearby?"

Janet scoops out ice cream for them. "If it's a letter, you can set it in my mailbox."

"It's a book I bought for Dad at that store your book club chose."

"Thank you for doing that."

"For buying Dad a book? Or buying something from the store?"

"Both. But I'm surprised you found a book there for him."

"It's all fiction."

Janet smirks with her. "Why don't you call him? It's not late there."

Alex breaks up chocolate chunks in melted ice cream.

"You never called him when he was in the hospital."

"No, I did."

"But you waited."

"I had work."

"And now you don't."

"Thanks for the reminder."

"I love seeing my daughter, but we all know you'd rather be with him than me. And that's fine."

"It's not that I don't love you, Mom."

"I know you love me."

"It's not like coming here to see you when I was younger was easier because I was with him."

"But I think you would've been more miserable with me."

"It doesn't matter now. What happened happened."

Janet wipes her mouth and gathers her napkin, bowl, spoon. "If you have this time off, you could deliver the book to him."

"But I still have to deal with everything else."

"Then do it from a place you want to be in."

The kitchen-sink faucet rushes on. Janet returns to the table, but Alex tells her she'll take care of the dishes. The nook in the living room brightens; Janet stretches out and reads. Alex flicks off the string of lights, flicks them on, off, on and says to herself, Who up there did I message? She looks into the sky—the black of night hours away. Anyone? Any place? She steps in front of the kitchen window; light shines down on her. She steps closer; her reflection fades away. Or do I have to wait until the right time and meet it halfway?

26

"Do you have plans today?"

Janet sets down her mug. "I was going to the nursery for plants on sale."

"Do it tomorrow."

"Why?"

"Let's get out. I want to get out. We can have a mother-daughter day out." She scrapes her breakfast into the compost bin. "There's those waterfalls we went to when I visited you once."

"I don't know if my knees can take the climbing."

"You were doing yoga this morning."

"That's maintenance at this point. And a reminder to keep at it."

"We don't have to hike far. I want to see water like that. And if we get back before the nursery closes, I'll take you."

Janet washes out her mug. "I'll get ready to go."

Alex reviews her emails but skips over replies from the utilities company and her apartment's manager. She changes, grabs the book, and starts a text to her father. <I need your address. I want to mail you something.> She adds Bigfoot and flying-saucer emojis and photographs the map inside, focusing on the section end to end he told her about, but covers the key and title. <I'll call you later. I'm with Mom. I know she told you. I was going to.> Coward, she scolds herself.

"I'm ready." Janet adjusts her visor and tucks her sunglasses in her shirt.

"Maybe we could swing by the post office too."

* * *

Janet drifts asleep when they hit the road. Alex balances driving and typing Post Office in her phone's map. Results pop around the road. She exits before the waterfalls and drives around but can't find the post office or a dropbox.

Janet snores awake. "This doesn't look like the park."

"I took a wrong turn."

"Where are we?"

"Off the interstate." She passes the marker on her map and double-checks the address: nothing but a scraped-over parking lot and streetlights stripped down to bolts and bases. She heads for the on-ramp.

"Are you hungry? You used to pass gas when you were hungry and needed to use the bathroom on our road trips. One time you'd let so much go Clarence pulled over in that van he used for his construction jobs. I thought he was having a flashback."

She checks before merging. "I need to concentrate, Mom."

"He said to me, 'I thought she removed all the finishes off my tools. Down to the metal. And then some.'"

"Thanks for sharing that."

"You also get gassy when you're stressed. I wondered if you were when you got here. You looked like it. It builds up."

She accelerates. "I bet the bookstore has something for that."

"I'm sure they do. You can ask Lew."

"Is that his name? The owner?" She closes her map and returns to the route for the waterfalls.

"Lewis Rosenfeld. A great scholar."

"Of what?"

Janet yawns. "Anything you can believe in."

· · ·

They line up behind vehicles idling outside the park and end up at the back of the lot. Janet cracks her knuckles, knees, and neck and tells Alex the ride irritated her hips.

"Do you want to sit?"

"I didn't come all this way to sit. But give me patience."

They inch closer. Sunlight and mist spray rainbows. People, dogs, and strollers pass them. Janet grumbles when a man her age cruises by propped on two hiking sticks and grumbles again when a three-legged dog hops by.

"Karl and I never made it here."

"Which one was he?"

"Four summers ago. His wife died in a car wreck. She was driving home from church when a teen on her phone ran into her."

"I'm glad I'm never had that when I was that age. You and Dad wouldn't have let me anyway."

"TV and radio were bad enough."

"Did you break up with him before coming here?" Alex clicks panorama on her camera and spans her phone across the rocks and waterfalls churning ahead.

"He broke up with me before coming here. He did triathlons. He was older than me. He told me the night before, 'I don't think you can do this. And I don't want to be with someone who can't.' He said it was important to him. He'd beaten cancer and being overweight for most of his life. The office life I never could hold down. Or jobs men like your father do."

They stop at the entrance and its stairs and the stones-and-dirt trail.

"You still have Karl's number?"

"Why?"

"We can take a photo of us at the top. Or only you."

Janet wobbles on the first step. "Maybe only you."

"No, come on, Mom. Let's do this. We got this view. We got this gorgeous day. We got this water rushing from somewhere. All the snowmelt. We're in the middle of all this change."

Alex extends her hand; Janet takes it. Switching from stairs to the trail, they climb into the roar and mist chasing light into the river below that sweeps water and light downstream. Halfway up, Janet wheezes and leans on a branch. Alex asks if she wants her to go back to the car and get anything. Janet says she needs to stay put but wants to see Alex wave when she reaches the top. When Alex does, she pulls out her phone and videos the waterfalls and sends it to her father who left a voicemail while they were on the road.

You call me back, Charlie Girl, and I'll tell you my address that way. That's only fair. Hope you and Janet are having fun. I'd like to be there.

The three-legged dog scampers by; a man kneels, takes it in, but never called it over.

Leaning over the edge, Alex waves, and leaning from trees, Janet waves back. Water between them breaks up and continues on.

They walk down the trail, and Alex suggests renting a canoe near the river, but Janet wants to get back.

"I'll take you to the nursery, if you think we can get there in time."

"We can. Their summer hours are later. What about the book? Are you mailing it?"

"I need his address."

"He gave it to me." She rubs her knees and stretches her legs. "But it's at home."

"I don't have to mail it today."

They pull up to the nursery. Janet says she may be a while. "Take your time," Alex replies, fidgeting with her phone. She dials her father but stops and jumps out of the car and wanders the plants outside the fence, and when she's among tall thickets, she hunches over, growls, and drags her feet and knuckles across dirt and gravel. She peers through branches until she scares a child on the other side. She retreats to the car, turns off her phone, and naps.

Janet nudges her. "Do you want me to drive? Charlotte?"

"Yes," she mumbles.

"Then you need to sit in the other seat. Scoot over."

"No. Not Alex. Yes. Charlotte." She shoots up.

"Let me help you out."

"No, Mom. I got it. I'm awake." She feels around for the ignition.

"Did you get ahold of your father?"

"No."

"After we get home, you can help me drop off the things I bought, and I'll get his address."

"I don't have to mail it right away."

"Where will you mail it from?"

She turns for Janet's neighborhood. "Wherever."

"You'll carry it with you wherever you go?"

"I guess."

"It's not much of a gift if he never gets it."

The car whines reversing into the driveway. Alex unloads the trunk. Janet heads inside and returns with a piece of paper. Alex switches on the car radio, types the address into her contacts, and turns up the volume when a song she hated years ago comes on. Louder, a voice inside her says. "It can't anymore," she replies. Janet peeks out. Louder. She tuns the dial the other way, but the sounds remain.

27

She idles outside the post office and counts people going in and out, but when time ticks closer to the lobby closing, she grabs the book from the backseat and heads in. The long line relieves her, but it moves quickly. She reaches the clerk at the window and apologizes for not preparing her package. The clerk offers an envelope or a box for mailing the book and rates for slowest to fastest delivery.

"Slowest, please."

"Very well."

"No. Fastest."

The clerk adjusts. "It should arrive in two days. Would you like insurance?"

"No."

"Fill out your name and address in the top corner."

She tugs the pen tethered to the chain and hovers over the spot. She writes *Alex* but scribbles it out; *Janet Rutherford* but scribbles that out. She settles on *Charlotte* but can't decide on the address. "Can I cancel this? I don't want to mail it yet."

"Let's go, lady," a man grumbles in the line.

The clerk says, "We have a kiosk for after-hours."

The dropoff door next to the kiosk squeaks open and slams shut. She leans on the table next to it. People check their mailboxes. Another clerk locks the lobby door and rotates the sign from Open to Closed. The line to the kiosk grows. She pulls out the book and tears up the envelope on her way out.

. . .

"Did you mail it?" Janet stirs a pot in the kitchen.

Alex drops the book on her bed. "Their computers were down."

"You can try again tomorrow. You could go to another branch. They have one of those kiosks."

"What's for dinner?"

"Pasta."

"I smell garlic. And pesto."

"I'll throw in chicken here in a minute." Janet slides the pot of boiling water to another burner.

"I'll do it. I want to help."

Janet slides over a knife and cutting board. "Want anything to drink?"

"Wine."

Janet beams. "How much?"

"Just start us off." She dices the meat. "I have a favor to ask. I know I came here unannounced and all that, but I was wondering if you could help me pay for something." She scrapes aside what she diced. "And by 'help' I mean you'd pay for it now, and I'd pay you back."

"Are you getting a job?"

"Yes."

"Here?"

"No."

"Are you going back?"

"No."

Janet slides over a glass of wine. "What is it I'd pay for now?"

"An airline ticket. To Virginia."

Janet spins her glass. "I'll pay for it. You don't need to pay me back."

"I want to."

"You need to go. I don't know why you've put him off, but you need to go."

"I'll pay you back."

"No, you won't. Because that doesn't matter. Go see him."

"Thank you."

"You're welcome." Silverware and napkins in hand, Janet starts for the back porch.

"And Mom?"

"Yes, Charlotte?"

She wipes off the knife, her name ringing through her. "Never mind."

· · ·

After dinner, she helps her mother clean up, and when Janet leaves for bed, she steps onto the back porch and moves emails from her apartment's manager, the utilities company, and job-search notices into a folder she labels TBD. She deletes an email from Kopolski's finance department informing her she's gone over her allotted amount. "Bill me," she says, turning off the string of lights. The evening chirps and hums. Silhouettes of birds fly into fractals of trees darkening with sunset. While she waits for her father to answer his phone, she wobbles in the chair.

His voice grates out, "Hello?"

"Dad, it's me."

"Charlie?"

"Were you asleep?"

"It's my medications. They make me loopy."

"How many do you have?"

"They're like shotgun shells in my cupboard."

"I don't need your address."

"You staying with your mom?"

"I'm gonna come see you."

"You coming to see me?"

She wipes her eyes. "I am."

"That's good. Because nothing the doctors have done have helped. And none of these pills do a lick of good."

"Maybe the book I'll bring will help."

"The picture you sent."

"Which one, Dad?"

"There was a map. And waterfalls."

"I sent you those two, yeah."

"All those points on that map looked familiar. But that water… Falling from somewhere I couldn't see."

"Mom and I went there today. I'll give that map to you in person. It's in that book. But the rest of it is a surprise."

"Something to do with Bigfoot."

"Maybe."

"I can tell. That map. But that water I couldn't where it was falling from. It had to start from somewhere and end somewhere. The point of that water is seeing it end or start."

"You're right. You got to see that in person."

"Charlie Girl?"

"Yeah?"

"You're coming here. To see me."

"I am, Dad."

"We'll have things to do. We'll make a list. Like we do."

"We'll figure all that out after I get there."

"You're coming to see me. My Charlie Girl."

"That's right, Dad. I am. Charlotte."

28

Janet drops her off at the airport, and Charlotte gathers her things, double-checking she has the book.

"Thank you for letting me stay with you."

"I'm glad you came. We hadn't seen each other in a while."

"I wish you could've seen me in my show."

"I'm thankful you weren't harmed in any way. You being a gorilla is better than you handling one. How did you do it?"

"I had help from my two castmates. Don and Pete. They were the vets. I was the rookie. They're great guys. They started that show. Before I came into it. And I had help from my supervisor Julie. She wanted the best out of all of us. And I had help from the audience too. If they weren't there, I didn't change."

They hug.

"Tell Clarence I said hello. And tell him I'm thinking of him." Janet climbs into her car. "Let me know when you get there."

She waves goodbye and, checking in at the counter, confirms her name on her ticket and luggage is Charlotte.

The plane takes off, and as she sleeps, she dreams about roll call from her first day as a new student. The teacher called out, "Charlotte Alexandra Long?" But she did not respond.

Mrs. Clark looked at her. "Charlotte?"

"Sorry. Here."

The classroom snickered.

"It's Alex."

"You go by Alex?"

"No. I go by Charlotte."

The class snickered again.

She sunk in her chair.

"Where did you come from?"

"Virginia."

Mrs. Clark reviewed a piece of paper. "I thought Mr. Garritt said..."

"No, it's OK."

The class gawked.

"Where in Virginia?"

"It doesn't matter."

"You'll have to tell us all about it when you're ready."

Charlotte covered her notebook and crossed her ankles while roll call finished. The classroom constricted.

Mrs. Clark wrote *Vietnam Era and After* on the chalkboard. "This was a major event for America and how we viewed our beliefs and ourselves."

"'Cause we lost," someone said from the back.

"We'll talk about that." Mrs. Clark picked up a book. "This is going to be our focus for most of the semester."

Charlotte looked up at the cover: a line of silhouetted soldiers holding guns in a field; helicopters over them.

"The author is looking back on his time as a soldier in Vietnam. What's interesting about the book is the narrator has the same name of the author, but he blurs that." Mrs. Clark set down the book. "As I reviewed our texts for the year I noticed we have similar themes in many of our works. Heroism, shame, loneliness, isolation. Trying to break out of what society or our families or ourselves expect. The burdens and hopes we all carry. And how we manifest those burdens and hopes into objects like a car, clothes, or a tattoo. If some of you are old enough to get a tattoo."

The classroom snickered.

"We call those things a talisman."

Charlotte wrote down the word.

"We'll see the themes of truth versus reality. What you've been told versus what's out there. Think about what you carry with you. Physically and mentally. We all have our journeys. How we got here. We came from somewhere. Where we're going. Who we want to be. Things from your journey you'll carry with you."

. . .

After she lands, emails and texts pour in. Kopolski's finance department confirms they invoiced her. She reads a text from her father saying he'll pick her up at the airport. Another one from him arrives: <Taking my time getting there. It's one of those days for me. But I'll be there.> She slings her luggage off the conveyor belt and scans the airport—no Clarence—and checks her phone. She dials the finance department and asks to speak to Bethany.

"I can't pay the invoice right now."

"You have thirty days."

"I doubt I can pay it by then either."

"Until you can, which by taking the credit card you agreed to this arrangement, you will incur delinquency fees."

"Do you have a payment plan I could get?"

"We're not a credit-card company. Or a bank."

"But you had the funds to make this happen. Like you are."

"Alex…"

"It's Charlotte now. Not Alex."

"Are you using a new identity to avoid what you owe Kopolski Traveling Amusement?"

"I can't pay this."

"You used the card to purchase airline tickets to Minnesota."

"I was told I could go anywhere."

"And by doing so you exceeded the amount we allowed to you."

"Can I at least get a thirty-day extension?"

"Hold please."

The phone clicks into a recording announcing the season, but the stops mentioned, Charlotte recalls, have been cancelled.

"We can give you a fifteen-day extension. Payments must be begin after forty-five days. If the total due is not received within forty-five days, late charges remain in effect until the total is fulfilled plus late charges accrued. Do you agree to these terms?"

"How long have you worked there?"

"Do you agree to these terms?"

"How long have you worked there?"

"Twelve years."

"Do you see another yourself with another twelve there?"

The phone silences.

"Do you agree to these terms I discussed with you?"

"I do."

A man hobbles into the airport and heads her way.

"Have a nice day, Ms. Long."

Her heart sinks as the man opens his arms, his cane off to the side, and leans like a bent stalk, and when she steps into his hug, his frame continues thinning: the sunlight thickened him and tricked her into believing that illusion. She clings to his voice rasping out, "Charlie Girl. My Charlie Girl."

"All the travel out there on the road made you skinny," he says.

"You're one to talk."

"Aren't sideshow gorillas big so they can be scary?"

"Not the person inside."

He wheezes lifting her luggage into his truck.

"Do you want me to drive?"

"You flew in. That's not how it works."

"Did you clean it? It's shiny."

"I parked it in the rain we had the other day."

"And the smell." She glimpses the shiny dashboard, upholstery, and cleaned-out ashtray. "It smells better."

"Little changes here and there."

"Which means you only smoke at home now."

Grinding his truck into gear, he smirks. "Only when I drink."

They pull into his driveway, and he brushes her off wanting to carry in her luggage, but he pauses halfway on the busted-up sidewalk leading to his front door. His neighbor on the other side of the quadplex shuffles out and chats with two men sitting in a golf cart labeled Maintenance. One of the men grabs a long pole and bucket and starts for the pool.

"You can swim over there." Clarence unlocks his door. "Residents are allowed one guest."

"I might do that. I haven't lounged around in a while."

"They don't have a bar." He steps in and greets his neighbor heading out. "Pierre's been here longer than me, and he's asked for one. And he keeps getting shot down by management. Don't you, Pierre?"

"I cannot give up. We can enjoy ourselves like adults should. Pierre Jones."

"Charlotte Long."

"She's my daughter."

"Welcome." Pierre untangles a Trinidad and Tobago flag on the pole outside his door.

"I gotta be honest, Dad. I wouldn't have expected him for your neighbor."

"There's a plant up the road that makes airplane radios. New as of two years ago. Boosted the economy a bit. And shocked what the old timers see around here." He clicks on the bedroom's light and struggles moving boxes printed with medical-supply companies. He looks away when she helps him. "Hope this is OK."

"It is. I don't how long I'll be here."

"Don't worry about that. But I snore more. A lot. Pierre and my other neighbor Evelyn let me know. In a good way. They were concerned. They're not much younger than me. Pierre is fifty-something. Evelyn has never said, but the shuttle that takes all the old folks to church or to the store picks her up and drops her off. I've already talked to the driver."

"About riding it?"

"Driving it." He taps his cane twice. "Hungry?"

"Yes." She comes across photos in the rooms: Clarence in his uniform or in overalls; his parents at a church picnic; his brothers; Janet holding Charlotte while sitting on a swing in a park.

"You want a drink?"

"I don't want to drink in front of you if you're trying to change that."

"I only drink on Fridays now."

"How much?"

"Less than I did." He gets out one glass. "It ain't a fast track. It's a lot of furlongs."

"How 'bout a Coke and Jack on the rocks? Please." She heads into her bedroom and digs through her backpack. "This is for you."

He slumps into a chair and opens the book; his hands fumble over the pages and map. "Ha! Didn't I tell you? From eastern Oklahoma through Arkansas, southern Missouri, and through that belt right there in between into here. Bigfeet. Look at all those markers." He whistles. "But Lordy, look at northern California all the way up through Oregon into Washington. Where'd you get this?"

"A bookstore when I was with Mom."

"Hippies?"

"You should see it."

"I don't need to. I was married to one." He kisses her. "Thank you. Let me get our dinner going. Pizza OK?"

"Pizza made by you sounds great. Pizza with you sounds great."

Chuckling, he unwraps plastic off a frozen pie. "I never said I was making it. Go put on music, would you? Living room. You'll see it."

She finds the turntable and sets on the LP she bought for him and keeps the volume low. Something clangs and clashes in the kitchen. She runs in.

Clarence grips the corner of the counter and pulls himself up. "Like I said…one of those days today."

"I'll get it, Dad," she says after he starts cleaning up his mess. "I want to."

"How did you end up at Janet's? Your tour didn't go that far north."

"No."

"Are you on vacation?"

The oven timer beeps.

"They fired me."

"Why?"

She downs her drink. "I couldn't see myself as anyone who needed them. It wasn't long term. None of those jobs are."

"So you're starting over with whatever you got. Whatever you brought."

"More ways than one."

29

He knocks on her door. "Charlie?"

She rolls over in bed and checks her phone: 7:11. "Yeah?"

"I left coffee on for you. There's another filter ready if you want. And I got eggs and sausage in the fridge. But I got to go to my appointment."

"Are you going to your doctor?"

"I'm power washing a patio and gas station today."

"Do you want help?"

"How fast can you get ready?"

Her bare feet wobble onto the floor; one side of her throbs. "On second thought, I'll take a raincheck. Sorry. I was out more than I thought. I need to take it easy."

"No problem. I'll be home for lunch."

After his truck rumbles out of the driveway, she pours a cup of coffee and, starting her laptop, slumps back into bed. Her screen's pixels break into quadrants; only the top left fills in. <Can I use your computer?> she texts him. My laptop is officially R.I.P. And my phone is too small for what I need to do.> He replies with his password, and before she logs into her email, she clicks one of his folders labeled Health. "That's a lot of medications, Dad. And recommendations." She scrolls to a recent date when his doctor suggested a lung-cancer screening. She rechecks the date—where she was and when he called her. "Multiple times," she mutters, clenching. The coffee bitter, she turns away.

She logs into her job-search account and adjusts her location, but before results load, she visits Kopolski's website. More than half of the tour has been canceled; nothing is listed under Jobs. She clicks News: the latest is the cancelled tour citing "financial difficulties and uncertainties after a reduction in revenue and staff as well as other concerns." She clicks on search-engine links related to the company. "From the Big Tops to the Small Tops: The Sunset on Traveling Amusement Companies" says one headline. Referencing finances, attendance, workers' rights, and "a shift in the culture at large," the reporter argues "this entertainment was for your parents and grandparents. Maybe you saw it with them, but your kids won't." The article ends with Chris interviewed.

> We've heard these doom-and-gloom predictions about our industry for decades. My father and grandfathers dealt with the same attitude during similar changes and challenges. And our position today is the same as theirs: we're more than numbers. Those numbers don't reflect what our guests will take with them when they leave us. You can't put a price on that. They'll take back who they

were at the moment they saw our shows, rode our rides, or interacted with our employees. They'll take back memories.

She zooms in on the last photo used in the article. The sunset silhouettes the hump of a roller coaster rising between sideshow tents and a sandwich board the photo's border clips at her handwritten GORILL.

She returns to her job-search results—all miles away from her current location and in industries she was told a college degree would keep her from working in. She expands her search outside her father's town, county, the state—visit him within a half or full day's drive. She imagines the map in the book she gave him and its trails and markers trickling out near the ocean where the land breaks into islands and the channel between them where ponies swim across.

The back door creaks open.

"You're back early," she says.

Clarence stuffs his gloves in his back pocket. "I got the patio done faster than I thought I would. You feeling rested?"

"A little more." She closes the browser; but behind it documents in his Health folder remain up.

"I got pretty good internet in the complex. Except around five in the afternoon. Folks start coming home from work, and I lose it." He glances at the folder. "You want to help me with the gas station?"

"Let me get breakfast."

"I'll check my email real quick. Make sure Serat is still on for today."

As she heads for the kitchen, she checks over her shoulder. Clarence moves the Health folder off the desktop.

"I'll make you oatmeal like I used to."

"That'd be great. Thanks, Dad." She gets out of his way before he digs through his cupboard.

"Golden raisins. Maple syrup. And a scoop of peanut butter. Made from peanuts down the road."

"I'll have to take some back with me."

"You leaving already?"

She scoops her eggs and sausage onto a plate and sits at the table. "Do you want me to stay?"

"I said stay as long as you want. I mean that. I haven't seen you in so long. It's not like when you could pop on over whenever you wanted."

"I could help you with things. Like today. The gas station. Or…if you need to go somewhere. I could take you."

"Like to Walmart for a new belt buckle?"

"If you need that."

"Or to the repair shop where I can talk to Leroy and RayQuon about how they've been?"

"You decide."

He dumps in oats and turns down the heat before it all bubbles over. "Or anywhere?"

"How bad is it, Dad?"

"What?"

"Your cancer."

"It ain't cancer."

"Does your doctor…?"

"It ain't cancer because the first screening was negative."

"The first one?"

"One negative. The other was inconclusive."

"Which is why your doctor wants you to have another one."

"He's not from around here."

"What does that mean?"

"I have to drive all the way to Roanoke for one day of the week if he's there or Charlottesville if someone from his staff is there or Richmond whenever they're there. Could be him or anyone."

"Why does that matter?"

He serves the bowl to her. "I don't want to spend the rest of my life driving here or there for a doctor. For something I know can't turn around."

"You don't know that."

"I do. And I don't care. I've lived a good life. And anything attached to that kind of doctor or that kind of living is not a good life."

"But what if you got more years out of it?"

"More years for what? To keep driving to a doctor? Or not drive at all?" He tops off his thermos. "I'd rather drive to someplace I haven't been to in a while."

"Not someplace new?"

"There's nothing new. People think that. But all that matters is what's in the past. It's what makes you you. Not the present or the future. People talk like that. You don't be who you want to be. You be who you were."

"But you don't change that way."

"Says who? The past doesn't change. But you might because it doesn't." He wipes off the counter and pops the top off an aspirin bottle. "Finish up, and we'll go to the gas station."

Her phone pings New Job Alert! She slides away her plate and bowl.

. . .

Clarence parks behind the gas station. "Come in with me. You can meet Serat." He says hi to four men sipping coffee at a table off the front entrance. He asks them if they're ready for Tech's summer football practice; only one is looking forward to the season "when it's over." He waddles down the aisles, and a cyclist slides over, chugging down a sports drink, his shoes clicking on the tile.

"How far you riding today?"

"Metric century."

"Now that is..." Clarence's face squishes as he taps his cane. "Sixty miles?"

"Close. Sixty-two."

"What's two more miles at that point?"

The cyclist lowers his sunglasses and clacks out of the store.

"Serat, I want you to meet my daughter. My one and only."

A little brown man turns around behind the front counter. "Nice to meet you. Serat Khumar."

"Charlotte."

"We're gonna start washing the outside."

"Very good. Thank you, Mr. Long."

"Yes, sir. My pleasure. We'll be in when we're done."

She exaggerates her drawl. "He ain't from around here, Daddy."

He chuckles, unloading gear from his truck. "He and his wife and four kids and his father live in my complex. Been here five years. You think my place is small? Imagine all them souls in there." He drops the hose and massages his hand. "Could you?"

She attaches it to the power washer.

"That too." He wheezes and plops against his truck.

She pulls on the washer, strains, then jumps in the bed and pushes but strains again—the power washer not moving. "I'll go get Serat."

"Get someone else."

She scans the parking lot. "Those four men in there drinking coffee are older than you. I don't think they can."

"Yes they can. They're all farmers and factory workers."

She walks in and returns with the four men. One of the men directs the other three lowering the washer off the bed and onto the pavement. Her phone pings A Newly Added Entry-Level Office Job in Boston Perfect For You; she deletes the update.

"How were you going to get this down by yourself?" she asks. "Is that why you have a cane?"

"It's a sore back and knee. It happened the other week. I'll be fine."

"It has nothing to do with your cancer?"

He yanks the hose and flips on the power washer, which rumbles the ground and jolts his body. The four older men dodge the spray while Clarence struggles directing it onto grime and moss on the building. He hits under the roof and knocks letters off signs. Charlotte dries them off and sets them in the truck bed. He closes in on a nest dangling like a lantern under an eave. The four men scatter when yellow jackets swarm out.

"Dad!"

He shuffles closer—the nest relentless—his leg limping behind him.

"Dad, they're out!"

The spray blows back his boonie hat. The yellow jackets explode.

"Back off, Dad!"

He smacks his neck and staggers; the hose clangs on the ground and twists around him. He leans for it but slips. People at the pumps gawk. One of the four men peeks out. Charlotte latches onto her father and pulls, but neither move. The hose whips about. A man from a pump runs over and flicks off the power washer; he and Charlotte pull out Clarence, dodging the hornets. She examines her father—swollen, red, half numb— thanks the man and apologizes to Serat who hopes Clarence recovers. "I'll come back and clean up," she tells him. "But it may be later." Her father wheezing but conscious, she drives them to the hospital.

. . .

The nurse calls for Clarence who tells Charlotte to stay put in the waiting room. She objects, but he disagrees and asks the nurse for a wheelchair. Children climb over chairs next to Charlotte; the parent apologizes and returns to the TV where two hosts and an audience wait near a runway where curtains peel back and reveal a wall of mirrors. A frumpy woman walks up to the mirrors. The black in the glass drops away, light replaces it, and a woman dressed in bright colors sashays out of the mirrors and onto the runway where the hosts and audience rise and clap. Charlotte dashes for the cafeteria where she loads her job-search account and moves the alert from the trash to her inbox. Entry level is perfect she thinks, reviewing Duties and Requirements, and tells herself the salary is good enough. But she hovers over the location. Her map calculates the time to drive from Boston to her father's house. "That's a long day to get there," she mumbles, sinking. But she saves this job, copies and pastes key words and phrases from it into searches for other jobs, and adjusts the locations; she saves results and returns to the waiting area.

Clarence rolls out. "Ready?"

"Are you?"

"Good as new."

She helps him into the truck. "Need anything while we're out?"

"Stop by the station so I can talk to Serat about this."

"I told him I'd clean up any mess we made. And pay for anything we damaged."

"We didn't make a mess. It was those yellow jackets. And we're not paying for anything."

"We broke off a piece of his siding. And the letters from a sign got knocked off."

"Are the letters broken?"

"They're in the back."

"Are they broken?"

"No."

He taps his cane on the dashboard. "Then we'll put them back."

"I'll drop you off then do it."

"You will not. I can do that. I can supervise you. Like my brothers did when I worked with them."

She starts the truck and pulls onto the road.

Before they reach the gas station, he falls asleep, and she keeps on for his house. She helps him into his bed where he falls asleep faster than in his truck. She loads garbage bags and the biggest ladder he has; grabs his welder's jacket, gloves, and helmet; and puts on jeans over her shorts.

She parks behind the station and teeters for the downed nest where she scrapes it off the ground chunk by chunk among a swarm of hornets. She unfolds the ladder and resets the letters on the sign and wipes off dirt. Before going into the store, she photographs the broken siding and grabs her credit card.

"We're happy to pay for this damage." She pivots her phone toward Serat. "Everything else is cleaned up."

"I wish your father a fast recovery."

She idles outside Clarence's house before driving to the library where she logs into her email. She attaches jobs' links to her Charlotte account but forwards them to her Alex account. She creates a new résumé and cover letter and applies to the jobs.

I am available at your earliest convenience for an interview. My schedule and interest in this position allows me to be in the area. I am available to begin work next month. I look forward to this opportunity and contributing to this position and your company.

She cruises the aisles and muses about getting a library card, but it requires proof of permanent residence. She stops at books about staring a new career and across from this a table with the sign Summer Scary Reads, highlighting the paranormal—all of the books proclaiming everything within is true.

"I've been holed in here since that hornets' nest. I want to get out."

She lowers her phone. "Where do you want to go?"

"Drive and see where the road takes us."

"How about a picnic somewhere?"

"I'll get the bread and goodies." He clangs around in the kitchen. "You want a cream soda?"

Her phone rings: Incoming Call – Unknown. She mutes it. "Sure." She grabs her wallet and ties her shoes, and when she gets into the kitchen, her phone buzzes: New Voicemail.

"How 'bout some chips? I got the good stuff." He pulls down a bag flavored dill pickle.

She nods yes while listening to the voicemail.

This message is for Alex. I'm Dave Knuteson with the recruiting department. We're contacting you about your interest in the data-entry specialist positions we have available. Call me back at this number when you have a chance, and we can schedule an interview.

"Something sweet?" He rolls over a tray of something gooey with chocolate, dates, and powdered sugar. "Serat's wife made it. He sells it at the station. I got an extra cavity from it the last time I was at the dentist. It's that good."

"You need to tie something on your finger to remind you to chew gum or brush your teeth." Looking up the area code and company, she mumbles, "Cleveland."

He grabs napkins. "What was that?"

"Are you ready?"

"Got it all."

"You look like when you took me fishing."

He adjusts his boonie hat and vest. "I'll get the rods and tackle."

"I was kidding, Dad."

"Not about how I look." He hands his keys to her.

She waits until he's out of the house and in the truck, double-checks she didn't delete the voicemail, and pretends locking the door takes her a long time.

* * *

"Take the exit for the gas station," he says. "I want to run in for the bathroom and check in with Serat."

"I took care of things."

"Not all of it." He grabs his cane and hobbles out the truck before it stops.

Serat shakes Clarence's hand; they talk while Charlotte calls back the number.

"May I speak to Dave?"

"He's at lunch. May I help you?"

"I'm returning his call about setting up an interview."

"My name is Patricia. I'm also with recruiting, and I can help with that. And you are?"

Before heading for the truck, Clarence chats with the four men drinking their coffee at the front table.

"Are you still there?"

Clarence hobbles toward his truck.

"I need to go. When's a good time to call back?"

"I'll be here until four Eastern."

"And Dave?"

"You can talk to either of us."

The passenger door squeaks open.

"Did you want to go inside and pee while we're here?"

"No."

The truck swivels as Clarence struggles getting in.

"You're gonna save it for the woods behind the pond like you did when you were a kid."

She starts the engine. "Did you see Serat?"

"Everything's OK. He said I can come back when I'm ready. 'You do good work,' he said. 'Accidents happen.' He said you did the right thing coming in. Thank you for that."

"Maybe you should get help next time."

"I don't have money to hire anyone."

"I don't mean that. I mean help. Someone from church."

"They're all dead or feeble."

"What about someone from your complex?"

"Nobody's young there."

"What about those four men?" She points at the table.

"I don't want to bother them every time I come here."

She stops short of the road. "How many times do you plan on coming here?"

"As many as it takes." He pops open a cream soda. "Want one?"

"I'll save it."

"For when you catch something out there?"

"Yes. I'll save it for a celebration." She pauses at the intersection. "When I catch something."

. . .

Mud cakes up the chassis and tires as the truck twists into a field near the water. The ground squishes as they hike across and pop out their chairs at the edge of the pond. Clarence sets their lures and teases Charlotte if she remembers how to do this. "You taught me. I better not have forgotten." He casts wide on his left; she casts short down the middle; the current swirls under afternoon unfolding around them.

His line bobs; he lets it go. "You could stay here. And help me."

She casts again. "I thought you didn't want help."

"You can keep the other bedroom. Until you find your own place."

"Here?"

"I'll pay you."

"You said you didn't have the money to pay help."

"You'd get a small cut. Being my daughter and all. Or you could do it for free. Being my daughter and all."

"I might have an interview with a company."

"Another place like the sideshow?"

"A healthcare company. In Cleveland."

He pulls out cream soda and a bottle of vodka and mixes them.

"What are you doing?"

"It's Friday."

"You said you stopped."

"I said I cut back to only Fridays."

Her line bobs, but she throws down her rod. "Why can't you stop?"

"It takes time."

"Have you tried?"

"It's one leg in front of the other."

"But you can do that and still be one leg in front of the other."

He coughs into his fist and spits a dark-red glob into the weeds. "Can we fish? I want to spend time with you. And if you're leaving for Cleveland…"

"I don't know if I am. I have to set up an interview with them first."

"Why haven't you?"

She stares him up and down—a pale rider waiting for a horse.

"Is the internet at my place bad?"

"No."

"I could pay for better service while you're here if that would help you."

"You don't need to do that, Dad." She picks up her rod and reels the line out of the water.

"You can stay."

"I know."

"You don't have to avoid this place."

She bursts into laughing.

"What?"

"I gotta pee. Like you said I'd have to."

He swigs. "Give me your line. When you come back, I'll have the catch of the day."

"How big will it be?"

"This when we leave." His hands hover in front of his legs. "But as the years go on, this." He expands his hands past his hips. "I'll be on the front page of the *Tri-Valley Reporter*."

"If it's still around by then."

"You'll have to come back from Cleveland and find out."

Branches rustle as she trudges through. She squats over a divot, checks the bars on her phone, and dials a number. She wipes off when Dave answers, but his voice breaks in and out. Asking if he can hear her, she walks back to the pond and drops her phone when she finds Clarence slumped and gasping.

"Dad! Dad!" She kicks away bottles.

He doesn't respond while she shakes him.

She drags him to the truck where he coughs awake and hacks blood onto grass and chrome.

"Stop. I can get myself in."

"I had a better signal back there." She starts the truck. "I'm going back there and calling emergency. If I can't get hold of them, I'll take you to county."

"Stop. I'm fine."

"You're not."

"I told you this happens. I get a build-up. This was a big one." He slumps back against the seat. "We bring any water?"

"We have cream sodas."

"Better than nothing."

She opens one and helps him drink.

"I'll get the gear."

"I'll get it, Dad."

She loads the truck and, backing up and driving forward, balances her phone and the steering wheel. She turns for one way, but Clarence stops her.

"Go for a drive."

"No."

"I said go for a drive."

"Where do you want me to go?"

"Take us on the country roads."

"They're all county roads from here."

"Exactly."

The interstate disappears behind them as she crosses it and drives them deeper into foothills and woods thickening along the road and mountains surrounding them like dark green waves capped off by flashes from a blue sky. The truck jiggles over rocky patches, but when it hits smoother sections, Clarence's wheezing subsides. Songs come and go on the radio, and Clarence hums melodies and chants lyrics while Charlotte checks him and her phone. The landscape spreads out, constricts, flattens, rolls into gorges and streams. Clarence hauls his legs out from under him and wobbles in the seat.

"Do you want me to stop?"

"Yes but only because I'm feeling better and would like get out and stretch."

She pulls off near a field where a tractor along the horizon cuts down grass and dirt and seeds spiral out.

Clarence slides out and without his cane hobbles toward the fence.

"Dad?"

But he continues on; the whirs of cutting blades circle back to her. She checks her phone until he jumps the fence. And running after him, she calls out like when she was young and lost near the den where he told her he saw foxes, and she feared she was too small for him to hear her in the woods and flinched as briar snagged her, but he pulled back the sharp halo, his knuckles bloodied, and cleared a path.

The mower stops; a figure rises off the seat.

"Dad, what are you doing? Come back to the truck."

"They ain't here." He spins in grass and sun and shadows of the mountains.

"Who?"

"There used to be horses here."

"It's farm country. Horses could be anywhere."

"It was here." Panic flushes him. "Right here. Under us."

The figure steps off the mower.

"We should go, Dad. This is not our property."

"There was horses on this side. And headstones on the other." He whips around. "They would eat the weeds growing up through the cracks of the stones."

"Hey!" the figure yells.

"Dad, come on." She tugs his arm.

"They buried soldiers there. Grays and Blues." He points at an oak shading the land. He staggers forward, breaking her grip. "And Mr. Martone. My junior-high music teacher. He's buried here. He was part of an old-timey country group that made it all the way to Nashville."

The figure strides their way.

"We got to go." She tugs again.

"And up there was someone who improved chutes for hog production. And behind us…" His arms fan out in front of a copse. "A hurricane made its way inland and blasted everything here. That's why it's all gone."

"It's always been woods, Dad." She gets him to the truck.

The figure retreats.

She starts the truck and heads for the interstate.

"That hurricane came inland. Off the ocean."

· · ·

They reach his home, and she helps him inside while neighbors peek out their windows. He tells her he can do it without her and teeters into the bathroom. She checks the time and calls a number.

"David?"

"This is."

"I need to withdraw my interest in the position."

"And you are?"

Clarence steps out, wet towels over his head and neck, and flops on his bed.

"Charlotte Long. But I applied with my middle name. Alex."

"I see it here."

"Can you keep my name on file if I want to apply again?"

"I'd be happy to. We're always looking for new team members."

"I've never been to Cleveland."

"We're a growing company."

"Is the company more than numbers? Like the bottom line?"

"We're more than numbers. Our employees mean the world to us."

"How long have you been there?"

"Eight years."

"Do you see yourself there for longer?"

"As long as they'll have me. And they let me know that every chance they get."

Clarence enters the kitchen.

She hides her phone.

He says he has an idea for them. "Let's go to the ocean."

"Anything else I can help you with?" Dave asks.

"You answered what I needed."

Clarence pours a glass of water. "I didn't know you were on the phone."

"You said something about the ocean?"

"Let's go there. While you're here."

"You want to travel after today?"

"I feel better." He downs his pills with the water. "We can go for a few days. Out and back."

She opens his cabinets and dumps out liquors. "I know you can buy more when we get back. And when I leave. But I'm not leaving yet. And until then this will be empty. And you can't have anything, not even a beer or a cheap wine cooler from a grocery store, when we're at the ocean."

"OK."

"And you go to the doctor when we get back."

"OK."

"I'll take you…as long as I'm here."

Before he shuffles off, he says, "Maybe that arcade with the zoetrope is still there."

31

Traffic slows at the edge of the beach; the pier disappears in sheen coming off sand and surf. Vehicles honk, nothing moving forward, but they don't wake Clarence stick-thin on his back, his seat reclined. Charlotte reaches for his shoulder—Make sure, she thinks—but he gulps awake and checks the saliva on his lips. She checks too: no blood. His seat creaks up. She creeps their car tighter on the rear bumper of the SUV in front.

Clarence puts on his sunglasses. "I'm glad we rented this. The truck would've been a tight ride."

"I'm glad we could get anything for the weekend."

They pass under red-white-and-blue banners and Happy Fourth of July streamers. Kids in the SUV stick out sparklers.

"We could go back and might make it in time for the parade back home," she teases.

"I can promise you it hasn't changed." He massages his knees and chest. "We'd still sit in the Food City parking lot and watch the fireworks. But maybe we could've done it in this and made everyone think I got a new car."

"They would find out."

"That's true. Word spreads fast like that."

"But they'd pretend they didn't know and ask where you truck was."

"They would. And I'd tell them a Bigfoot hit it when I was tracking it late at night."

"And you would've captured it and put in your truck, but it got away."

"Like when we went fishing the other day. Or I found out that Bigfoot was just a guy in a suit."

A sparkler drops. Clarence opens his door and bangs it on the nearby car. He apologizes and picks up the sparkler. The kid in the SUV looks around, crying. Clarence relights the sparkler and hands it to the kid. Charlotte tells him to hurry up. "They're moving up there." She turns on her blinker, but the car Clarence hit won't let her over.

"Let her in," Clarence growls.

The driver flips him off and rolls up his window.

Clarence jiggles the driver's handle.

"Dad, forget it. Stay in."

He wheezes sitting.

The honks around them increase.

"You can't do that, Dad."

"They can't do that."

She misses the exit and drives the long way around the beach, sand and sun and sheen shifting into asphalt and neighborhoods, for their hotel.

. . .

They check into their room; Clarence drops to the foot of the bed and pants.

"Dad?"

"Give me a minute."

"The front desk apologized for the last-minute change." She opens the curtains. The view faces the city and interstate, not the ocean. "They said they can credit us or give us a voucher for our next stay or while we're here."

"What's the voucher?"

"King of the Sea All U Can Eat."

He coughs and checks his spit. "It's still here."

"That's where you sat me on that statue."

"The King of the Sea, Charlie. Not any statue."

"I remember the aquarium. Huge."

"All those fishes you wanted to touch. I turned around for something, and you had one leg in. You were headed for the baby sharks."

"You had your hands full with me."

"Good thing Janet never found out. Unless you told her?"

"No."

He scrolls through his phone. "We could eat a big lunch now." He thumbs over images tied to a star on the map. "The arcade is still here."

She leans closer. "We should go tonight."

He starts for the bathroom. "Let me cool down."

She scrolls through images of the arcade. "The zoetrope might be gone, Dad."

"They wouldn't do that," he shouts over running water. "I saw it."

She stops on a photo but doesn't tell him it's from a link titled "Changes Coming to the Boardwalk Arcade."

"Ready?" He towels off his neck and grabs his pillbox.

"I'm starving."

"Good thing it's all-you-can-eat. We can get the voucher from the front desk, but it's still my treat. All of this is. We'll eat, take our time, maybe have a drink. Soft drink for me. Hard for you. We can walk around. Make our way to the beach and boardwalk."

"You're OK to walk?"

"I didn't come all this way not to."

She lets him leave the room first then turns back toward the window and light filling it from somewhere.

· · ·

They beam at each other when they grab the seashell handles and open the blue-gold doors with portholes: the restaurant is the same as when they left it. Clarence adds it's the same as when he left it before Charlotte was "a wish that Janet and I got answered."

The hostess asks if they have a preference.

"Away from the bar."

"As close to the aquarium as possible."

"Right this way."

Waves on the ceiling glitter and ripple alongside a whale, dolphin, shark, salmon, and octopus. At a table behind them, a bell dings twice, and waiters and waitresses bring out a cake with a trident stuck in the middle and sing happy birthday to a boy. Employees load ice in the buffet's cold section and steaming trays in the hot.

They tell their server they need a minute. Charlotte skips to the statue of the King of the Sea looming over it all and sits on his knee covered in barnacles, seaweed, and waves. Clarence holds up his phone and tells her to say "yesteryear." She does, wiping her eyes. They pause at the wall of photos new and faded and with and without dates and names and messages.

"Did you put the old one up there?"

"No. I had it," he answers. "But I didn't come across it when I moved."

"We have a new one."

"We do." He texts the photo to her. "But this one's all mine. Not for anyone else."

On their way back to their table, Clarence stumbles and bumps another table, spilling drinks. Coughing, he apologizes before hobbling into his chair, wincing, and his phone's alarm beeping, taking his pills.

"I can ask our server if we can get this to go."

"Fried catfish, hushpuppies, and slaw will set me straight." He slurps down his ginger ale. "You can't up and leave all this. It's dine-in and stay. Not take-out and go away." His voice fades as he stares across their table and the room and toward the seahorses the King of the Sea rides out of the waves.

. . .

Buildings block their view of the ocean when they step from the restaurant and meander. Clarence rests in a shade under a shop's awning. Three Uncle Sams on stilts strut by. Crowds gather here and there, towing blankets, coolers, umbrellas, food, drinks —vivid colors among red, white, and blue. Charlotte scans for a break in traffic and, pulling up their location on her phone, suggests taking a side street to the boardwalk. Clarence tells her to put away her phone. "We'll walk until we get there. Look around. It's there." His frail hands trickle about the sun-charged air. "It's close."

They start, but he wobbles and retreats to the shade.

"The heat," he says. "It's out there too today."

"The other street is more in the shade."

"That takes us away from the beach."

"We can get to it."

"I want to walk but not over there."

"Let me run in and get us something." She cruises the store's aisles and, returning to him, tugs down a wide-brimmed black hat with a skull and crossbones on the front and hands an umbrella to Clarence.

"It's not raining," he says.

"It's a sun umbrella."

"I don't plan on lounging on the beach."

She pops open the umbrella. "It's not that big. But it works. There weren't many left."

He looks over the great white shark's mouth printed on the outside. "How much I owe you?"

"My treat. But you can buy us the shark teeth, cutlass, and treasure chest if we need a little more than this." She adjusts her pirate hat.

"We'll save that for the Halloween race they have down here."

"I'd come back for that."

"They don't have sharks in Cleveland."

They walk into the sunlight and pause at shops where Charlotte buys a Wish You Were Here postcard for her mother; at a mini-golf course where she pretends she's captured a dinosaur and Clarence, circling them, pumps his umbrella; at the go-karts snaking around where Clarence yells at the drivers, "Trade some paint!" when they charge into the corners and straightaways; and at the Seaside Circus and its sandwich boards announcing Music * Magic * Mayhem. A crowd bursts from a red-and-white striped tent, laughing, sweating, big-eyed. Charlotte stops near the sign.

Step Inside And See Our Wolf-Man!
Watch Him Change Into A Wolf Before Your Eyes!

Clarence digs out his wallet. "Want to go in?"

"No."

"Might be fun."

"I said no, Dad."

"You could get up there and show them how to do it."

She peers inside the tent: a glass box in the middle of the floor and a forest and full moon on a curtain surrounding it. "I know how they do it."

"I'd like to to see it. I never saw yours in person." He shuffles for the ticket counter.

"It's all fake."

"It's an illusion, Charlie. That's different."

"I'm not going in."

He pauses.

"Go see it on your own. I'm not going."

"One, please," he tells the employee. He lowers his umbrella and walks in.

More guests file in behind Clarence. The tent closes. A howl ripples through the air and into Charlotte who faces the ocean and silhouettes of people and boats disappearing in water and light. She walks toward the long shadows cast by buildings across sand and surf while thunder rumbles from the tent behind her.

The flap bursts open. The crowd emerges—but no Clarence. She rushes in but finds him chatting with the Wolf-Man.

"There she is. Do you want to meet her?"

Charlotte strides out.

Clarence hobbles after her. "Charlie. Wait. I was talking to him about your act. He said it's the same."

"Great."

"They're not hiring."

"Did you ask him that?"

"He said things have picked up for the summer. They're the busiest they've been."

"Good for them."

They stroll down the boardwalk. On the other side, a high-school marching band practices.

"He burst out of that box he went into."

"I know."

"He was moving back there. All tortured from being cursed. Then he burst out. The story goes he was at the wrong place at the wrong time."

The band strikes up a tune.

She covers one ear. "Do you want a snack?"

"It was scary at first. Fun-scary. My heart raced. But I knew that wasn't really him. I waited it out and talked to him. And when I did he wasn't scary anymore." Clarence balances against the wall across from the tent and wheezes. "Corndogs? Popcorn? Cotton candy? What could we send a picture of to Janet?"

They trudge down the boardwalk, dodging a parade setting up.

"We're close," he says.

"To what?"

"The arcade with the zoetrope."

"I don't know, Dad."

"Look at the lights atop the shops over here. They're old. Like from the turn of the century." He looks down an alley. "It was down this way."

She loads her phone's map. "I don't think it is."

"Put that away. Let me find it."

"I'll get us our snack."

He lowers his umbrella and disappears in the alley's shadows.

She pays for their snacks and lines them up on a bench near the pier and sends a photograph of it all to her mother. <Dad and I are at the beach today. We got all this before the fireworks and parade tonight. Happy Fourth to you.>

Janet sends back a red-white-and-blue frosted sponge cake. <Sounds like a good day. I'm glad you got to do that with him.>

<Did you make that?>

<I did.>

<Dad would love to have a bite.>

<Tell him it's my old recipe he used to "help" me with. His help was taste-testing it while I made it.>

Charlotte pulls up the map on her phone then the search she saved about the arcade. The alley livens up. A busker plays her guitar while teens run by, lighting sparklers and firecrackers and tossing poppers. A silhouette slumps against the wall. "Homeless sack of crap," one of the teens says. Poppers ricochet like gunfire. Charlotte walks toward the silhouette who wheezes, coughs, spits. "Is he drunk? Or a pedophile?" the teen girls ask, getting out their phones and skipping away. A crowd circles the silhouette; someone asks if he needs 9-1-1 and kicks away the shark-mouth umbrella.

Charlotte runs. "Oh my God...Dad. Dad!" She wipes blood off his mouth and cradles him until the ambulance arrives.

. . .

The monitor hiccups beats. Charlotte shoots up.

"It does that." The nurse checks Clarence's bed. "It's part of the rhythm." She updates her notepad before leaving.

The TV flickers live coverage of parades. The respirator throbs louder in Charlotte as she scoots closer to Clarence. She touches his hand, the tubes, his ID bracelet, the scars on his wrist. Buildings on the TV dim. An orchestra warms up, but the feed cuts to actors dressed as Washington, Jefferson, and Lincoln and ragtag farmers firing at redcoats. She peers out the window. Gold, red, silver, and green fireworks shatter over the ocean. Silhouettes buzz along the boardwalk. One by one, shops and restaurants and hotel rooms fade to black. She answers her phone.

"How's he doing?"

"Not good, Mom. He's in critical. The nurse has changed buckets of blood he coughed up. They're talking surgery. The doctor said things aren't looking good."

"I got a flight booked. But the earliest I can be there is Monday."

"You may want to save that."

"Don't talk like that."

"He's not good, Mom." She turns down the TV as the national anthem buzzes, the orchestra brass glistens, floodlights illuminate buildings, and fireworks burst. The parade along the boardwalk picks up. The TV's clock winds down.

"Now's not the time to debate if I should come."

"You may be early." Her phone pings with job alerts. "Or I'm late to it all."

"I'll be there and stay as long as it takes."

Her head dropping, chilling, she whispers, "Hurry, Mom." She steps out of the room, but the air is no less suffocating. Janitors, late-night administrators, candy-stripers, nurses, doctors, security swirl around her. Monitors beep on the floor; machines breathe for someone. Nurses rush into a room down the hall. The rest walk away but don't leave; the hospital's terminals take them back to where they started. The door to her father's room closes. Charlotte asks the nurse at the station if she has time to step out. "If we take him to surgery, we'll notify you." Thanking the nurse, she touches her pendant, can't punch the elevator down fast enough, and flings open the stairwell door.

She runs toward the ride-share before the driver slows and confirms he's picking up the right passenger. Cheers from the parade swell in the distance; fireworks explode over the ocean and leave a ghostly residue on waves churning black. "Faster," she begs the driver, but traffic and blockades slow them and reroute them away from the boardwalk. She scrolls over her map. "Take a left." The map rotates. "No, right."

"I can't get us closer," driver says. "It's the parade and all that."

"Get me to here." She shows him a pin on the map.

"You want off there?"

"Just get me there."

"It'll be blocked off too." He idles while a cop directs traffic. "That's off the parade route."

"Then get me as close at you can to the boardwalk."

"Into the ocean?" He glances in the rearview mirror.

"Just get me there."

The driver cuts through a neighborhood and slams on his brakes. A circle of families hang out in the middle of the street and fire off rockets the night cloaks until small squares of white parachutes billow out and slow the descents. The driver backs up and retraces streets. The car icon on Charlotte's map reverses. A text cuts through: <Your patient is in pre-surgery.> She leaps from the car and runs through the neighborhood, checking her phone, but she follows explosions in the air illuminating the ocean and the roofs of shops along the boardwalk. Closer to them she slows, noticing turn-of-the-century lightbulbs, and turns for the alley where her father slumped against the wall. She passes surf shops, vendors, bars, a bookstore, a coffeeshop, spools of saltwater taffy, and the fortune-teller machine behind the glass, her voice floating from the speaker *What is your name? What is your future? Step closer and I shall tell you.*

Around the corner, the arcade flashes before her, larger and filled with modern games. She walks in—not deserted but not full—among beeps and blips of games she does not remember and rows of screens flickering like movies; she reads the overhead banner Winter Expansion & Remodeling Complete!

Her heart pulses when she stops at a brass finger pointing around the corner for a museum. The hallway is dark except for fireworks. She reaches a room labeled The Arcade of Yesteryear: dark wood walls; an ocean wave etched on the door's glass; a sign painted on the wood floor promising Wonder and Amazement in the Palm of Your Hand. She turns the knob—locked. She kicks it; it doesn't budge. She glances at the security camera before stepping outside and picking up a rock. She cocks back her arm and aims for the seashell etched above the doorknob; she hurls but misses her target. Pressing against the glass, she peers in. Fireworks and the parade crescendo; blue-purple flashes from video games—all of it backlighting shapes within the room: towers, boxes, circles. Yellow explodes over water and brightens cylinders in the corner across from her. She skims down the row of zoetropes, passing Runner, Walker, Boxer, Batter, Pitcher, Bird, and stops at Horse.

A text buzzes her phone: <Your patient has been scheduled for emergency surgery.> She checks the time and runs out of the arcade. She calls for a ride, but the icons on her map float far away from her. The parade twists down a street leading to the oceanfront; bands, crowds, fireworks pierce the night. Waves curl silver-black-blue in front of her. She compares the fastest routes by car back to the hospital, but holiday traffic will block time. The ocean air is the last thing cooling her before she runs.

And while she runs, the hospital miles away, her memory returns—the zoetropes off to the side in the arcade and the man out front on a unicycle shouting through a megaphone, "You, sir, and you, young lady, step right in." The brass sign above one said Horse, and she tugged her father's hand before letting go and running over to it but couldn't turn the lever without a coin.

As soon as he named his birthday present to her—"The ocean"—she ran for the calendar and counted the days until then and X-ed them out with all she wished: a pier, whales, seals, starfish; her father standing behind her; waves rolling under a blue sky—nowhere a cloud—shimmering and cold and frothy and slapping around her like her father described when he left for good but, before he did, he told her, he went to the ocean and watched it roll in and out and waded into deeper waves, telling her, "It takes away everything."

The night's tones and tremors flood her when she jaywalks and a car lays on its horn and the driver curses her. Fireworks from a nearby house whizz off. She checks her map—a right there; a left two blocks down; the hospital less than a mile away—but turns it off and runs.

And stepping out of the ocean that day, she did her best describing something that followed them onto the roads leading from the beach; into a dream where her father said he was on a boat with red masts and tattered sails and its sole purpose was shipping flowers back and forth across the sea to anyone who would take them, but no one did; into one more day with him—washing dishes, suds on their arms and noses, the rhythm he kept while scrubbing, singing aloud if the circle would be unbroken.

The hospital glows at the top of the hill. An ambulance pulls in, its lights flashing. Staff roll in the gurney. A car squelches behind the ambulance; a man bolts out and runs alongside the gurney. Charlotte wheezes, her legs and back tight, her lungs spent. She receives a text but doesn't read it. A window on her father's floor darkens. She trots into the hospital and up the stairs to the floor where she asks the nurse where she needs to go. And as she moves toward the elevator, she moves into the memory that followed them that day from the arcade. They walked through the etched-glass door, the arcade's windows open, a breeze coming in off the ocean and lifting their hair while they stood at the zoetrope and he slid in a coin and told her to look into the slots. He turned the handle; the black top spun—light blinking inside the slots; the black-and-white photos quickening within. She leaned closer to the horse galloping with no one on its back. He told her it can never get away from her no matter how far away she is.

ACKNOWLEDGEMENTS

To everyone who reads and supports me and my work—thank you.

And to H.

ABOUT THE AUTHOR

William Auten is the author of the novels *October*, *In Another Sun*, and *Pepper's Ghost* and the short-story collections *Inroads* and *A Fine Day Will Burn Through*. Learn more at williamauten.com.